The
Salem Village
Greens

The Salem Village Greens

HARRY ARTHUR GRACE

Copyright 1987 by Harry Arthur Grace. All rights reserved.

For information address: *Vyoupoint*
8625 Rugby Drive
West Hollywood, CA 90069
(213) 657-2398

Library of Congress Catalog Card Number: 87–90050
ISBN 0–9618–08306 (Hard Bound)
ISBN 0–9618–08314 (Paper Bound)

To
Tekla
and
to
All the Inhabitants
of
Salem Village
for
Fulfilling Their Promise
to
Joseph Green,
"to Continue to Live in Peace . . ."

1 Nicodemus?

"What a sad sight it is to see," I clapped my hands over my ears to stop the booming voice from waking me until I had slept off the rum. His words still pounded through my fingers. "Eight firebrands of Hell hanging there!"

'A bad dream.' I swatted mosquitoes from my face as I shivered from the late September shower. 'Better get up.' I struggled to my feet, but my knees buckled and I pitched headfirst into the brambles.

As I picked thorns from my palms, that same voice echoed from the tree that sheltered me. "What a sad sight it is to see eight firebrands of Hell hanging there!"

Mired in the slippery turf, I slid farther down the hill as a horse-drawn cart hurtled toward me. Luckily, the jade shied at the tree and forced its mistress, a girl no more than twelve, to rein the cart's mad dash. As she did so, a lanky preacher skidded down the path, grabbed the reins from her, and halted the cart's plunge. A chubby preacher then minced his way toward them. Before the trio separated at the foot of the hill, the fat, flush-faced minister faced the crest, shook his fists above his head, and again exploded, "What a sad sight it is to see eight firebrands of Hell hanging there!"

Curiosity forced me to look toward the hilltop, but the tree blocked my view. Peering down the road, I was relieved to see the thick-set minister leave his companions while the other led the girl's horse and cart in the opposite direction.

'Some holiday!' I berated myself as I scanned the darkening hill for fear that another reckless rider might surprise me before I could control my legs.

'My horse . . . I've lost my horse!' Squinting as dusk fell, I groped toward the hilltop, but slipped into the cart's rut. "The Devil take it!" I kicked at the hole with my free foot, dimly sensing that it held a clue to the loss of my horse and the afternoon's events.

My self-pity was quickly broken by the sound of hoofs bearing down on me. "The Devil take you!" I screamed and threw myself into the shrubbery to avoid being trampled.

"Hold or I shoot!" The horseman reined short of the furrow. "I've seen you before, stranger. Who are you? What brings you here?"

"Joseph . . . Joseph Green," I stammered, pleased he was not a minister but afraid he might report my blasphemy.

"Ah, I remember," the rider menaced me with his musket, "you're the young fool who helped push the cart out of this rut . . ."

"I came to Salem to speak to Goodman English about a position aboard his ship." I squirmed to avoid his musket's aim but he tracked me. "He wasn't at the wharf . . ." My memory returned under the force of my challenger. "When I couldn't find him, I stopped by a tavern . . ."

"Beadle's."

"That's it." I shook my head to clear its stupor. "I . . . I drank too much. I . . . I spent all my money."

"No matter," his musket waved my words aside, "what brought you to Gallows Hill?"

'I do hereby resolve, through the Lord's mercy, to become more moderate in my drinking,' I prayed as I studied my inquisitor whom I judged to be older and taller than I. "When my money was spent, I headed back toward Cambridge. Have . . . have you seen my sorrel?"

My challenger, who reminded me of a centaur, glowered his answer. My clothes, albeit shredded by the brambles, were far better than his homespun russet. His silence increased my dread.

"In any case," perhaps if I talked he would lay his weapon aside, "I rode west from Salem Town, down Prison Street, up Main, across the Town Bridge, and into the open fields." I smiled, hoping for some respite, but he continued to stare. "Then I saw a crowd ahead of me."

"Headed here—to Gallows Hill."

"As you say, *sir* . . ." maybe flattery would help.

"Don't call me 'sir.' I'm no college boy!" He lay his musket across his lap and leaned toward me. "Never mind your tale—you may be innocent, but you *are* a fool! How long has it been since Reverend Noyes passed this way?"

My blank look irritated him to raise his musket.

"Surely you saw a fat preacher shout blasphemous remarks from near that tree?"

"You mentioned Gallows Hill," I countered, "has there been a hanging today?"

"See for yourself," he gestured toward the hilltop. "Had it not been for the three murderers who passed you . . ." He wheeled his horse in a slow descent of the muddy trail. "Forget what I said."

"Have you seen my sorrel?"

"No!" he stood in his stirrups. "Forget about your horse, Green, but don't forget the names of those murderers: Samuel Parris . . . Nicholas Noyes . . . Ann Putnam." Finding surer footing down the trail, he called, "I suspect your horse enjoys the pasture atop Gallows Hill."

My relief at the horseman's departure caused me to slide into the rut again. Soberer than before, my misstep brought to mind the afternoon's events.

The crowd, a cart in its midst, had blocked me from my homeward route. Dismounting drunkenly, I was pushed toward the cart and dropped my reins. Crushed against its rear, with people around me jeering its occupants, I was rocked back and forth until the rut-locked wheel sprang loose and the cart rumbled upwards. I escaped the mob by crawling to a nearby tree.

'Not much more I can do until I find my sorrel,' I hugged the trail's steepening edge. At the crest, I searched the clearing for my horse until my eyes became transfixed by what seemed to be candles dangling from their wicks. The apparition lasted only a second before the scene's horror struck me. 'Those are *bodies*,' I counted, 'eight bodies hanging like hares that have been sprung!'

The faint moon vanished. The blackness matched the terror in my soul while protecting me from the awful scene. 'Pray God these are not the remains of those people in the cart I helped push today.' I retched, filling my mouth with bile. As I recovered, a body moved, and I passed out.

*   *   *

"Welcome, Nicodemus," a woman whispered behind me as I came to. My only relief was that she had mistaken me for someone else.

"We were expecting thee. We knew by the Scripture that thee would arrive to do thy duty."

"You . . . you're sorely mistaken." I shook off her words, "My name is Joseph." An inner sense warned me to reveal no more.

"Doth someone accompany thee, Deborah?" a man's voice droned amid the trees before me.

'That accounts for the movement,' my brain calmed my heart as I stepped aside to seek my horse.

"Tis Nicodemus," the woman grabbed my arm above the elbow, "come to help."

I jerked to free myself and correct her for misnaming me, but failed on both counts. 'It's some consolation that others are here,' I rationalized and spun to face the woman. My comfort was shattered, however, when the returning moonlight glistened from her naked, ash-covered body.

'God help me!' I shut my eyes and shrank away. 'I'm trapped with nowhere to hide!'

In spite of my fear, I forced myself to look at her. Her face was blackened such that the whites of her eyes and teeth gleamed like the *ignus fatuus* along the hilltop. I did not notice her partner until he stood beside me.

"Thee have met my wife?" he covered her with his cloak. "Then thee need not squint. Welcome to our night's unpleasant duty here at Golgotha."

'Golgotha? Gallows Hill?' I tried to convince myself that the past few minutes were only a drunken dream. The pain when I pinched myself told me my experience was real.

"Let us be about our task," the man commanded. Placing his palm between my shoulders, he edged me toward the swaying bodies. Although I dug my heels into the ground with each step, he forced me ever closer to the trees.

"See here—I only came to find my sorrel."

"Apologize not, Nicodemus . . ."

"Apologize? What for? It's God's truth!"

"Thee blaspheme!" He shoved me forward. "My dear wife walked naked today through Salem, her face blackened by ashes, to ridicule the barrenness of the town's religion—a faith that could hang eight innocents!"

As I tried to run, the man caught the nape of my neck, and I realized I had to wait for a better chance to escape.

"Know, too, that when Reverend Parris arrived in Salem Village he demanded Deborah and I abandon our Quaker belief."

"Admonishing Ranters is to be expected . . ."

"And when thee refused," he spoke tearfully, "Parris had thee stripped, tied to a cart like the one which dragged these innocents here today . . ." Mention of the cart pained me that I had had a part in tormenting the eight whose bodies I approached with each reluctant step. ". . . and wheeled thee through the streets of Salem Town and Village."

Feeling his grip relax, I struggled to rid myself of the couple and their heretical ideas. The suddenness of my movement might have plummeted me down the hill had not the woman grabbed my leg and stayed my fall.

"And so, Nicodemus, Deborah's nakedness is not new to these ignorant Farmers."

Released from her rescuing grasp, I felt obliged to be led closer to the corpse-laden trees.

"Before we proceed with our mournful chores," we paused in our walk, "we are the Joshua Buffums."

My sigh of thanks for not having to confront the bodies was put into words when his wife offered me a bite of corn cake. Relaxed, I greedily washed my dry throat with a gulp of cider from the Buffum's flask. Strength returned to my legs as I prepared to leave.

"Now that thee are refreshed, Nicodemus, 'tis time we began our Christian duty." The Buffums bowed their heads to pray in silence for the victims and I bowed mine to pray for myself.

*   *   *

Braced between them, I reached the row of trees to stop beneath the twirling body of a woman whose bare feet dangled inches above my nose.

"Martha Corey," Joshua Buffum intoned.

Guiding me to the second body, Deborah mumbled, "Mary Easty," and so we plodded down the gruesome line until I sighed, "Eight," just avoiding Mary Parker's heels from swinging into my face.

"Twenty-one!" Joshua corrected as he fumbled for an object a few feet to the side of the last tree.

"I count only *eight* . . ."

"My husband means that these poor souls follow upon five hanged a month ago and another five a month before."

"That's still not twenty-one . . ."

"Two are deathly ill and will surely die in jail, their chests ruined by the damp," Joshua grunted his annoyance as he grappled with a makeshift ladder. "Take hold' "

I shuddered when I realized he addressed me rather than his wife.

"The other, Giles Corey, rest his soul, was the bravest of the lot . . . Enough banter—let's get on with our duty!"

"My horse!" I spotted the animal grazing greedily, heedless of my discomfort.

"Forget thy nag! He'll await thee when thy night's work is done. Mount the ladder," Buffum insisted, "we'll begin with Mary Parker of Andover."

When I moved too slowly, he pushed me aside and cautioned me to steady the corpse's bare feet while he slowly cut the rope that held it. The body toppled, however, and Deborah jumped to catch it, placing it gently on the ground.

"Samuel Wardwell," the Quaker bowed as he perched on the ladder beside the next body. "Confessed to the false charge of witchcraft— then bravely recanted, which was his undoing." The heavier body taxed my muscles when the rope was cut, and I again needed his wife's help to prevent its falling to the earth.

"The poor man might have escaped this undeserved fate had he been allowed to confess as he stood atop this very ladder," she added, wrapping the corpse in linen.

"Sheriff Curwin would have none of that, Nicodemus!" Joshua indicated he wanted me to move the ladder to the tree that held Wilmot Reed's remains. "No indeed! Fearful lest Goodman Wardwell sway the mob, the sheriff blew tobacco smoke in his face, causing him to cough in the midst of his confession—a sign the crowd took as an affirmation of Samuel's guilt."

"The Devil you say!"

"Careful, careful! That was almost the very blasphemy held against yonder corpse."

I was so chastened by the Ranter's warning that I took her husband's knife and climbed the ladder to relieve the tree of 'Mammy' Reed's body. Whenever accused of witchcraft, the Marblehead fisherman's wife protested, "I know nothing about it," Buffum informed me as I sliced the rope too quickly and the corpse fell into the pair's waiting arms.

I tried to atone by more carefully attacking the strands which held the body of Mary Scott, late of Rowley Village. 'Good Lord, they fetched this woman from beyond Boxford to bring her to this fate!' It frightened me that had Reverends Parris or Noyes heard me I might be summoned from Harvard College to face a similar reckoning.

"Suppose *thee* were condemned to death by a confessed liar, Nicodemus?" the Ranter taunted as he took the ladder. "Such false witness brought Widow Pudeator to this sad end." The dull knife caused her corpse to spin, no matter how much Joshua tried to steady the rope, and forced me to concentrate all the more.

"Jonathan Best, her main accuser, had been whipped as a liar, but she might have been freed had it not been for the antics of young Ann Putnam . . ."

The sudden snap of the rope startled me such that the woman's body slipped through my hands until I caught it beneath the armpits and found myself staring into her dead but open eyes.

"I'll take her," Deborah snatched the body from me as I vomited corn pone and cider over the precipice.

"Thou hast a squeamish belly," Buffum forced the knife into my hand as I climbed the ladder, careful to turn my head from Elsie Parker's face.

"Drink is thy curse, Nicodemus," the Quakeress again miscalled me. "Mariner Parker's endless drunkeness at Beadle's," I managed to saw through the rope, "led Elsie to denounce him publicly, as John Westgate testified at her trial."

"Not entirely on his word, thee will allow," Joshua lay the body on linen for his wife to wrap. "One of our own people, the Quaker hatter, Samuel Shattuck, shares guilt in the crime against this Salem woman . . ."

Engrossed in the grim undertaking, I prepared to remove Mary Easty's body from its tether.

"Pass to the next tree!" I complied with Joshua's command and steadied the ladder for him as he climbed, puzzled as to why we would leave a body behind.

"Here are the remains of a woman turned from sinner to saint," Deborah readied herself to help me. "Having borne a mulatto child out of wedlock, who lived with her all these years, she confessed and became a stalwart Christian, showing a devotion ended only by the noose which choked her dying prayer."

"Hold Martha Corey's body carefully, Nicodemus," the Quaker warned as he descended. "Only the Lord knows how Reverend Parris and Deacon Edward Putnam prevailed in bringing her to this tragic end."

We placed the seven linen-wrapped corpses in the crevasses among the rocks and covered them so that neither bad weather nor marauding animals would bare them, as the Buffums said had happened to Reverend Burroughs' corpse.

"Gallows Hill has become our Golgotha," Deborah lamented. "When we witnessed the disgrace done Reverend Burroughs, we two agreed to retrieve and bury anyone who might suffer from the ignorance and superstition of these Farmers."

"Thee are free to leave, Nicodemus," the Ranter handed my horse's reins to me, "thou hast fulfilled thy duty."

"I have two questions," my boldness surprised me. "First, should we not care for the poor soul whose body hangs behind us?"

"Her own people, the Nurses, will do that," Buffum almost smiled. "Your second question?"

"When you first called me 'Nicodemus,' I told you my name was Joseph," my voice rose as I mounted my horse. "Why have you persisted in this misnomer?"

"The last shall be first," Deborah ignored me and pointed instead toward the buried dead. "The burial of Martha Corey was thy last duty—make the comforting of her soul thy first concern!"

'My first concern?' My first concern was a speedy, safe return to HC. I knew my second question would remain unanswered and let my sorrel pick its way down the trail to the road. Thoroughly sobered from my ordeal, yet puzzled by the Friends' meaning, I promised, 'I will be more moderate in my drinking, gambling, and blaspheming, for Providence has protected me this day, assuring that I have done my duty, once and for all, to Salem—and to Martha Corey.'

Relieved by my prayer, although wrong on both counts, I dozed in the saddle, my relaxed grip allowing my horse to grope down Gallows Hill in search of water to quench its thirst.

*   *   *

The sound of water lapping against a shore woke me, and so I tightened my grip on the reins and dismounted to scoop a handful of brackish water.

'Lost again, but dawn is near. I had better wait for the light to find my way to Cambridge.' As I became more accustomed to the fog, I spotted a mill across the river, connected to my bank by a bridge a short distance to my right. 'I'll cross and find some shelter against the morning frost.'

The sound of heavy breathing caught my attention as a party of men made its tortuous way down Gallows Hill, their panting caused by an object they were bearing. Fascinated by the trio, I failed to notice the horseman until he towered behind me.

"Joseph Green again!"

Startled, I almost screamed a reply, but obeyed his signal to keep silent while he pointed toward the group edging toward the riverbank.

"You've found your horse, but are still not bound for home," the stocky rider who had accosted me hours before accused.

"I fell asleep in my saddle—I've lost my way."

"The road to Boston lies above us. Bear right or you'll head back to Salem."

Relaxed at the thought of an end to my terror, I sprang into my saddle only to have the stranger grab my reins.

"Not so fast! Since you're still around, there's work for us atop Gallows Hill. It's not yet dawn, so let's be about it . . ."

"But . . . but I've spent the night up there!"

"A strange place for a boy to spend the night, alone with eight corpses."

"I wasn't . . ."

"So," he released my reins, "the Buffums returned and you volunteered to help them?"

''Hardly! They forced me to lower, wrap, and bury seven . . .''

''Only seven?'' He controlled my horse with his. ''Of course, the eighth must be the one those men are carrying to the river. We'll draw nearer in case they need help.''

Crowding me at the river bank, he found us shelter within earshot of three men who stood with bowed heads around the linen-wrapped victim.

''The Ranters insisted we leave her.''

''They knew her family would fetch Mary Easty's body as it did her sister's, Rebecca Nurse. We'll dismount while they hold their ceremony.'' His voice trailed off enough that I could hear a man read from what sounded like a letter.

''Unable to plead our own cause or to have benefit of counsel,'' snatches were all I could make out, ''our being unaware of any guilt or other scandalous evil against our Lord . . .'' In spite of my concentration, the morning breeze made listening difficult. ''We plead that spectral testimony requires other, concurring legal evidence . . . .''

The reader ended and joined his companions in silent prayer. ''Isaac Easty,'' my solemn companion whispered, ''read his wife's letter to the Court.'' His tone became surly, ''Unfortunately, my brother's— Sergeant Thomas'—note did more to kill her than *her* letter did to save her!''

The ceremony continued beside the gently rocking shallop in which Mary Easty's body had been laid. As an older man drew a document from his cloak to read in a more faltering manner, my nemesis identified himself as Joseph Putnam.

''I know the accusers to be wily and subtle, and so beg you to be charitable to others whom they accuse,'' the reader began.

''Francis Nurse, Rebecca's husband,'' Goodman Putnam advised, ''reading from Mary Easty's last letter.''

''I know that *I* must die,'' tears streamed down my captor's cheeks, ''albeit I am clear of this sin, and so I plead with you,'' Joseph Putnam squeezed my hand, ''shed no more innocent blood!''

Isaac Easty and the third man seated themselves in the shallop as Goodman Nurse pushed it into the river and boarded it.

''Diabolical!'' Putnam released me. ''The judge was so unsure of her guilt he asked the assembly, 'Are you *certain* this is the woman?'

At that,'' he clenched his fist, ''my niece, Ann, threw a fit to seal Goody Easty's fate!''

The dawn was full, the fog had lifted from the river, but I waited for Goodman Putnam to remount, afraid of anyone whose mood could change so quickly.

''You're lucky I didn't kill you yesterday for the part you played in propelling these innocents to their deaths,'' he led our horses westward. ''I'll leave you here, at Strong Water Bridge. Pray we never meet again, Joseph Green . . .''

His musket at the ready, he galloped off. I waited until he was well out of sight before I urged my horse toward the safety of Harvard College and prayed we would never meet again.

*   *   *

'Slap . . . slap . . . slap,' the sound of the North River sloshing against Mary Easty's shallop kept me wakeful as I tossed in the sweat of my dormitory bed. The same nightmare had tormented me since my return to HC. No longer could I enjoy springing hares, their dangling bodies reminded me too much of Gallows Hill. I hid my head under the cover without relief. I could still hear 'rap . . . rap . . . rap.'

''Joseph? JO-SEPH GREEN!''

The sound of someone's calling me as he tapped gently on my door only added to my nightmare the specter of the centaur come to fetch me.

''Joseph,'' my caller's voice softened, ''this is Reverend Brattle. Come to my chambers for supper this evening.''

Fully awake, I applied myself to Latin and Greek, both of which I hated, for I was afraid that the 'Father of the College' would surely confront me about both subjects when I visited him.

''How is your dear mother's health?'' my mentor refilled our jacks with ale while his maid cleared the empty trencher from the table.

''Quite well, although she worries about my brothers at sea. She fears for their lives at the hands of pirates or the French.''

''Well she might! Your brothers are in the vanguard of New England—not unlike the farmers north of Salem.''

This was a clue that our discussion might focus on my truancy of the past fall rather than my poor scholarship.

"Tell me about your Salem adventure," I declined his offer of tobacco, having not yet succumbed to that addiction.

"I was feeling sickly, unable to concentrate on my studies, and so I rode to Salem to see if Phillip English would take me aboard his fleet."

"Shame on you! That would have been a terrible blow to your mother after all the trouble she and your late brother, Percival, went through to support your education." He puffed impatiently as I tried to change the subject from Salem to my studies.

'If you tell him your tale, it may relieve your nightmares,' I chastised myself and told him about everything except my drinking and gambling. 'Think of the affection former students hold for this man who nursed them through the pox, almost dying in the process. Trust him to understand!'

The bayberry candles burned out, Master Brattle paused from his note-taking to light new ones, "You've been through a lot for a sixteen year old . . ."

"Seventeen—last November."

"You witnessed more tragedy in one day than most of us in a lifetime. But you failed to overhear Mary Easty's advice to the Court, which some of us, such as my brother, Thomas, and I committed to memory. 'You are going the wrong way . . . You must examine the afflicted persons very strictly . . . You must keep them apart from one another for some time . . . You must assure yourselves that none of them has lied.' And then," he emptied the ashes from his pipe, "she gave the Court her blessing . . .

"While you were chasing about Salem, running away from your responsibilities here and to your family, Sheriff Curwin seized English's property! Providence protected you from implication in that sad affair . . ."

'I promise, Lord, not to drink to excess,' I prayed as my host rose to dismiss me.

"Let us hope that having told your tale you will no longer suffer nightmares," he consoled. "Your frown, however, suggests there's something on your mind?"

"The Quakers insisted on calling me Nicodemus—in spite of knowing my real name!"

"You're not well-versed in Scripture." He showed no disapproval.

"The Gospel of John, Chapter Three." He scribbled a note to me. "It describes our Lord's meeting with a wealthy young man who questions him relentlessly."

"I recall the passage—vaguely."

"Rather than take offense," Reverend Brattle pointed at me, "Jesus said that to truly serve God and Man, Nicodemus must be reborn, confess his sins, and so be accepted into what we now call our covenant."

I squirmed, as much to avoid his lecture as his accusing finger. Although I had been baptized, both of my parents having been reborn, I was far from ready to give up my pleasures, let alone confess them publicly and await the congregation's approval.

"Later, when Jesus was on trial, this same Pharisee protested the proceedings." He reached for his Scripture. "Does our law permit us to pass judgment on a man unless we have given him a hearing and learned the facts?"

"Mary Easty's letter!"

"Nicodemus' appeal also failed and our Lord died on Golgatha."

The image of Jesus on the cross shaded into the eight corpses hanging from Gallows Hill and sent a shudder through me.

"And so, when our Lord's secret disciple, Joseph of Arimathea, retrieved His body from the cross, wrapping it in linen, he was joined by . . ."

"Nicodemus!"

Reverend Brattle let my discovery affect me before he nodded confirmation.

"Last fall, *you* were Nicodemus . . ."

"And Joshua Buffum . . ."

"Served as Joseph of Arimathea." William Brattle clasped my right hand, "Don't try to understand all we've talked about. Leave some of it to time and Providence. Pray privately each day. Study the Scripture. Above all, Joseph, think of Eternity—or face damnation."

I returned to my quarters and slept without a nightmare for the first time since Salem. My studies came easier, albeit I remained weak in Latin and Greek, and upon graduation happily accepted a teaching position at Roxbury Latin School, to the delight of my mother, Ruth, whose only concern was that I could not bring myself to confess my sins and join the covenant.

2 Be Converted or Damned

"Crack!"

The sound of the boys' heads as they crashed together, their necks in my grasp, caused both to bawl, but gave me little satisfaction.

"Blasphemy! That's what you've willfully committed," my knuckles whitened on their napes.

"We . . . we only won . . . wondered, Sir . . ." I pinched the stronger boy's neck all the more, but this gave his partner more courage.

"Whatever *is* sinful about becoming an adult?" the weaker one blurted, maddening me such that I cuffed him across his ear.

"The Commandment reads: 'Thou shalt not commit adultery,' " I raised my fists in rage. Heaven knows what restrained me—I might have killed them.

"Sir, please, Sir Green, Exodus 20:14 . . ."

"*I* know the Scripture. *I* assigned you to study it!"

"But, Sir," his classmate begged, "the passage gives no explanation . . ."

"Study, then, Leviticus 20:10, and pray the Lord and I forgive you for your sin of blasphemy!" I swung my leg at the bolder boy, missing him, as the two ran from my room. Even a strong draught of rum and a pipeful of tobacco failed to calm my nerves. 'Surely life at sea could not be worse than having to teach these unruly rascals! At the very worst, I would never have entertained such thoughts as these scoundrels mouth. The best of them are rotten at heart . . . .' I threw my lecture notes into my desk and told myself I might as well

have another rum and go fowling outside Roxbury before the Sabbath
began.

*   *   *

"Sir Green," I recognized Pastor Walter's call and quickened my
pace to avoid him.

"Joseph!" The call became a command. I fidgeted with my catch
of pigeons until he was abreast of me. "Can it be true—the tale your
pupils reported? I deem you over-reacted to their honest inquiry."

"There's no honesty in those boys, Nehemiah. Had I known about
the confusion Master Barnard left for me, I'd have chosen a sea chap-
laincy over Roxbury Latin School!"

"You're flushed with anger, Joseph, a blasphemy any day, and
worse so near the Sabbath! Besides, the boys sought instruction—you
only gave them punishment . . ."

"I *did* instruct them!"

"To study Leviticus by themselves? Without your wisdom? That's
hardly worthy of you. Why couldn't you have tutored them like John
Hancock tutored you at college?"

Never in the mood for a lecture, whether from my father, teachers,
or ministers, I turned my thoughts to my upcoming pigeon dinner,
washed down with a few tankards of ale.

"Will you share some of my catch?" I offered.

"I'd choke to death on pigeon shot just before the Sabbath, but at
least *I'd* be prepared for Eternity—*you* would be damned for all
time!"

The Roxbury pastor fumbled in his coat, avoiding my stare as I
fumed, and handed me a book.

"Read *A Preparation for the Lord's Table*, it's among Cotton Mather's best." He hesitated as he left me by my door, "You could die
at any time—perhaps in a fowling accident—and you can't repent on
your death bed!"

Entering my room, I threw the book on my table and poured myself
the first of too many jacks of rum. Drink, and perhaps the fear that I
might choke on a piece of pigeon, caused me to throw my catch away
and go to bed supperless.

Thus I was in no condition to cope with the boys I caught dancing
the next Sabbath. The noise of their singing and swearing drew me

to their room, but they reacted to my lecture as poorly as I had to Pastor Walter's. Disgusted with them and myself, I thought I would browse Reverend Mather's book—instead I found myself engrossed!

"I must be converted or damned," I wept to Reverend Walter in his study the next day. "I must either turn from all sin, and give myself up to Christ or else I must be damned!"

"Let not the Devil persuade you to tarry any longer, Joseph," he advised, not warned me, "do not put off 'til tomorrow—for you're never sure of tomorrow!"

Thus began my conversion, aided by my pastor's gentle prodding and my private study of Cotton Mather's *Companion for Communicants*. Meantime, I drank only an occasional ale with food and stopped smoking my junk altogether.

"You call temperance a 'burden?' Is that what makes you so flushed and angry whenever we talk?" Nehemiah asked as we sat in his parsonage.

"I have the right to be angry! My family's poverty delayed my entrance to college," I had never admitted this to myself, yet I blurted it to him, "and I was further humiliated by my low standing upon graduation—twentieth in a class of twenty-two!"

My pastor nodded more in encouragement of my confession than in agreement with it.

"Furthermore, I find myself in the wrong career! My own teachers were exact opposites at Cambridge Grammar School. Elijah Corlett had no control over the boys, he lacked any shred of discipline. Sir Hastings, on the other hand, was *all* discipline and couldn't teach at all—the Devil take them!"

"Fly to God, Joseph," my confessor smiled, ignoring my blasphemy, "get into Jesus Christ. He, not *you*, carries all our burdens."

Unwilling to accept my excuses, Reverend Walter insisted I study Thomas Doolittle's *Treatise Concerning the Lord's Supper* before we met again, after which he said he might consider accepting my confession.

"I have *not* prayed to God in secret, nor have I read the Scriptures daily," the confession I made to him was the same I would make to the Roxbury Church. "I have not kept the Sabbath holy, nor have I listened to sermons and lectures . . . ."

"Enough! Enough! Joseph, you are merely reciting the right words—

with no real meaning!'' Nehemiah Walter's customary ease with me became stern. "What does this passage mean to you? 'Forgive us our trespasses as we forgive those who have trespassed against us.''

"I have learned to forgive others . . .''

"Your father, John, for the poverty in which he, as an humble tailor, raised you?'' His upraised hand cautioned me. "Your teachers and your predecessor, about whom you have so bitterly complained?''

"If there were anything to forgive them for, Pastor, I have long since done so.''

"But have you asked to *be* forgiven? After all, you were an equal part of their failures. Had you been a better son, a more worthy pupil, you might now be a better teacher—you might even be ready for admission to the covenant . . .''

Reverend Walter dismissed me to let me brood over my sin of vanity, my other secret sins, and to think of Death, whether to be spent in Hell or Eternity.

It was not until the end of May, 1696, that my confession was acceptable to the pastor and congregation of Roxbury, a day of thanksgiving for my mother, Reverend Brattle, and myself.

Almost four months to the day that I had joined the church, I woke with the worst hangover ever!

"I return to drink like a dog to its vomit,'' I ashamedly admitted to Reverend Walter that same morning, expecting him to chastise me, as I surely would have scolded a pupil who had backslid. Instead, he began the Lord's Prayer and invited me to join him.

"I desire to return to God, as a poor prodigal;'' I stood again before the congregation, "and to be humbled before God that I have so long served the Devil and the lusts of my own heart. *Deo volente!*''

The warmth with which I was readmitted to the covenant encouraged me to accept invitations to preach and lecture in and around Boston. 'Think of Eternity' became my major theme, although I saw my true occupation as teaching not preaching, my anger at my pupils having been converted into love for them. It never entered my mind that each pulpit appearance I made drew me inexorably toward Salem Village. Had I any intimation, my dreamless sleep since my conversion might have brought on nightmares.

*   *   *

Asleep in my room at Roxbury, my right ear resting on Revelations Chapter 6, the pounding of what seemed horses' hooves stirred me. As the noise increased, the four horsemen merged into one, 'That diabolical centaur!' I tried to scream myself awake, which only served to bring the rider closer.

'That's no horse—some pupil's knocking on my door.' I rose on my forearms, "Begone! I'm preparing my lecture. Come back later, if you must . . ."

"Joseph Green?" A solemn voice, decidedly not a boy's, intoned. "We summon you to Salem Village . . ."

'Pray the Devil's work has not resumed!' My stomach griped as it had five years before on Gallows Hill. 'Pray I'm not called for some foolish accounting or contrived sin, Lord, I *have* been reborn and kept faithful . . .'

My mind raced faster than my feet as I rued ever having helped the Quakers that evil night.

"Master Green?" the more distinguished visitor of the pair opened as I ushered them into my room. "We are sent by vote of . . ."

'Lord have mercy on me.' The second visitor's military bearing increased my fear of arrest such that I failed to hear the speaker's words. 'Am I to share Reverend Burroughs' fate—commanded to return from Wells, Maine, to be hanged in Salem?'

"We are sent by vote of our church," I was attentive now, somewhat relieved that the church had sent them rather than the Court, and fought to control my inner trembling from becoming visible. ". . . in Salem Village, taken after a fast this October, to find ourselves a minister." He settled into my desk chair. "We invite you to preach this Sabbath."

Relieved, because I had no intention of leaving my school for any pulpit, let alone theirs, I served them beer. "Is not Simon Bradstreet presently your preacher?"

"Sadly," the taller visitor replied, "he tarried with us a bare six months and left early this year."

"And Nathaniel Rogers," interjected the military-looking villager, "preached only from February 'til September," he put his mug on my desk and extended his hand. "I am Captain John Putnam, head of our militia," his grip was strong. "My companion is Deacon Edward Putnam—Deacon Ingersoll's too ill to travel."

'Putnam, Putnam—how many villagers are Putnams?' My mind

raced as we chatted about their ride and the approaching winter, 'Neither of these is the Putnam I met, Providence be thanked!' I smiled to think of the centaur's apparition, a smile my visitors took, mistakenly, as my having agreed to preach to them.

"I warn you, Master Green, we expect a Taranteen attack some time this spring," Deacon Putnam offered.

"We're well prepared," Captain Putnam assured, "for the Indians by land or their diabolical allies, the French, by sea!"

Their manner calmed me, albeit I would count the hours before I could return to Roxbury, 'I want nothing to do with the French Fleet or I would have gone to sea with my brother, Edward. Nor may I let on how the very thought of Indians frightens me, the captain wouldn't tolerate that!'

"I would be honored to preach to you next week, you see me preparing such a sermon now," I motioned toward the opened Scripture, "and you may so inform your church."

"By the way," the deacon donned his coat; his companion opened the door, "please accept lodging with Reverend Gerrish of Wenham after your sermon." He looked uneasily at the captain who explained. "Samuel Parris, of whom you may have heard, has refused to vacate the parsonage."

So the visitors, whose entry had frightened me, frightened me at their exit! 'Will I be forced to face Reverend Parris?' The idea distracted me from further study, my only recollection of that pastor was his mad dash down Gallows Hill to stop the runaway cart. 'Putnam! That was her name—yet another Putnam!'

I tossed and sweat although the night was far from warm. Only when I recalled her name, 'Ann!' was I able to fall asleep. Sleep, however, brought with it that long-forgotten nightmare of a centaur's charging down upon me, musket at the ready. And so I woke, lit a candle, and wrote my sermon on the apocaplyse.

'When God finally destroys the Devil, pray that I may be raised among the Righteous.' I found this simple prayer comforting me on my ride to Salem Village. So, too, did having my musket in hand, wary of being waylaid by marauding Taranteens.

*   *   *

The incessant head-wagging of one woman distracted me from my sermon, but the tithingman had only one girl's head to tickle with his rod's squirrel tail, and so I felt my preaching was successful. No matter how carefully I searched the men's pews for the figure of my centaur, I could not recognize Joseph Putnam. 'Just as well, my curiosity is satisfied. After Wenham I'll be on my way.'

As I made my way across the Old Planters Farms, I had no premonition that I was on the first of countless visits to the Gerrish's.

"Greetings, Master Green," the young woman, almost as tall but slimmer than I, her face remarkably unpocked, opened the parsonage door. "We're about to sup. Mother's in the kitchen. Father's still at meeting."

"I'm obliged for your invitation . . ."

"Nonsense! What happenings have you witnessed in Boston?" she beckoned me to sit in the Carver chair. Angered by her abrupt manner, I pretended to warm myself by the hearth.

'Perhaps I'll shock her into civility,' I watched the turkey dangle from its winding cord. 'I'll tell her of the man I saw whipped forty lashes, a rope tight around his neck, condemned to wear a two inch cloth with the letter 'A' for having committed adultery!'

"The other day, in Salem," she blurted, setting two trenchers on the table, "a villager was punished for incest: lashed forty times, with a rope around her neck. She must forever wear a two inch 'I'—a just punishment, you must agree?"

I searched for a suitable reply and knocked the excess tobacco from my junk as a minister entered the room. Smaller than I, he had a commanding appearance, much the same as his daughter's.

"Father, Master Green is about to tell me of recent events in the Bay!"

"Tell your mother I'm famished," we shook hands, "as I'm sure our guest must be." He seated me beside him, a trencher of turkey and beans between us. "You see our humble condition—I've never recovered from the ravages of King Phillip's War—albeit Wenham has been good to us . . ."

"The parish *could* be more generous!"

"Enough, Beth! Nanna," he called his wife, "join us and meet Master Green."

"I can't abide Indians," I glanced at my musket near the hearth, "the father of one of my schoolboys was fined forty shillings just this week," I nodded toward his daughter, hoping the news would satisfy her, "for selling cider to an Indian!"

"Nonsense!" Beth almost choked on a spoonful of beans, "not cider—you must mean beer."

"No difference—cider and beer bring the same penalty," I defended, "It was cider!"

"That's unfair," she looked to her parents for their support, "we keep cider in an 'Indian Barrel'—for any who want to help themselves . . ."

"Beth . . . Elizabeth," her father interceded, "cider can be just as potent if left too long."

The tension broke when a young man about my age entered the parsonage and almost tripped over my musket. "I'm Beth's brother," he laughed as he sat across from me sharing a trencher with his sister. Goodwife Gerrish then left for the kitchen while Elizabeth cleared the table scraps into a voider.

"Let me pardon myself," her brother rose almost as quickly as he had sat, "two Josephs are enough for a chat—you don't need a third."

"My children are a quick-tongued lot, I fear," Reverend Gerrish lit our pipes, thereby missing my silent nod of agreement. "To return to what I mentioned, King William's War had a lot to do with Salem Village's troubles. What I mean to say is that Reverend Parris was a merchant, trading between here and the Barbados, and driven to poverty by French pirates." He puffed reflectively, "I do believe that Sam's failure in business led to his attempt to redeem himself at the expense of his parish."

"Diabolical French and Indians," was all I could muster, any topic about Salem Village having only remote interest to me. I knew, however, that politeness demanded I pay attention to my gracious host, who obliged me by filling my tankard.

"Why else would he humiliate Deacons Ingersoll and Putnam—such stalwarts of the church?"

"No sooner did Samuel Parris arrive," Elizabeth talked her way from the kitchen and seated herself on a stool beside her father, "than he suspended both of them for more than a year. They had to re-earn their standing in the church!"

"Making up for his poverty?" I recalled the bitterness I had felt at my own impoverished childhood.

"He even sent his daughter to safety after she'd been among the first to accuse others of witchcraft," his daughter's head wagged her disapproval.

"Beth, Beth! The gal was only nine years old . . ."

"Well, I don't fault *her*—but I *do* fault Sam for letting his slaves, Tituba and John Indian, take the blame!"

"Perhaps, Master Green," Joseph Gerrish leaned toward me, "you will take care to educate the young," his head pointed at Elizabeth, "for fear you'll pay the penalty of having them express themselves."

"Then," I found myself protecting his daughter whom I detected slightly flushed from his remark, "you believe the tragedy can be blamed on fear of a French invasion and Indian raids rather than Reverend Parris?"

"*I* don't!" Elizabeth jumped to stoke the fire.

"Blameless? No, Sam was not entirely without blame. However, he was strongly supported by Cotton Mather, and later by Nicholas Noyes of Salem Town . . ."

"There's more to it than that." The over-stoked fire roared an accompaniment to Elizabeth's anger. "All the while the Farmers were negotiating with Samuel Parris, they were knee-deep in squabbles among themselves . . ."

"Theological disputes?" I hoped to add something.

"Theological disputes!" Elizabeth triumphed at my expense, "*Property* disputes!"

"Sadly true," her father confirmed, motioning his daughter to refill our mugs. "Topsfield and Beverly claimed lands Thomas Putnam and others felt they owned. The Porters and Nurses sided against the Putnams . . ."

"I fail to see the significance of such disputes to the church," weary from the discussion, I hoped I might bring it to an early end.

"Let me, Father," Elizabeth took the tone to me that I often took when catechizing a stupid boy. "Sergeant Thomas Putnam, clerk of the church, was married to Ann Carr . . ." She held up one finger, "Her sister, Mary, was married to Reverend James Bayley, but she died soon after." Up went the second finger, then the third. "The Putnam-Bayley link was also a marriage between Property and Religion . . ."

"Elizabeth," uncomfortable with my discomfort, her father brushed her hand aside. "Bayley was accused of not keeping the Sabbath, not catechizing," he frowned at his daughter, "not holding family prayers, all of which the Putnams felt led to his wife's early death . . ."

"I wonder?"

"All right, Beth. Bayley became so bitter he refused to return to preach this past year, 'though he was invited shortly after Goody Parris died."

"You help me understand why Salem Village has such a bad reputation throughout New England," I shifted, my back toward Elizabeth. 'One invitation to preach to that contentious lot more than satisfies my curiosity.'

"Sadly, his wife did not live to hear her husband's greatest sermon," the tremor in Elizabeth's voice made me feel I had insulted her, and so I stood, stretched my legs, and sat to face her, fascinated by her varying moods.

"Using the Sixth Commandment as his text," her tremor was replaced by reverence, "Samuel argued that the Lord forbade all anger without cause . . ."

"Quite an interpretation of 'Thou shalt not kill,' " for a person so easily angered, I felt deeply about the issue—or had I begun to feel for Elizabeth?

"The Inhabitants felt they were all guilty for Elizabeth Parris' death," Reverend Gerrish cleaned his pipe into the fireplace, "perhaps they were right." Fetching the Scripture from the mantle, he then led us in evening prayers.

"You'll have my bed," young Joseph re-entered, "I'll sleep in the garret."

"Please, make no fuss about me," I acknowledged Joseph's nod while I addressed his mother. "I'll be off to Cambridge before bevers."

"Perhaps you'll bring me more exciting news from the Bay next week, Master Green," Elizabeth's parting remark startled me.

"Dear me! I forgot!" Reverend Gerrish chuckled, "a messenger from Salem Village met me at the church, that's why I was late—you're invited to preach next week . . ."

"And welcome to stay with us again," his wife added loud enough for her departing daughter to hear.

The knowledge that I would return to Salem Village made my night's sleep less comfortable than it might have been. My long ride home the next day was made more comfortable, however, by the knowledge that, Providence willing, I would again visit with Elizabeth, whose manners—vacillating between brash and sentimental—strangely attracted me.

*   *   *

Providence willed otherwise . . .

"Reverend Parris has vacated the parsonage," Deacon Putnam yelled as I approached the meeting house rail, "but you're to lodge at Deacon Ingersoll's ordinary."

Distressed by the deacon's information, I expressed my anger by detailing the agony of a man from Cambridge as he suffered a whipping on the pillory, followed by having his tongue bored with a red hot iron. It was a story I had intended for Elizabeth, but it fit my sermon against the evil of blasphemy. In fact, the more livid my description, the quieter the Farmers became, including that older woman of the week before who put aside her scribbling to glower at me.

"A very telling sermon," Deacon Putnam congratulated me. "Tabitha Deal commented on your sincerity—rarely does a sermon quiet that woman! You will bless us with your presence next Sabbath?"

"*Deo volente!*" I gambled that I might see Elizabeth, although the farthest thing from my mind was to encourage the villagers to offer me a position, a thought that chilled me as I saw a horseman approach—the centaur of Gallows Hill.

"My half-brother, Joseph," the deacon's graciousness disappeared as he walked away from me.

"Daniel Andrews would have a word with you in the ordinary," as had been the case five years before, his musket seemed to command me. "You and I had *our* talk the night those eight innocents were *murdered.* . . ."

"Blasphemy! You know the penalty . . ."

"Murder!" his horse nudged me to the door of the ordinary.

"You visited Wenham last week," the stiff, older man, whom I took to be Daniel Andrews, began without further introduction. "My property abuts John Leach's near the Wenham line."

"Yes, I was entertained . . ."

"Hear that, Putt! Mister Green was *entertained* and on the Sabbath!"

"You, you understand what I mean." I fumbled my way behind the pair to a rear table.

"Not at all. Not at all! What *do* you mean, Sir?"

"Cousin!" Joseph Putnam touched my inquisitor's arm while he looked at me. "We Farmers have undergone an eternity of confusion brought on by speakers' using words with private meanings, Samuel Parris in particular."

The cider warmed me, although it seemed a little spoiled, and so I only sipped it while the waiter filled our trenchers.

"Cousin Andrews has served our parish well, serving as tutor . . ."

"But I fled during the trials, while you, Putt, fought Parris, your half-brothers, and your shittabed niece . . ."

"Daniel," I realized they had been over this ground many times, but why were they staging this scene for me? "You'd been served a warrant, your house searched . . ." The older man waved to change the topic and so Putnam turned to me. "It's taken the Inhabitants five long years to get Reverend Parris to leave."

"He has turned the minds of prospective pastors against us," Sir Andrews softened, "taken the church to court for money he said was due him, a suit he won, and through one or another trickery managed to stay on until Deacon Ingersoll bought him out."

Putt refilled our mugs with cider whose taste was tangier than before. 'I must be careful lest I profane myself with drunkenness,' I cautioned myself but gulped more to calm the dryness of my throat. The effect, however, was to upset my stomach. 'Is it the sour cider or the distasteful conversation that makes me feel ill?' The rumble in my belly offered no answer.

"Surely, gentlemen," I felt that talking might ease my discomfort but it only added to it, "you have forgiven your former pastor his follies?"

"Follies!" Andrews banged his fist on the table and spilled whatever cider remained in our mugs.

"*Murders,* that's a better word than 'follies,' Master Green," Joseph Putnam's intensity frightened me as much as had his musket.

"I remind you of his final sermon, against 'murder' in any of its forms," I brushed their objections aside, "including that of character assassination!"

"A superb lesson," Sir Andrews admitted but his companion was so furious he rose from the table, supported by his clenched fists. "Remember, Putt, John Tarbell was so swayed he wondered if we'd done right by Sam Parris?"

Without a further word, Joseph Putnam motioned his cousin to follow him out the door, annoyed when Daniel Andrews stopped to have a final word.

"Were it not for Sam's angelic wife, Elizabeth, we Farmers might have rid ourselves of him and his diabolical doings much earlier."

'Murderer,' Putnam's lips formed the unspoken word for my benefit, his cousin having preceded him from the ordinary.

I knew a dream-filled night awaited me and chose to face it on an empty stomach. Forcing myself to vomit, I steadied my wobbly knees by leaning against the shed behind the ordinary. The cold November night did not, however, dispel my fears, albeit it cleared my head.

'You're not going to sleep without nightmares, and when you wake you'll still have the ride to Cambridge.' Decided, I bade goodbye to Deacon Ingersoll, explaining that my Roxbury students expected me early the next day, and spent most of the night in my saddle en route home. Whenever sleep overcame me, relaxing my grip on my musket, the spectre of Joseph Putnam alerted me. Try as I might to shift my thoughts to Elizabeth Gerrish, the controversies surrounding the ministry in Salem Village consumed me.

"The serpent, its body coiled round and round the tree, taunts the squirrel with its gleaming eyes . . ."

"Relax, Joseph," Reverend Brattle, to whom I had come for counsel, poured us cider and offered me a corn cake. "Continue with your dream when you feel up to it."

"In the upper branches of the same tree, the squirrel frolics from limb to limb, trying to avoid that piercing stare from below . . . Does that mean something?"

"It's hard for me to say. Do you recognize anything about the squirrel?"

"Yes, yes, I see my former roisterous habits in him—but they're behind me now!"

"Are they? Of course, you no longer blaspheme, break the Sabbath, and so forth," it comforted me to know he understood that I had kept the covenant, "but have you not preached at Salem Village since this nightmare began?"

"Twice—no, three times in December, after each of which my nightmare got worse until . . ."

"Until?"

"What made me seek your help was Salem Village's invitation to become its pastor!"

"So, Joseph, the squirrel must decide whether to frolic in the tree . . ."

". . . or leap into the serpent's jaws!" I choked on too large a swig of cider, "that doesn't leave me great choice!"

"This is a year for choice-making about Salem Village, once your mind is free of apparitions, my young friend."

"You mean like Judge Sewall's confession at the Old South Church?"

"You're paying better attention now," he served me salt pork and beans as I poured the ale. "He stood before us all to beg God's pardon for himself and all concerned in the frenzy."

"Wasn't he moved to confess because of the sudden death of his daughter a few days before?"

"Who knows how Providence works? Could it be that *you* are lured toward Salem Village by something—or perhaps someone—rather than by morbid curiosity?"

I had told him about having met the Gerrishes, but it came as a surprise to me that Elizabeth might appear as the serpent of my dreams. That the squirrel represented me, I had no doubt. I could also visualize the Inhabitants, especially Joseph Putnam, Daniel Andrews, and that crone, Tabitha Deal, personified in the serpent. But I found it hard to admit I had such mixed feelings about Elizabeth: alluring, yes; but as repugnant as a snake?

"Your mind wanders, Joseph, perhaps we should postpone our conversation."

I agreed with his suggestion, promised to concentrate on the real issues behind my decision, and meet with him the next evening in his rooms. As I might have expected, my dream was not of a squirrel and serpent, but of the future I might share with a woman so attractive yet outspoken as Elizabeth.

"It worries me, greatly, I might add," Reverend Brattle set the tone as he drew deeply on his pipe, having seated me beside him at his desk, "that you are so prone to nightmares. Your dreams are filled with spectres—centaurs, serpents, and so on—such as my brother, Thomas, and I have strongly essayed against."

"I've read your letter addressed to the 'Salem Gentlemen' in which you inveigh against spectral evidence such as that used in the witchcraft proceedings.''

"But you stand on the threshold of becoming pastor to Salem Village, a community whose Farmers are filled with superstition, and all the while *you* dare entertain spectres of one sort or another! Believe me, you must put such superstitions behind you if you are to be worthy of your calling. Study whatever you can of the New Science. The Lord gave it to us to use toward His ends. Of course, you'll find some of your colleagues, like Nicholas Noyes . . .''

"One of the 'S.G.' to whom your letter referred?''

". . . opposed to any knowledge which has arisen since he went to school. You, however, must not see Reverend Noyes as your foe, no matter how resentful he may be toward the church in Salem Village. Like the Mathers, Nicholas deplores most of the newer churches and almost all their young ministers.''

'At only twenty-two, who am I to contest with any ordained minister?'

"Divided though the ministry may seem, the Church stands alone against Satan, whose current spokesman, John Locke, insists that government be predicated upon ownership of property . . .''

"Rather than upon membership in the covenant?''

"Exactly!'' He poured me a tankard of cider while he reviewed his notes. "But you'll not deal with philosophers like Locke, not among your isolated villagers. Instead, these great issues will appear to you as small spats within families, between farmers, and within yourself.''

"Like Phillip English's seizure of Sheriff Curwin's body earlier this year?''

"Typical of what you may expect. Curwin had confiscated the High-Flier's property five years ago during the trials and English waited to get even. This is the kind of fire you'll have to douse while the Mathers and Brattles in Boston, and the likes of Noyes and Wise in your area . . .''

"John Wise?''

"The same. Once imprisoned by the governor and warned that his only right as an Englishman was not to be sold into slavery; later, the scourge of Samuel Parris,'' he smiled, "you didn't know that, eh? Now the foe of Nicholas Noyes.''

"Perhaps the pastorate is too much for me to handle?''

"Ridiculous! I didn't mean to *dis*suade you but to *per*suade you—but not out of ignorance about the situation throughout New England, and especially its outlying parishes. You now know what conflicts to expect: Commerce versus Religion for supremacy; charterless New England versus Old England; growing numbers of people moving to the hinterlands needing new churches and pastors and opposed by old-timers; and, worst of all, a church and ministry fractionated by the New Science's inroads against spectral evidence—false witness—and superstition."

"I shall accept the call." I rose to leave.

"You never really had a choice, my friend, except to equip yourself for settling the disputes which undermine Salem Village and which will surface in diabolical ways."

"Will Providence be my only ally?" I pled. "Except for yourself? How about Daniel Andrews?"

"A well-educated rhetorician, known for having defended Reverend Bayley against the charge of blasphemy—but also the man who made sure that Deodat Lawson was never ordained by the church . . . I don't mean to smile on your misfortune, but Andrews is no sure ally."

"With pastors as difficult as Reverends Noyes and Wise there . . ."

"Add John Hale, author of *A Modest Enquiry into The Nature of Witchcraft*—he's nearby, at Beverly . . ."

"I, I was thinking of Joseph Gerrish, too."

"He's knowledgeable about past events, was rather neutral during the trials, and probably knows more about another nemesis, the Indians, than anyone else. Otherwise, you can eliminate him, too." Reverend Brattle threw my coat over my shoulders, chuckling quietly, "Now, were you to suggest Gerrish's *daughter* as your partner . . ."

"How . . . how did you know?"

"You, like Nicholas Noyes, are an idler—a bachelor!" He laughed, "You'll find we discuss more at ministers' councils than you've been led to expect!"

"I confess, I have some doubts about Elizabeth . . ."

"Expect her to have as many about you. Now, go home, compose yourself, say your prayers, and read the Scripture. You're as ready as you'll ever be to meet the Salem Village delegation tomorrow night."

Although my head was filled with the pros and cons surrounding the pastorage at Salem Village, my sleep was the calmest I had experienced in weeks, made so by having read and reread Hebrews 7:2. And so, when the deacons arrived at my lodgings that night, I was at peace.

"Gentlemen, I accept your invitation to serve as minister," they bowed their heads, "in the spirit of *peace,* which according to the Scripture is the meaning of 'Salem'." I waited until they looked me in the eye, never having felt as much in command of myself. "My terms are: first, that *you* continue to live in peace," I paused, "or I shall be free of my obligation to you and will leave."

I wondered how Daniel Andrews might have reacted had he been among the delegation.

"Second, that I receive the parsonage and its land as long as I live," remembering their difficulty with Parris, I added, "*and serve* among you, with sixty pounds salary for my first year and seventy pounds thereafter," following Reverend Brattle's instruction, I emphasized, "besides strangers' money." This clause, innocent at the time, would later cloud my relations with the church.

"Finally, should I then decide to remain in Salem Village, something of my own." I worried that I might have sounded too much like the Trader Parris but rationalized that the contract was one of both Commerce and Religion.

Their acceptance of my terms led me to begin my six months' probation in January, 1698.

'Six months in which to become ordained by Salem Village! How long to become betrothed to Elizabeth Gerrish?' I celebrated after the deacons had left with enough canary to dispel any thoughts but those of Elizabeth from my dreams.

3   Do Nothing Rashly

"Whoa! Whoa, Pastor!" Captain Putnam fairly pulled me from my saddle. "You almost knocked my fence down . . . Now that you're here, give me a hand with this rail."

"But, but . . ." I tugged the reins from his grasp, "Shouldn't we be off to Haverhill?"

"*As ma*," he laughed, "not yet! If you're worried about Frontenac and his murderous Taranteens, have no fear." He helped me dismount, handing me a split rail to hold. "I've more than two dozen scouts in the field—they advise me to wait."

"Well I came prepared to march with you to Haverhill," I slapped my rapier proudly.

"Foolish, Master Green, utterly foolish!"

Silently, we fixed the fence, our heated feelings warming us against the morning chill.

"About Haverhill . . ."

"Pastor, you've been with us briefly, not yet admitted to our fellowship. If you persisit in butting into affairs that don't concern you— you may yet be denied admittance . . . It's happened before!"

'Is this the same gentleman who was so quiet when he visited me at Roxbury Latin School?'

"Your harping about Haverhill sounds like Goodman Gedney who prosecutes the war from the safety of Salem Town! I'll have you know, *I'm* in command of the militia. When I say, *as ma,* my word is law . . ."

"I only meant to help," I calmed my horse and prepared to remount.

"Ever since that renegade, Thomas Morton, taught the Taranteens to use guns, we've been under brutal attack. You wouldn't understand— you've been safely tucked away in Boston." He hammered at the rail we had set in place. "Well, I'm not about to risk men's lives in some foolish foray against a slippery enemy. You, Pastor, have concern for their souls, but I'm *sog mo* here—my concern is for their very lives." Holding my horse's reins, he shook his hatchet at me. "Only a few years ago, Captain Lathrop led his men into an ambush—the massacre at Bloody Creek. Our village cannot tolerate such folly. As commander of the militia, I refuse to be panicked by the likes of you!"

'Why is my horse so much calmer under the captain's hand than mine?' I waited impatiently for him to release me.

"Why, when I was your age, not yet thirty?" I nodded. "We had a handful of savages surrounded. 'We are dead!' their leader cried to our delight. 'Let us sell our lives dearly!' With that," his shaking hand startled my horse, "they fought their way out of our trap . . ."

Freed from his grasp, my horse began to chew at the stubble.

"You stopped here on your way to Wenham, I suspect." He tossed my musket to me. "Ride East to Jonathan Putnam's then head North 'til you reach a fork. Be sure to bear right or you'll be out in the woods, where you could lose your *wha gakw!* He doffed his cap and laughingly pulled at his wig. "Pass Daniel Andrews' house—you know the rest of the route."

Heeding his instructions, I tugged my horse from its grazing.

"If you see any hostiles," he shouted through cupped hands, "use your musket! Otherwise, you may be the first killed hereabouts since Deacon Putnam's servant, Nicholas Reed, got scalped ten years ago!"

Long after his homestead had disappeared from sight, his guffaws rang in my ears. 'Why have militia if not to deploy it against the enemy? Aren't the people of Haverhill as much our neighbors as those from Ipswich or Beverly? I'll devote a lecture to the militia,' my distress lessened as I considered a suitable Scripture, but the tug of my horse broke my reverie. We had reached the fork, the animal heading to the right while I urged him left. 'Defeated by a dumb brute!'

I gave the horse full rein toward Wenham.

"What brings you here, your horse in such a lather?" Elizabeth stroked its snout.

"News of the Haverhill Raid," I twisted the truth; I needed little excuse to see her again.

"We're in no danger. You should've checked with Captain Putnam—he's *sog mo* for the village." I handed her my musket and dismounted.

"*Sog mo!*" my voice betrayed my distress. "*You* use that pagan tongue?"

"*Nedarenandwe,*" her tone suggested she enjoyed my discomfort. "Yes, 'I speak man . . .'"

"Speak man? Whatever do you mean?" What I had hoped would be a pleasant conversation was becoming another confrontation with this woman always a jump ahead of me.

"The Taranteens acknowledge no ancestors. When they said, 'I speak Man,' the phrase means they speak Abenaki." Her hand brushed mine, intentionally I was sure, as she tied my horse by the house. Her touch caused me to let my guard down.

"If you know so much, why is it these savages are called 'Taranteens?"

"The early colonists were befriended by an Indian named Atironta," her soft-spoken words did little to assuage me, "I guess 'Taranteen' was as close as they could come to pronouncing his name."

Having been embarrassed twice in one morning, my gruffness encouraged rather than discouraged her.

"Colonists from New York call them the 'Owenagungas.' Why, I'm not sure . . ."

"Do I smell fresh bread?" Elizabeth reached the door and entered before I could help her.

"You *do* manage to arrive at mealtime." She forced a chuckle which did not calm me and pointed toward the dutch oven in the fireplace. "The French, however, call the Indians after their main river, the Kennebec."

My humor began to return as I carried the steaming oven to the table. Beth took the moment to write a note from a book she had left on the table.

"The French slurred Kennebec into 'Canibas,'" exasperated, I juggled and almost dropped the oven as Elizabeth concluded "or 'Kani-bals . . .' Steady, steady, Joseph. That's all I can tell you—the rest you'll have to learn for yourself."

The hot bread dripped with fresh butter, made more tasty by a few mugs of cider. Although I had left the village intent to alert Captain Putnam and assure myself of Elizabeth's safety, the morning's events left me in no mood for small talk. My deepest worry remained upper-most in my thoughts: how the Church would vote over my forthcoming confession. I had hoped to discuss this with Elizabeth but kept my fears to myself. Consumed by my own thoughts, I mentioned that I had better get an early start home.

"Don't expect the Abenakis to warn before attacking," she coun-seled with unusual seriousness as she stood beside my horse. "Keep your musket ready. Remember, they travel in small, family-size groups . . ."

My slight tremble made my horse wriggle and further stimulated my hostess.

"You know, Joseph, their Great Spirit, Gluskabe, promised to drive us 'White Eyes' from New England."

"Surely, you don't *believe* that," my grip on the reins brought a neigh from my horse and a laugh from Elizabeth.

"Why, Gluskabe once bent the sides of a church bell so it couldn't warn our 'people from whence coming from yonder' of a dawn attack!" She slipped the note she had written into my boot. "Here, read this when you get home . . ."

'If there's anything I don't need to hear before my journey, it's this Satanic story! As if I don't have enough bother with the Farmers' upcoming vote. She thoroughly confuses, yet strangely intrigues me.'

Before I could compose myself, Elizabeth had slipped inside the parsonage. Embroiled in my thoughts, I missed the fork leading to Meeting House Road and was well past the Phillipps' place beside the Wooden Bridge before I retraced my path and headed to Ingersoll's ordinary—arriving far too late for supper.

As I jerked off my boots in disgust, Elizabeth's note fell to the floor. Curious about its contents, yet reluctant to read it, I said my prayers and read the Scripture first.

'If in a soldier rashness be so precious,
Know in a general 'tis most pernicious.'

I smiled in appreciation of Elizabeth's selection from Anne Bradstreet's *Melancholy*. 'Even in my solitude, Beth has the last word.'

*   *   *

"Goodman Andrews!" I clutched the pulpit to restrain my rage. "Declare, once and for all, are you or are you *not* satisfied with my confession to this congregation?"

My outburst startled the tithingman such that he whacked Tabitha Deal with the knob end of his pole rather than tickle her with its squirrel tail. Goody Deal, who had taken me aside before my last lecture to say that the Haverhill Raid was a Special Providence brought upon New England for its support of the Anti-Christ, rubbed her head— a severe penalty for having fallen asleep during Andrews' tirade.

'I'll deal with the tithingman for his grievous error—albeit he broke the monotony of Daniel's pedantry and may have helped my cause.'

It bothered me that I had been so careful to lay a foundation for acceptance by the Farmers in a visit with Goodman Andrews the past week. At that time, his vote for me seemed assured—now he opposed accepting my confession!

Elizabeth had arranged for me to meet with her tutor at her father's parsonage. While she made whistle-belly-vengeance, simmered the sour beer, added molasses, hops, and a sprinkle of bread crumbs, he challenged me.

"Are *you*, Master Green, in a conjugal state?"

Caught off guard, I showed disbelief that he should begin with such a question.

"We already suffer one bachelor in this patent. Noisy Noyes, whose idleness and unwillingness to assume conjugal responsibility an*noys* us," he smirked, "We would not tolerate a *green* idler . . ."

With Elizabeth out of earshot, I assured him I had decided to marry, after counsel with William Brattle and correspondence with my mother. Whom I might ask to become my wife was not his business, although most Farmers suspected it would be Joseph Gerrish's daughter.

A rhythmic thumping from within the closet beneath my pulpit drew my attention back to the meeting. 'I'll talk with Ben Hutchinson tomorrow about his son's misbehavior.' The stomp of my foot momentarily quieted the boy.

"Does Master Green agree," Andrews, ignoring my call for a vote, continued, "with Thomas Hooker?"

'We've covered that topic.' I refrained from criticizing him aloud, 'I assured you of my belief in his doctrine during our ride from Wenham to your homestead.'

"Do you agree, as you stand in our pulpit, that a minister is created by the congregation—and not beforehand?"

I scowled disapproval at young Ann Putnam for toying with the ornament on her pew, the squeaks distracted attention from the issue.

"I do, Goodman Andrews . . ." Before he questioned me further, I added, "that ordination signifies only the approval by the congregation—nothing more."

My reply drew an assenting nod from Goodwife Deal. 'I must not enrage Daniel or others may join him in opposing my confession.'

Catching sight of the Putnam gals' passing herbs through the slits in their pew reminded me of the scene I had witnessed upon entering Andrews' home the past week. With no school in the village, children were sent to him for catechizing and tutoring. As we entered, they lined up before him, toes abutting a crack in the floor, prepared to recite their lessons. Upset though I now was, I was impressed by him then, as he criticized them the way he was criticizing me.

"You *are* a good Ramist," Andrews sought agreement from other Inhabitants, "your logic allows me to diagram your sermons with ease."

Ignoring approval from either side of the meeting house, he lectured about the importance of using simple language, citing Sam Parris as a bad example. In doing so, however, he lost Goodwife Deal's support.

'The last thing I want is for the Farmers to base their vote for or against me on the record of my predecessor!'

The approach of darkness caused some of those who lived farthest from the meeting house to prepare to leave before the vote, 'If darkness falls before the vote, delaying members from their journeys, it might further discredit me. Do be more considerate, Daniel . . .'

He had been most considerate when the swineherd's horn interrupted our conversation at his farm.

"My worry," I cautioned him at the time, "is that I sometimes take a formal approach to God. I treat Him more like a stern superior than a loving friend.'' We goaded his pigs into the shed before the sun set.

"Sometimes my mind brings me very good frames, only to have them dispelled by Satanic ones . . .''

Goody Andrews dismissed my worries with a grin as he led my horse to me.

"In spite of the aid I've received,'' I mounted as he handed me my musket, "I confess I suffer from ephialtes . . .''

"Plain style!'' Andrews bellowed then as he did now before the assembly. "Plain style! I object to your language, Master Green. Your use of fancy words, ephialtes instead of nightmares, suggests you may be a merit-monger!''

Thus said, he had whacked my horse and plummeted us down the road. 'If only I could whack him now,' I bemoaned, embarrassed by his betrayal of my confidence.

As if in answer to my prayer, Joseph Putnam made his way to the pulpit with corn as a partial fulfillment of his rate. Putt's action fazed his uncle.

"Master Green,'' Daniel Andrews modulated his voice, his arms outstretched to me and then the congregation, "I am satisfied with your confession. I call upon my fellow Inhabitants to approve your joining our covenant . . . We await your blessing.''

Before my closing prayer had ended, pews banged, crickets toppled, and the Farmers rushed for the door. John Deal stuffed his paper-wrapped money in the box and left his wife to finish her scribbling.

The noise of the congregation's exist echoed off the sounding-board which swung perilously above my head. Fearful that it might fall, I chased the Hutchinson boy from the pulpit closet and climbed down the stairs of the empty meeting house.

Before I shut the door and dismissed our armed sentinel, I read aloud in thanks the motto inscribed on the octagonal sounding-board, *"Deo volente!''*

*   *   *

'Your forthcoming ordination,' I reread my mother's recent letter on my way to Wenham, 'makes you worthy of anyone's hand in marriage, albeit your father was but an humble tailor . . .'

A comforting thought, since I had committed myself to getting married, but followed, as so often in my mother's manner, by her addendum, 'Even Rev. Gerrish's daughter, of whom Rev. Brattle speaks so highly . . .'

'Approach this decision logically,' I cautioned myself, 'as you would a lecture. Pose a question to yourself, then list answers for and against Elizabeth.'

Letting my horse pick its way along the route it knew so well, the foremost question was whether Beth's education would help or hinder my ministry.

'Schooling is reported to have driven more than one woman insane. It could happen to her. She's already outspoken with her own family—what's to stop her from upsetting members of your flock? And what about her preference for Anne Bradstreet, when she might read Michael Wigglesworth?'

"Whoa!" I reined my horse too abruptly as I tried to shift my thoughts to a more positive vein. Fortunately, he forgave me and continued his pace. 'Education makes Beth a helpmate. Her choice of reading fills gaps in your own knowledge, a valuable trait for a minister's wife, especially as isolated as you are from Boston.'

"Aha!" My horse took my outburst as a signal to trot. 'But isn't she already too close to the Farmers . . . the accusing gals of '92 are all about her age? On the other hand, she had the wisdom not to join them—that's in her favor!'

Sight of the Wenham parsonage hurried my thoughts. 'You two are equally willful, although her confidence makes up for your foolhardiness . . .

'Is not her trust in Indians foolhardy?' It disturbed me that she was at ease about the Taranteens, especially that she spoke their tongue. 'That may be to your advantage: she knows the patent well. You have yet to prove yourself in these surroundings.'

The sight of Elizabeth, standing beside the well-sweep, upset my careful calculations as a glow of warmth overwhelmed me.

"You chose a wonderful day for a ride," she gushed as she mounted the pillion behind me, securing her feet on the wooden bar. "Take the southern fork, through the Old Planters Farms. The Selectmen of Salem oversee the common fields to assure that everyone contributes to the fencing."

She had me at a disadvantage. I had either to shout into the wind to make myself heard or turn in my saddle and break my horse's gait.

"That's why the commonage has only two rails per fence while each farm is likely to have five—such as the one you saw at the Andrews' . . ."

"You've learned of my visit?" I shouted.

"And *more!*"

I slowed my horse in anticipation of my rider's next words, but she was strangely quiet, and so we broke into a trot. 'That's another point against her. Unlike my dear mother, Beth stops in the middle of a sentence to disquiet me.'

"Phew!" I broke the silence. "That stench of rotting fish! Doesn't the smell bother you?"

"Without those stinking fish, we'd have no crops from this barren soil for food or export." Her soft pat on my back, intended to calm me, irritated me. I supposed she had sensed my tension, for she spoke quietly, her mouth as close as she could get to my ear.

"Father thinks you should know that Tabitha Deal's been rumoring that the Taranteen Raid was a special providence . . ."

"A special providence . . . of what?" Jerking around in my saddle forced my horse to stumble and Elizabeth clutched my chest to avoid falling.

"Because of Cotton Mather's ex-communication of Mercy Short."

"She deserved it!"

"For adultery, wasn't it, Joseph?" Rather than risk another stumble, I let a nod suffice. "Poor Mercy . . . Captured by the Indians at Salmon Falls in '90, ransomed later, and then become deranged . . ."

"Ah, yes! But also saved by Cotton Mather—'though she failed to eat for more than two weeks."

"Poor Mercy, to have suffered yet another disgrace, and at the hands of Cotton . . ."

"Wait, Beth, that's no way to talk! Why, Reverend Mather's *Humiliations Followed With Deliverances* is an excellent warning to all backsliders . . ."

"I blame John Emerson, too. Imagine, claiming that 'spectral Indians' were seen at Salmon Falls. It's nonsense like that which disturbs people such as Goody Deal!"

Silent with exasperation, I continued west of the Great Pond until we intercepted the Ipswich Road where Elizabeth asked to rest. 'You've committed yourself to marriage—but is *she* the right woman? She seems to ally herself with sinners rather than saints.'

"There's the Herrick home," she pointed eastward, "on the other side of Alford's Hill." Beth picked a wildflower, the midday sun twinkling in her eyes. "I remember when they cleared this area, felled the trees, and piled them to dry. The bonfire they lit could be seen for miles! A year later, they burned the stumps, but it took another year before the roots had rotted enough for planting to begin."

'Now you're witnessing another Elizabeth,' I admired, delighted in the change of topic. "Such hard work, but worth it to see field after field of corn and onions. Which way now: across the Horse Bridge to my village or to Beverly?"

"I chose earlier, you choose now."

'If you're seeking someone like your mother, Elizabeth is not the one! She wants nothing more than to be your equal, neither lesser nor better than you . . .'

Never having visited the saw or grist mills along the Bass River, I chose Beverly. Helping Beth mount her pillion, a thrill ran through me, although I wasn't sure my horse liked the double load.

"Let's stop at Exercise Conant's, Joseph, he's having a horse race today!"

'Is there anything that goes on in this patent of which she's unaware?' My doubt slowed us such that we arrived just as the race ended.

"Congratulations, Deacon Woodbury," Beth hailed, then whispered, "don't you wish you could ride so well?"

We bore toward the right, past the Rayment farm, toward Captain Dodge's sawmill. Although I had no way of knowing it at the time, this would only be the first of her many criticisms about my horsemanship, most of which I deserved and yet resented.

"The village stocks and pillory are in bad shape, Beth."

"Negotiate with the sawyer. He's just come from Old England. Unlike his predecessor, who was pilloried and forced to pay double for overcharging, he's an honest man." She let herself down without my help, "The lumber's local; the logs come from the West Indies."

After I bargained with the sawyer, I suggested to my partner that we omit visiting the gristmill.

"I'm surprised so many men are working at the sawmill . . ."

"Why not, Beth? You know, idleness . . ."

"The constable should have turned them out to cultivate the fields or mend the commonage fences . . ."

"Land! LAND! has been the Idol of many in New England," I pointed upwards for emphasis.

"That doesn't sound like you, Joseph."

"A quote from Increase Mather," we laughed, allowing my horse to carry us north past the Balch farm. Nearing Conant's again, squeals announced a pig-run in progress, Beth's squeeze choked me in delight.

Entering Wenham, we found the leather-aproned blacksmith repairing farm implements. His rafters were hung with hoes, hinges, and plows, but my eye caught sight of an object my brother, Percival, had described to me many years before.

"Look, Beth! I haven't seen a bilboes since I visited Boston wharf as a boy."

"They used to be plentiful hereabouts, the stocks and pillory have replaced them, though. See, they shackled the offender's legs and then padlocked them—quite effective for aboard ship . . ."

'Does she know everthing?' I shook my head and struck it on a globe of hollow iron that also dangled from the roof. Elizabeth's warm words and warmer hands soothed my bump.

"I suppose you know what *that* infernal device is?" I groaned, exasperated with my clumsiness and Beth's know-it-all attitude.

"No," she puzzled, turning the globe about. "It's got iron straps, and here, toward the ceiling, a lock and bolt." Offering her hand to shield me from another stumble, she admitted, "I can't say I've ever seen such a device."

Recovered from my blow, my pride was enhanced by knowing something she did not. I said it was often used in Old England but rarely here.

"Don't tease, Joseph. Tell me for what crime it's used!" Waving toward the threatening sky, I helped her mount and we finished our ride in silence.

'You've painted yourself into a corner. Providence willing, you'll be headed home before she remembers that contraption.'

Dismounted, my horse's reins in my hand, Elizabeth begged, "Tell me! What *was* that globe on which you hit your head?"

"A brank," she put her hand on mine to stop me from mounting.

"Go on . . ."

"It was put around a person's head, sometimes with a piece of spiked iron inserted in the mouth and locked." Beth frowned. "The offender wore it for as long as the Court determined."

"How horrible!" she released my arm. "I suppose no worse than having an ear lopped off, or being stocked, pilloried, branded, or whipped . . ."

Uncomfortable at the conversation and the rapidly approaching dusk, I lit my pipe and shielded it against the drizzle.

"Speaking of crimes, Master Green—tobacco smoking brings a two-shilling six-pence fine . . ."

"Come, come, Beth—that law's as hard to enforce as the one against wearing wigs."

"Joseph," she reached for my reins but I held them higher, "you've put me off again. Without further ado—for what crime was the brank used?"

"If your curiosity's got the better of you," I coughed a cloud of smoke, "to punish a scolding woman!"

"Oh ho!" she pranced away from me. "And did you bang your head on that contraption purposely," she sprang to my side, "just to instruct *me?*"

The drizzle fell from my cap onto her forehead as I bent to kiss her.

"Shame on you!" she laughed, running through the downpour to the house. Turning at the door, she was bound to have the last word, "Sailor Higbe recently spent two hours in the stocks—for kissing his own wife!"

"In *public* . . ." I defended, my horse growing restless.

"His *wife*—whom he hadn't seen in three years!"

". . . on the Sabbath!" We shouted such that I was afraid we might be punished if someone overheard.

"His *wife*, Joseph, W-I-F-E!" Elizabeth disappeared inside the parsonage.

Although I was drenched, my horse seemed to delight in the rain, seemingly going out of its way to splash me through each puddle, yet bearing me home before the Sabbath fell.

'Do nothing rashly,' I read from my Commonplace Book of the previous year, 'but do all things with advice and consideration.'

'Your impetuous kiss, rash though it was, sealed your commitment to Elizabeth—Ramist logic notwithstanding.' Blasphemous though I knew it to be, I chuckled to myself as I read the Scriptures before going to bed.

*   *   *

John Deal winced, never whimpered, each time the whip bit into his bare back. When I asked why he had missed the past Sabbath's services, he said he had fallen into his well the day before—no excuse for his absence from services. How the church members might have felt had they known that Tabitha had pushed him into the well, I couldn't be sure, that information never came to light during the deacons' questioning. Therefore, following my Thursday lecture, he suffered his punishment.

Had I known of Tabitha's treachery, I would not have chosen my text from 12 Ecclesiastes. "Never trust your enemy," I aimed the passage at Goodman Deal, "Do not have him at your side, or he will trip you up . . ."

John squirmed when he listened but sat upright as I continued. "If disaster overtakes you, you will find him there ahead of you, ready, with a pretence of help, to pull your feet from under you!"

That's what had happened: pretending to help her husband, Goodwife Deal had purposely tripped him.

"Then he will nod his head and rub his hands and spread gossip," I shifted my attention to the women's pews where Tabitha sat without scribbling, "showing his true colors . . ."

'Putt'll accept the duty of dog-whipper,' I assured myself as I ran my fingers over the nail holes on the meeting house door, most of which attested to his prowess at hunting wolves and bears whose carcasses he had nailed there. 'With winter coming on, women will bring dogs to warm their feet; Putt's just the man to keep the beasts in line.'

"As you wish, Pastor," he agreed a few weeks later at the ordinary where we were the last to leave before the Sabbath. "Now I've got to rush home and shave before dusk."

"One more puff and we'll both be off."

"I may seem outspoken, Reverend, but you ought to poll the Inhabitants as soon as possible," I appreciated his warning, "to find if they want you to remain as their pastor."

Before I could thank him for his confidence, he had galloped off, leaving me with thoughts of Deodat Lawson and John Burroughs, ministers whom the Farmers had failed to ordain.

The church took only minutes to answer Deacon Edward Putnam's call for a vote. Two "Nays" resounded: Captain Putnam's and Goodwife Deal's. Over an hour was then spent arguing about how much firewood I was to receive.

'Sam Parris stumbled on this same issue,' I cautioned myself, and so when they offered me 30 cords a year, I accepted, saying it "was sufficient, if not generous."

Reverend Gerrish cautioned me to withhold my answer for a few weeks, so as not to seem overeager, and so it was early October before I responded.

"Whereas you have applied yourselves to me and ask that I continue in your ministry," I was pleased the Gerrishes had come to hear my acceptance, sitting in the foreseat in front of the pulpit, "assuming that peace continues among you, with the grace of God, I humbly accept the offer to become and remain your minister."

The ministers' council set my ordination for early November. Reverend Walter dismissed me from the Roxbury Church and whispered a few words of advice, "Do not sit still while the waters are still troubled."

At first I thought he referred to the fact that my election had not been unanimous. Reverend Noyes dispelled that idea when he declared that the "Nays" had "tarnished but not hindered" my ordination, a comment which drew a sigh from Elizabeth.

"On behalf of Salem Village," Nicholas gloried in presiding, although my ordination weakened his dominance of the patent, "we admit you to our communion based on your confession."

Pastor Walter prayed, after which John Hale of Beverly gave me the charge. Reverend Gerrish was the first to lay hands on me, reserving for Nicholas Noyes the privilege of extending me his right hand in fellowship.

"How good it is and how pleasant for brothers to live together," we sang Psalm 133 in unison, except for the silent Goodwife Deal.

I gave the blessing and implored the Lord to keep us in His mercy, healing the wounds we had inflicted on one another . . . 'Is it my imagination, or did John Deal wince?' And giving me the wisdom He had bestowed on Solomon.

"Reverend Gerrish," I caught his cloak while others milled about the ordinary.

"Thirty cords of wood are hardly enough to see you and Beth through the winter," he commented before I could ask him about his daughter. "Come, Nanna," he beckoned, "we'll enjoy a drop of canary before heading home."

"No kissing in public," Elizabeth quipped.

"I'm at peace with myself and all mankind . . ."

"It's time you were," she pursed her lips in a silent kiss and drifted into the crowd.

"*You* are worthy," Reverend Noyes' voice drew my attention, adding in a more confidential tone, "I can't say as much for your Farmers. The farther people scatter, the more parishes they demand, like yours, and the weaker becomes our Church."

"I would suppose the more congregations, the larger our membership, and the stronger . . ."

"You're as *green* as your name," his outburst surprised me such that I almost spilled my canary. "We've broken our covenant . . ."

"Wouldn't 'modified' be a better word?"

"*Mortified* expressed *my* meaning. I'm mortified when a child of unbaptized parents joins our covenant." He passed his empty cup for me to fill. "The next thing you know, we'll disgrace ourselves by accepting Coleman's *Manifesto* . . ."

"Allowing a person to join in communion without a public confession of his experience of rebirth?"

"Worse than that: allowing *all* baptized males to vote for a minister!" His eyes narrowed. "How many might have voted against *your* ordination if Coleman's heresy were in force now?"

'Had my ordination come in September, Cotton Mather's annual visit might have provided Nicholas with an ally.'

Uninterested in continuing our conversation, the Salem minister excused himself, leaving a half-empty serving of wine, to relieve himself in the shed before his journey to town.

Alone in my room, I dismissed both the factiousness of a less than unanimous vote and Noyes' contentiousness by rereading the Scripture for the day.

My final thoughts, however, were neither of Elizabeth nor her father's casual acceptance of our marriage, but of Reverend Walter's whispered aside, "Not to sit still while the waters were troubled."

*   *   *

Samuel Parris introduced himself to me indirectly when I read his entries in the Church Record, the last of which was dated October, 1696, three months after his wife's untimely death. In the year that followed, he had refused to vacate the parsonage, engaged as he was in a fierce dispute over the money owed him by the Inhabitants.

Putt, the youngest dissident, led the attack on Parris, declined to pay his rate, and petitioned the Court to void the contract with the forlorn minister. Daniel Andrews' hand could be seen in the petition, citing John Tarbell's complaint that called Parris 'the Great Persecutor,' and adding, 'that had it not been for him,' John's mother-in-law, Rebecca Nurse, 'might have been still living, and so freed from execution.' Understandably, Goody Nurse's son, Samuel, also signed the petition.

When the Court found in favor of Samuel Parris, Deacon Ingersoll bought his land and parsonage back and my predecessor ingloriously left the patent.

'Don't sit still while the waters are troubled,' I repeated to myself as I read Parris' report of banishing Samuel Nurse, John Tarbell, and Peter Cloyse from communion. 'How dreadful! Banishing Goodman Cloyse, a signer of the original covenant in '89. Was it because he was Goody Nurse's brother-in-law or because he and his wife bolted out of the meeting house during Parris' tirade against Rebecca?'

When Thomas Wilkins supported his in-laws, Parris banished him as well.

'I will act this Sabbath.' Studying Parris' notes, I found the way to begin.

"Turn from evil and do good," I quoted from Psalms 34:14, as had Samuel Parris in his greatest sermon, 'Meditations for Peace.' Sergeant Thomas Putnam showed no sign of recognizing the passage, but Ben Hutchinson, seated well behind him, seemed to squirm when he heard, "Seek peace and pursue it!"

"Samuel Nurse," I pointed to the pew he might have occupied near the sergeant's, "John Tarbell . . . Thomas Wilkins."

Putt sat upright. Goodwife Deal groaned.

"I desire you to manifest by the usual sign of raising your hands that you are not dissatisfied with the brethren I just mentioned," the meeting house quieted, even the birds kept to the rafters, "and wish that they would rejoin the church as full communicants."

I allowed a moment for my plea to receive consideration and then recited from Parris's second text, Romans 12:18 and 19. "If possible, so far as it lies within you, live at peace with all men." I spoke softly, "My dear friends, do not seek revenge, but leave a place for Divine retribution."

To my delight, with neither undue reluctance nor speed, hands were raised in assent. When I called for those opposed to readmission of the three families, no hands appeared, and so I added that whatever the specific charges against them had been, "They were to be looked upon as nothing and let fall to the ground, buried forever . . ."

The last grain of sand slipped through my hourglass signalling pews to be slammed upward, crickets to be kicked along the floor, and my parishioners to bolt from the meeting house, the clamor so bad it shook much of the stored corn from its rafters.

I bade the nearly frozen sentry a good day, assured him we would meet at Deacon Ingersoll's training field later in the week, and turned my attention to the tithingman about to disperse a threesome for loitering.

"Brethren," my shout to the three allowed the snook to chastise the Deals for their hasty and noisy departure from the service.

"A bold gesture, Reverend," Daniel Andrews proffered.

"Quite bold," supported Captain Putnam.

"Let's not tarry on the Sabbath," Putt smiled, "I'd hate to have to grace these stocks."

"Master Green," the captain shuffled awkwardly, "consider my vote against your ordination as nothing. Let it 'fall to the ground, and be buried forever."

"Magnanimous of you," Goody Andrews offered his hand, as did his nephew and I.

Wary of the tithingman's return, the three split and rode off, leaving me to trudge through the snow to the parsonage, warmed by the glow of friendship.

On Training Day, Captain Putnam took me aside, grieved by new French provocations at sea that had followed the Haverhill massacre, and suggested a day of thanksgiving for our fine harvest.

"Note, Master Green, tracks of the Taranteens' *a'gamaks*," he pointed his rapier toward the four-foot-long, foot-and-a-half wide marks left by the Indians' white cedar snowshoes. "Their shaman was so pleased with the money we gave him for their help during the harvest, he gave me this *madaodos*—it's carved whalebone—as a token of good fortune.'' He pressed it in my palm, ''Accept it on behalf of our friendship.''

Before I could thank him, he had turned his attention to drilling the Farmers, exhorting them to imitate Putt's horsemanship if they were to defend us against enemy raids. A few minutes later, satisfied with our efforts, he dismissed us, and I made my way to Wenham.

''The Church Records show your father signed the ministers' petition against Parris,'' Beth and I sat beside the fire as she polished their pewter porringer: first, its shallow inner surface, then its flat pierced handle, finally its base.

''Indeed he did, I'm proud to say,'' she returned the gleaming piece to its place on the mantle while I adjusted the trammel so that the boiling pork and beans would be well above the fire. ''Unfortunately, Reverend Noyes refused to sign . . .''

''He always sided with Parris . . .''

''. . . and against John Wise, whom Sam feared might favor the accused.''

''Congratulations, Reverend,'' Nanna Gerrish hastily removed the bannock, filled with a mixture of cornmeal and water, from the fireside, ''I commend your bold action of welcoming the three brethern to communion.''

''Agreed,'' her husband added, ''a *very* bold action—and only two weeks after your ordination.''

I ate my milktoast with embarrassed pleasure while listening to the Gerrishes exult.

''Bold actions, such as yours,'' my host addressed me as the women cleared the table, ''belie Ned Ward's thesis about us Puritans! Your quizzical look tells me,'' he tamped his pipe as I refilled my tankard with rum, ''you haven't read his book, *A Trip To New England*. Maybe that's just as well. He says we're all cheats and make poor husbands! Claims our bad habits come from living too near the Indians,'' he pointed his pipe at my tankard, ''and using too much rum and tobacco.''

''Father failed to mention,'' Beth entered with my coat, ''Ward also claimed New England women were ripe by age 13 . . .''

I knew her comments were aimed at me and tried not to overreact.

''That's what he wrote,'' her father laughed, ''and became hags by age 25!''

Nanna Gerrish made her wishes known by locking her husband's arm in hers and hastening him upstairs while I stammered my thanks for their hospitality.

"Bold! Rash! That's what I've been hearing you called all week," Elizabeth groused while I prepared to leave. "How can you be so bold in matters of the church and so meek in matters of the heart?"

Looking over her shoulder, to be sure we were alone, I wrapped my open coat around her and kissed her with all the passion I could muster.

"I'm bundled to a fare-thee-well," I laughed as we broke our embrace.

"Bundling! A bold suggestion, Master Green," she stared at me, arms akimbo. "Or might you agree with Richard Baxter, who forbids all sexual relations unless for the purposes of offspring?"

"Since my beliefs about such matters may be too rash for you," for once I was really enjoying our repartee, "I would agree with Baxter that until such time as we are man and wife, you avail yourself of ice cold baths and maintain a vegetable diet!"

"Boldly said," she stood tiptoe to kiss me, "Ride carefully . . ."

Cantering home, the thought of bundling warmed me. Each time the image crossed my mind, blood surged throughout my body, occasionally ridiculed by my horse's snort.

4   If Ever Two Were One . . .

"Doom the seats!" Captain Putnam protested my suggestion.

"Whatever for?" demanded Deacon Edward Putnam.

I waited for our host, Deacon Ingersoll, to comment, but he only wagged his head feebly in disapproval.

"It's come to my attention that some of our elderly, especially widows, sit to the rear of the meeting house," my raised hand stemmed their interruptions, "while others, less deserving, such as Tabitha Deal or Ben Hutchinson, sit more forward than their standing warrants."

Social standing was a tradition I had never liked but had to accept. Ignoring me, the deacons grumbled among themselves. 'Were it not for my dead brother's tutors, John Hancock and John Leverett, who promised my mother they'd pay my way through Harvard, in memory of Percival, I might have joined my brothers Nat, Sam, and Ed as tailors—rather than be embroiled in yet another church dispute!'

"Deacons, the Church Record shows no reseating to have taken place in recent years—clearly against our covenant. Your families will, of course, continue to occupy the prestigious foreseat, from which you may help me control our sometimes riotous Farmers." Their tension eased, as I knew it would, when they realized I was not about to embarrass them as had Samuel Parris.

"Reverend Gerrish will announce the banns this Sabbath," I grinned, "and so the seat to the side of my pulpit should be reserved for Elizabeth . . ."

". . . and whatever number of children might ensue," Deacon Ingersoll's soft-spoken manner brought chuckles from his fellows.

"A welcome end to your idleness, Pastor," Captain Putnam added.

"Then we shall follow the rules: preferential seating to the elderly; then to those offering service in the militia;" that gained the captain's vigorous support, "finally, according to how much each family contributes in taxes."

"Will the boys still sit below you, on the pulpit stairs?" Deacon Putnam gave the captain a piece of paper on which to sketch.

"To be sure!" Deacon Ingersoll squeaked, "That's where the Sons of Belial belong!"

"Let's not forget two pews up front—for the blacks." The captain showed his sketch, marking the men's forwardmost pew, 'B.M.' and its mate on the women's side, 'B.W.,' for Black Men and Black Women.

My job done, my help no longer needed, I left the three to reseat our membership and retired to my study. I chose my text from Isaiah 58:9–14. My concentration was, however, disturbed with anxiety about how the Inhabitants would react on the coming Sabbath.

Apprehensively, before the conch shell was blown, I made my way to the meeting house. As men filed in, followed by their womenfolk, Captain and Deacon Putnam informed them of their pews.

Sergeant Putnam, whose family had been so virulent in accusing the Nurses of witchcraft, showed no aversion as he sat beside Rebecca's son, Samuel, in a forward pew. Nor did Thomas's wife, Ann, express more than a shrug as she sat beside Goodman Nurse's wife and the Widow Houton.

'Solemn—befitting the Sabbath,' I congratulated myself and turned to mount the pulpit stairs only to stumble when a roar burst from the men's pews.

The outburst, I later discovered, resulted from a prank by Ben Hutchinson, perhaps because he had been reseated by the dooming.

A stranger from Old England asked where he might sit. Both deacons having made their way to the foreseat, Hutch told the visitor to sit in the pew usually reserved for Bill Mills, pointing to the one marked, 'B.M.'

The Sabbath-shattering tumult came, of course, when the Englishman found his pew filling with Negro slaves!

By the time I recovered my footing, the incident had passed, and so I witnessed John Putnam greet John Tarbell, while Widow Walcott, mother of an accusing gal, offered to share her cricket with Widow Preston, Rebecca Nurse's daughter.

Goodwife Deal's late arrival made her a perfect target for my wrath at all latecomers.

"Next Sabbath, Tabitha," I scowled, "my sermon will be in two parts: the first, for those on time, shall pertain to saints; the second, to sinners! Make your choice!"

A Hutchinson boy laughed and so I banished him to sit beside his mother and sisters—a punishment which had always had a sobering effect on me.

"Ruins will be restored by your own kindred . . ." I read from the Scripture. "You will rebuild broken walls," a process already begun, "if you keep holy the Sabbath . . ."

Whether it was my sermon, the text I had chosen, the dooming, the B.M. incident, or the Hutchinson boy's punishment, I could not be sure. In any event, at the end of my three-hour sermon, no pews banged, no crickets clanked, and no one bolted for home.

'It's eerie—almost sinister,' I reflected as I drew nearer to Joseph Putnam, the last to leave.

"Nice of you to let us out in time to ride home before dark, Pastor," he turned his head from me, hoping I might not notice his tears.

"Next Sabbath, Putt, make sure you're among the saints," I thumped his horse with my cap, "not among the sinners."

*   *   *

"Before I comment on the letters you gave me to read, Joseph," Elizabeth greeted me the Monday after our second banns had been announced, "I want to read you this meditation by Anne Bradstreet. It seems appropriate to your recent actions:

> 'A sore finger may disquiet the whole body,
> But an ulcer within destroy it . . .''

"Beth, dear, I fail to see . . ."
"Quiet, let me finish," she reread the first passage and ended:

> "So an enemy without may disturb a commonwealth,
> But dissensions within overthrow it."

"You know," I confided, delighted by the passages she had selected, "when I confronted the deacons about reseating, I wondered, in the language of your poet, whether my own 'dissensions within' were not the cause of my proposal."

"Good! A touch of humility tempers boldness," she smilingly served us beer and corn cakes, "but only a touch! You're the only hope your poor mother had: John, killed by Turks; Nat, lost at sea; Tom, become a blacksmith . . . You owed it to Ruth to follow in Percy's footsteps."

"I was so slow at studies, so slow I was sent to Cambridge Grammar School and didn't enter HC until I was sixteen."

"Were you ever sconced?"

"Don't remind me!" My letters had opened the door, there was no way out but to admit I had been fined, more than once, for playing cards on the Sabbath. "At least I avoided expulsion—the punishment of Joseph Webb, a few years earlier . . ."

"Fagging seems to have upset Cotton Mather at college," she pursued a topic I would have preferred to have dropped.

"Not me! I was so poor at Latin and Greek I rather enjoyed upperclassmen who interrupted my studies to have me run errands for them."

"Then what bothered you most?"

'Why press this dreary line of thought?' I tamped my tobacco so hard my pipe stem broke. Beth fetched me another from her father's collection, holding it until I answered.

"Each newcomer had to make a speech or sing a song in front of the others," I tamped more gently. "If he were witty, or his talent impressive, he was applauded and served beer . . ."

"You failed!"

"Miserably! Not only was I forced to drink salted beer," the memory of its taste ruined the aroma of my pipe, "I was also tucked."

The tilt of her head told me she was unfamiliar with the punishment.

"Pinched under the chin until I bled . . ."

"Poor dear," Beth took my pipe, relit it, puffed, and gave it back.

"The telling hurts less than the tucking!"

"Sorry to have pressed you," my wife-to-be laid a trencher of Indian corn, kidney beans, and salted venison between us. "I just had to know."

"Cleanse me of any secret fault," I prayed aloud before we ate, "hold me from the sins of self-will, lest they get the better of me. Then I shall be blameless and innocent."

We ate without conversation.

"Enough self-criticism, dear," Beth prepared our blankets for bundling by the hearth. "I'll read you what Goody Bradstreet wrote about the subject . . ."

'If you must,' I sighed, still averse to her choice of authors, 'you will!'

"Sweet words are like honey,' it's from the same selection as before, 'a little may refresh, but too much gloats the stomach."

Nanna Gerrish bundled us under the heavy blankets sewn on three sides and down the middle. She then bade us a good night and led her husband upstairs.

"You know," my partner caught me as sleep was about to overcome me, "I admire the Taranteens' manner of marriage—it's simple, yet beautiful."

"Another time, Beth . . ."

"After the couple's mothers have discussed the matter," her elbow jabbed me through the blankets, "the man throws his blanket into the girl's wigwam . . ."

Having no way to escape, I squirmed to face my future bride.

"Unless the girl throws it out—they're engaged!"

"I can't move my hands, let alone throw off my blanket—or I just might, banns or no banns!"

"Be serious. Let me finish," she kissed my forehead. "When the woman approves, the couple slips into the forest to find a boulder to call their own. Kneeling beside it, they exchange vows . . . and that's it."

"Unlike the Papists and High-Fliers, our weddings are simple, too. But why seek a boulder, not a tree?"

"I knew your curiosity would get you!" she giggled. "Because a boulder, like a loving marriage, outlives a tree."

"Too pagan for my taste," I brushed her cheek with my lips as we sank into our blankets. 'Will her fascination with Indians' ways pass—or endanger both of us?' My wayward thought disturbed me, but when I turned to discuss it with her, she was fast asleep.

"Did you see my Father wink the very moment Reverend Hubbard pronounced us man and wife?" my bride worried as she added eggs and heavy cream, spiced with mace, nutmeg, and molasses to the ale and sack.

"I saw him blink, not wink. A swallow dropped a kernel of grain in his eye—what else could he do?"

"I hope no one will take Father's reaction as a spectral sign of disfavor upon us," her hand was so unsteady I relieved her of pouring the sack-posset for our guests.

Edgy though I was in anticipation of our wedding night, our guests were enjoying themselves so much they continued to tarry at the Gerrish home.

"If we go upstairs before they leave," I joked, "they're apt to haul us down again, regardless of your condition of dress . . ."

"You mean *un*dress . . ."

Father Gerrish's wink forgotten, (but not by Tabitha Deal), we served food and drinks to others, careful not to overindulge ourselves.

Nanna finally stepped in and politely bade our well-wishers goodbye. Collaring her husband, who might have preferred the revelry to continue, she shooed him to their bedroom, leaving Beth the job of warming our bed with coals from the fire and me to bank it for morning.

By the time I entered her room, my bride was already tucked in. I undressed, lifted the covers, and crawled beside her. Our fervor consumed us as we groped for one another, laughing at the clumsiness of our passion. The heat left by the bedwarmer was multiplied by our steaming bodies, forcing us to throw our carpet to the floor as our gropes became caresses.

Kissing Beth's lips, our legs intertwined, was more than I needed to become fully aroused. I dropped my hands to her breasts, fondled her nipples, and received from her wordless lips full confirmation of her pleasure. When I placed my mouth over her left breast, rolling my tongue around her nipple, she gasped, pulled my head back to kiss me, and almost tumbled us to the floor. Warily, we slid to the center of the bed, Beth on her back, I kneeling between her legs.

"Bold—but gentle, Joseph," she nipped my nose.

We were both so moist I lost a little firmness as I entered her. The thrill sent a spasm through her body, her arms wrung my neck, her mouth sucked my tongue. The passion of her excitement slowed me until I gripped the slippery mattress with my toes, and entered her fully for the first of many loving times.

"I . . . I can't hold back any longer," I warned, my legs tingling from toes to knees. No sooner did she smile than we felt a final surge throughout our bodies and panted with satisfaction. 'I'm glad I drank only two tankards tonight—a drop more would have profaned our love.'

"Oh, Joseph, I've been anticipating this night since we first met," my bride lay beside me, hugging me with her arms and legs.

And so we spent our wedding night: sometimes side by side, sometimes one atop the other, rarely under the bedclothes, although it was mid-March.

"You've read from the Forty-Fifth Psalm" she smiled before we went downstairs for bevers the next morning. "Now, listen to what Anne Bradstreet wrote, 'To my Dear and Loving Husband:'

> 'If ever two were one, then surely we.
> If ever man were loved by wife, then thee;
> If ever wife was happy in a man,
> Compare with me, ye women, if you can.
> I prize thy love more than whole mines of gold
> Or all the riches that the East doth hold.
> My love is such that rivers cannot quench,
> Nor ought but love from thee, give recompense.
> Thy love is such I can no way repay,
> The heavens reward thee manifold, I pray.
> Then while we live, in love let's so persevere
> That when we live no more, we may live ever.''

"Beth, dear Beth, those sentiments are enough to . . ."

"Down to bevers, Joseph—we'll be the last to arrive anyway."

The fire I had banked poorly in my haste had to be relit by Father Gerrish with his kit of flint and steel. He had even broken the ice in the basin so we could wash, and sent his son to milk the cows and slop the hogs well before Elizabeth and I appeared.

"Thank you, Father, for the turkey-leather psalm book you gave us," I feigned a casual attitude and tried not to stare at my bride as she pressed the cheese, watched over the soap kettle so that its whale oil and butchers fat did not overflow, and otherwise tried to appear nonchalant. Each time she came near me, we touched hands, 'At this rate,' I reacted to the stirring in my yard, 'we may not make it through the day without finding ourselves in bed again . . .'

*   *   *

After a lustful month in Wenham, my parsonage was ready for us. It became my duty to relight the fire and break the basin ice before my wife rose.

"Joseph, I have bad memories of this parsonage," Beth shivered while she worked the cheese press. "Imagine, only seven years ago, right where I'm standing, young Ann Putnam and her friends began the sorcery that killed so many innocents."

"In your pregnant condition, I'd prefer you dwelt on happier thoughts. If you can't find solace in the Scripture—fall back on your poet's words."

'Lord help us if Beth falls prey to superstition,' we ate our porridge hungrily. 'First, rumors of Father Gerrish's winking at our wedding; now, Beth's anxiety about events in this house . . . I'll lecture the Farmers again about such drivel.'

Tired though we were from our efforts to restore the dilapidated parsonage, we found time before prayers to enjoy the bliss of marriage. As a result, I slept dreamlessly, so soundly I failed to hear the sound that woke my wife.

"Joseph," I groped where she had lain; not finding her, I woke.

"Ann Putnam's here to see you . . . Young Ann."

"Pastor," the skinny nineteen-year-old cowered at the foot of the stairs.

"What brings you here this May night, Ann?" my wife offered her a tankard of cider which she sipped.

"Father's very ill,"she bowed toward me. "Will you visit with him?"

Elizabeth sent Ann ahead to assure the Putnams I would follow. I walked, Scripture in hand, past the Hutchinson, Darling, and Rea farms to the sergeant's. We prayed together, the church clerk and I, through his last hours. He died just after midnight.

"You know, dear," Beth remarked, while I took my turn at stirring the soap kettle, "Thomas Putnam's cryptic letter about 'a wheel within a wheel' led directly to Mary Easty's death . . .''

". . . and that of George Burroughs," I responded too hastily, frightening Elizabeth, who was unaware that I had immersed myself in the events of '92 in case the Devil should return to confound us. "The accuser has now joined the accused."

"He was only forty-seven . . .", my wife broke into tears. I let her cry it out, feeling I might make matters worse.

Within two weeks we were again awakened—again by Ann.

"My mother . . ."

"We'll go together," Beth insisted, "I know her mother very well, she and Nanna were very close."

"If you must, but take a whiff of tansie first . . ."

Beth complied, because she was well aware that tansie prevented miscarriage.

At the Putnam's, she helped young Ann calm her terrified siblings and made porridge for the next morning. Alone upstairs with Widow Putnam, I prayed with her until she died.

We walked two-by-two at the funeral, women first, behind the under-bearers and their casket, to the family crypt behind Putt's farm. The tithingman assured that none of the orphaned children ran abreast or ahead of the coffin. The bellringer's second tolling notified those of us in attendance that Goodwife Putnam's life had ended at thirty-eight—"cut off amid her usefulness and growing respectability"—I phrased it.

After the funeral, my wife squeezed my hand repeatedly on our sorry walk home, the funeral scarf Young Ann had given me tucked up my sleeve.

"Joseph," Beth wobbled toward me late that October, "take this medicine with you when you visit Ann today—it'll relieve her sleeplessness. I bruised some anise, steeped it in red rose water, and put it in these bags."

"What am I supposed to do with them?"

"They're small, see? Bind one in each of her nostrils—if your prayers are answered, they'll ease her insomnia."

Ann, a better patient than I would ever be, accepted my ministration without question. 'As to the remedy's success for her insomnia—that remains to be seen—perhaps it'd work for me . . .'

Difficulty sleeping, often due to nightmares, was a condition from which I had suffered before my Gallows Hill misadventure and moreso thereafter. Since my marriage, however, I had usually slept dreamlessly.

My sleep was dramatically broken the night of November 27, 1699, when the village midwife, Goody Hutchinson, delivered Elizabeth of the first of our nine children.

"I baptize you," I hesitated, 'Ann, Anne, or Anna?' My wife's quizzical stare settled me and I continued, "Anna, in honor of my Mother Gerrish."

Although filled with enormous joy for Beth and me, I grieved for Ann Putnam who watched, hollow-eyed, from her almost empty pew.

*   *   *

"It's not proper! In fact, it's downright unwise! Rash, to say the least," Anna balked at nursing while her mother berated me. "Surely Margaret Jacobs could be married by Pastor Noyes in her own church. Your marrying her will only add to the animosity between you and Nicholas."

"I've accepted John Foster's request. That's all there is to it . . . ."

But would that be all? Margaret had been an accusing gal whose testimony had hanged her grandfather! Then she recanted and confessed she had been deluded—by Nicholas Noyes. Because or in spite of this knowledge, I wasn't sure which, I performed the marriage in our parsonage. Beth acted the ever-gracious hostess, as if she were not perturbed with me or fearful of the consequences.

"The apocalypse is coming!" screamed Goodwife Deal during my first sermon of 1700. "Cotton Mather has declared this to be so—its signs are all about us!"

My sermon warned about the evils of divination, although Goody Deal cited as 'evidence' Father Gerrish's wink at our wedding, the Putnams' untimely deaths, and my 'usurpation' of Nicholas Noyes' prerogative by marrying the Fosters.

"Gamar Deal," I pounded my fist, "your satanic habit of trying to foretell events or distort innocent happenings to the Devil's purpose makes *you* the usurper—you usurp the place reserved only for Divine Providence!"

"You're too harsh with Tabitha," my wife commented while nursing Anna. "She's a most unhappy, distraught woman . . . besides, she only expresses aloud what many other Inhabitants may also believe but fear to say."

"I don't criticize her disrespect for *me*. I rebuke her for defaming the Sabbath ceremony. Anyhow, I'll not give her the satisfaction of a public forum for her tantrums—that mistake led to the terror that once wracked this forsaken village."

"Not so violent, you'll upset Anna." The baby obliged with a hearty belch. "Remember, scissors and sieves are found in every house—mine are beside the spinning wheel."

"It's not the tools themselves," I contended, "it's misusing them to 'divine' the future. Only the Lord knows what's in store for us. Anyone who tries foretelling—with scissors and shears, riddle and shears, or whatever tools—violates the First Commandment: Not to usurp God's rightful place."

We let our dispute drop, but events continued to irritate my flock.

In the middle of my sermon on the Sabbath following our first anniversary, the sentinel burst into the meeting house, his clanking armor arousing even my sleepiest parishioners.

"A fire—a diabolical fire's broken out on the fence!"

With Putt leading the way, the Inhabitants emptied the building to see Ben Hutchinson douse the fire.

"Another sign," Beth heard Goodwife Deal confide to Ann Putnam, "that 1700 will be the apocalypse."

The following Sabbath I again inveighed against divination.

"Brimstone's raining on Salem Town!" A rider hammered on the parsonage door, startled Anna from her nap, and forced Beth to catch her fingers in the spinning wheel.

By the time I had made my way to the ordinary, Goodman Deal, visibly upset, claimed the event was a sign of Doomsday. So many Farmers were drunk, I commanded them to leave, but they continued to mill about, some shouting obscenities at me.

As Providence would have it, Putt pushed his way through the crowd, elbowing Ben Hutchinson, and catching him before he fell to the floor.

"Have you heard the latest from Salem?" Anxiously, the crowd moved toward Goodman Putnam.

'Could he have been the faceless rider who fled my house?' I found it hard to believe that a man so cool in other crises could panic now.

His tethered horse in a lather, and human nature being so fickle, I prepared myself for the worst.

"Some fools are spreading false rumors about brimstone falling on Salem!" His language roiled rather than appeased the crowd. Acknowledging me with a nod, he added, "A pity Salem Town hasn't heard your recent sermons, Pastor . . ."

Sullenly, the Inhabitants dispersed, their tankards of ale half-drunk.

"Do you know who the rider was that spread this satanic rumor, Pitt?"

A shrug was his only reply.

When I returned to my study, I set my prepared text aside and chose Ezekial 13 for another sermon against superstition.

"Their inspiration comes from themselves; they have seen no vision," I bellowed, glaring at those Farmers who had almost drunk themselves into a stupor. "Your prophets have been like jackals," I interposed, "like the jackal who rode past yesterday, spreading false alarm."

I studied each face but none showed shame.

"Is not your divination a *lie?* You call it the word of the Lord," still no sign of shame among the assembled menfolk, "but it is *not* God who has spoken . . ."

As I shifted my focus toward the women, I intoned, "These are the words of the Lord God: 'I loathe . . . you women," Goodwife Deal squirmed, then sat upright as I repeated, "you women who hunt men's lives." Sighting along my outstretched arm, as if aiming a musket at her, I concluded, "*You* bring death to those who should not die . . . by lying to this people of Mine who listen to lies!"

In bed that night, the Sabbath over, exhilarated by our lovemaking, which had resumed once my wife healed from childbirth, Beth congratulated me on my sermon.

"It was well-received, dear, I could tell by the furious note-taking."

"Did I treat Goodwife Deal unfairly?"

"Much as I hate to admit it, I was wrong. You not only quieted her, for the time being, but isolated some of her would-be listeners who shunned her after the service."

My wife's perceptions were confirmed at the next town meeting when not a word was mentioned of the 'signs of doom.' Under Captain Putnam's leadership, I was then voted to receive whatever money strangers contributed at services.

"In response to your confidence in me," I seized the opportunity afforded by their vote, "I propose a committee be formed to investigate building a new meeting house."

A low-flying bird sprinkled grain in my eye, which I forced myself to accept without blinking.

Over and over, I preached in favor of a new place of worship until the July meeting agreed: it would be paid for in cash and completed within two years.

*   *   *

"Drenched!" my wife's belly shook as she greeted me, a new life stirring in her womb.

"My horse escaped—I had to walk home from Ipswich . . ."

"Well, your prayers brought the rain we sorely needed. Unfortunately, your horse foraged among Hutch's apple trees. Ben returned it to our shed—after he chastised me for your carelessness."

The drought behind us, and my neighbor placated by my apology, my catechizing of nearly forty youngsters was interrupted by Putt's musket pounding on our door.

"Another dead sheep, Pastor," he kicked the carcass. "Looks to me like the work of a wildcat."

"That's three I've lost this year."

"Tell you what, we'll make it a contest between you and me—to see who's first to kill him!"

"No wagering," I cautioned jokingly.

"Fair enough," he wheeled his horse, "whoever wins will nail the beast's head to the meeting house door . . ."

"The bounty to be given to the church!"

Raising his musket in agreement, he galloped off.

At dusk, in late September, Beth prevailed upon me to take her for a ride. Heavy as she was, she grasped me tight about the waist, complaining about the locust-like appetites of my catechism class— when disaster struck!

"Hold tight," I screamed as my horse shied from the wildcat's charge. Beth's added weight, however, snapped the rawhide that held her pillion and she tumbled to the ground.

"A bad bump, Joseph, nothing more," she forced a grin as I crouched warily beside her, afraid she might be hurt, and equally fearful that the wildcat might attack again. Consoling her as I gently rubbed her head, we chuckled as my horse abandoned us for the safety of its shed.

"I swear, Beth . . ."

"Careful, dear, that's blasphemous . . ."

"I swear I'll kill that cat even if I have to postpone other chores . . ."

"Why not let Putt handle him?" she was unaware of our wager, "he's a better horseman and an excellent marksman."

Elizabeth's remarks stimulated me a month later when I spotted the animal's tracks in the hoar frost, tracked him, and felled him with one blast. Putt was the first to congratulate me as I nailed the beast's head to the meeting house door, although my wife felt I had taken an unnecessary risk.

"Dear," she nudged me in the middle of the December night, "don't waken Anna—come downstairs with me."

Huddling barefoot in the snow, we stood in awe of the glowing sky.

"I pray no one mistakes this midnight light for a sign of doom," I whispered as I described the aurora borealis in my Commonplace Book.

"Why should they? It's a sight well-known to the Taranteens."

'Small consolation,' I scurried into bed to warm her body with my own.

"After all, Joseph, 'Abenaki' means 'the people in the glow of the midnight sky."

'Glow . . . glow,' the word played tricks with me as I tried to return to sleep. 'Glow! Of course! I'll insist the Farmers vote money for at least 20 buckets, iron hooks, and poles in case of fire . . .'

5 Make Her Soul Thy First Concern

'January 11, 1701,' the tear-blurred entry in my Diary reads, 'my wife was delivered of a stillborn son.'

As we left the village burial place, Putt took me aside. "I hate to bother you at a time like this, but William Raymond's plot over there reminds me that Goodwife Deal's been saying his death from a falling tree was a sign of God's wrath . . ."

Grateful for his company, if not for his untimely news, I dismissed him with a sigh and prayed aloud.

"I desire to acknowledge the hand of God in all, and quietly submit unto him, and I think that I never did once murmur against God for this stroke; but have cause to say that God has punished me far less than I deserve."

The snow quickly blanketed the fresh-turned grave, while my friend muffled his sob with the pretext of brushing snowflakes from his mouth.

"I desire to bless God that he has taken me into that covenant," I fought back unseemly grief, "which includes my seed also—and that he spared and restored my wife."

The brief ceremony over, Putt and I separated, the snow covering our tracks so fast it seemed we had never made the lonely trek.

"Whatever is this concoction, Joseph?"

"Thin-sliced rhubarb, steeped overnight in sack and strained," cautiously, she sipped from the tankard I held to her lips, finding it tasty, she gulped the rest.

"And to what purpose was that?"

I hated to admit it was prescribed for melancholia, nor could I lie to her, and so I busied myself with Anna.

"I'll not press you for an answer, dear. I know you feel as sad as I about our loss." Her forced smile became a frown, however, when she asked, "Will Tabitha take our tragedy as an evil sign of God's wrath?"

"From the talk at the ordinary, most people take it as a sign for us to organize to rid ourselves of wildcats!"

"Then . . . my fall from the horse . . ."

"Putt and others believe the wildcat carries the blame," I kissed her. "Now rest and let the medicine help you."

Beth continued to feel miserable, preferring to suffer alone than in my presence, and so I threw myself into prodding the Farmers about the meeting house.

"I'll give ten pounds to prime the pump," I handed the sum to Deacon Ingersoll, "can't we finish it in less than two years?"

"We appreciate your unwarranted generosity, Master Green, but Watch House Hill must be leveled before we begin construction— those nearest the hill will be responsible for that job."

The deacon's contribution, well beyond what was expected, was the land across from his ordinary. When a dispute broke out between Joseph Herrick and his neighbor, Edward Bishop, the project hit its first snag.

"Goody Bishop claims I injured him by paying only three-quarters of the money I promised," Herrick opened, seated beside me at the parsonage table and glaring at his neighbor.

Because their earlier, private talk, produced only further animosity, and a later meeting with their neighbors only added fuel to the fire between them, I was their final recourse before the issue would come before an open meeting.

"Why didn't he pay you in full?" I fetched more ale so that Beth could stay upstairs with Anna.

"He asked me to build a leanto behind his house, his old one have rotted, and we set a fair price for it. Now, he's got his leanto— but I'm short a quarter of the promised money!"

"True?" I probed.

"Three quarter's true . . . ." Herrick nodded thanks for his refilled jack.

"The truth is whole!" Bishop blurted.

"Explain yourself, Goodman Herrick," I invited, tiring of their attitudes.

Herrick insisted Bishop had skimped on the pitch such that his animals were as well-off outside as inside the structure.

On the pretext of having to prepare my sermon, I left the dispute undecided and showed them to the door, warning them we would resume our discussion at a later date.

The Inhabitants, well aware that the quarrel had stymied progress on the meeting house, prepared for the issue to come before a general meeting—an event I was determined to avoid because it challenged my skill as a mediator.

"Then there came into the king's presence two women . . ." I chose my sermon's text from First Kings 3:16–28. My wife warned against the passage, feeling it aggrandized my own part too much, especially its concluding verse: "When Israel heard the judgment which the king had given, they all stood in awe of him; for they saw he had the wisdom of God within him to administer justice."

Her warning was echoed by Ben Hutchinson who accosted me from his pew, "Do you really believe, Pastor Green, that this feeble sermon will resolve the quarrel between our brethren?" Deacon Ingersoll seemed to side with his adopted son, who concluded his attack on me by asking, "Do you truly believe that King Solomon's wisdom applies to *your* part in this dispute?"

"The Scripture, Goodman Hutchinson, reports *God's* wisdom—not Solomon's! I warrant you'd better read your Scripture more carefully in the future. Yes, I fully believe the light of Providence will shine on our neighbors—unless clouded by such smoke as you might blow their way!"

When construction resumed that week, Putt reported to me that Herrick had challenged Bishop to stand inside the shed during a downpour. Thoroughly soaked, the rain having gushed through the roof, Bishop agreed to retar it and received his full payment from Herrick.

Hard as Hutch was to please, he tipped his Monmouth toward me as he hastened past us to join the gang at work on the meeting house grounds.

I strolled across the road toward the parsonage, my heart singing praise for the Lord's merciful intercession in man's affairs, only to be startled by screams from the upstair's window.

Bolting up the short flight of stairs, I burst into the bedroom to find my wife rocking Anna on her lap, and singing lustily, "Take warning now by me,

For I must die . . ."

I shuddered, Anna giggled, and Beth wailed the refrain.

"Take warning now by me,

And shun bad company,

Lest you come to Hell with me,

For I must die!"

"What kind of blasphemy is *that*—and for a child?"

"The 'Ballad of Captain Kidd,' silly." Elizabeth propped Anna to her feet, and after the two-year-old toddled from the room, threw herself into my arms, knocking us onto the bed. "I learned it from the woodsmen as they replenished our supply," she tickled my ribs.

"Stop, Beth—you know what tickling does to me!" I tried to move but she had me pinned. "Do you mean you went outdoors in this February weather?"

"I needed the exercise. What's more, I wanted to be sure of the wood count!" She rolled beside me. "They did us fair—and only a day after you told the Inhabitants we were almost without fuel."

As we lay together, promising wordlessly we would lie in each other's arms that night, she bubbled about the woodmen's news.

"Captain Kidd's been hanged at Newgate for pirating an English ship. He refused to name his master. However, after the first noose snapped, he confessed his sins and pled for salvation just before the second noose did the trick."

"At least he made his peace . . ."

"The woodsmen say that Boon Island, in the Isles of Shoals, holds his treasure from the *Quedah Merchant*—guarded by a ghost which shines like a glowworm . . ."

"Enough of this," I let on as if disturbed while helping her from the bed. Walking downstairs, hand in hand, the closest we had been in ages, I added, "When you lullaby Anna, dear, choose something more appropriate, preferably from the Scriptures."

"Say from the Song of Solomon?"

Although she again had the better of me, I was overjoyed my wife had shaken off her melancholy, 'With the help of Providence—aided by a few jacks of sack.'

The passion which our tragedy had dampened seemed greater because of it. I worried that she insisted she accompany me wherever my ministry demanded, but she assured me that as long as the rawhide straps were sturdy enough to hold her increasing weight, she would be my constant companion.

Thus it was, following Cotton Mather's annual lecture in Salem, we observed a thief's branding, the letter 'T' burned into his cheek, after which he was sold as a slave for five years to cover the cost of his crime.

Riding homeward, we retraced the route of years before, past the sawmill to gain the sawyer's assurance he would expedite completion of the meeting house whose turret had been raised that summer, and leisurely past the many taverns along the Ipswich Road.

Autumn found us both very busy. I pressed cider from our abundant apple orchard; Beth taught Anna to dip candles. Amid chores like these, the Farmers debated how much each would pay for the new meeting house. The most disgruntled was Hutch, who felt his rate was too high, albeit he lived closest to it.

'These factious Inhabitants part with their time and money only after the most severe bargaining. At least they're at peace—probably as peaceful as they'll ever be.'

My private peace was shattered, joyously, one midnight in late December by Beth's piercing scream! With only time for me to fetch Goodwife Hutchinson, my wife gave birth to a son.

"I baptize you, John, in honor of my father," I announced that Sabbath. Father Gerrish held his grandson in his bearing cloth while I broke the ice atop the christening bowl and warmed the water in my palm so as not to chill the baby. John, however, howled as the water touched his forehead.

Preceding the baptism, my sermon was based on Paul's second letter to Timothy, beginning at the fourteenth verse. 'There's no better time than now to propose the Farmers establish a school,' I had convinced myself.

As Paul had warned Timothy about the Scripture's use, I also emphasized, "For teaching truth and refuting error . . . for reformation of manners and discipline in right living . . . so as to be efficient and equipped for good work of every kind."

When the Inhabitants obliged by voting to hire a schoolmaster, 'in some convenient time,' I vowed the time would be no later than John's readiness for education.

*   *   *

"The meeting house is not yet built—and now you've pushed them into building a school!" Elizabeth pulled John from her breast and burped him over her shoulder. "Too rash, Joseph! Don't push these people too far, too fast . . ."

"I only recommended what Providence might think best."

"Best? For whom? Your recommendation for a new place of worship was in everyone's interest. But your demand for a school seems more self-serving." She passed the baby to me and turned her attention to Anna's jealousy.

Neither we nor the congregation discussed the school further, the new meeting house consumed our attention. Without complaint, Captain Putnam doomed the seats, and by midsummer all joined in whitewashing it, careful not to damage its casement windows. In late July, Mr. Whipple colored the pulpit and the project was complete.

"Building the Church-material seems easier than building the Church-spiritual," I complained to my father-in-law as we paddled our gundalow toward another long-winded ministers' council, this time to discuss the Beverly vacancy.

"Replacing a minister as strong as John Hale is never easy. Witness how hard it was for the Inhabitants to settle on you." We glided calmly, careful not to splash one another.

"What makes filling a vacancy so difficult," he turned to explain, "are the controversies within the Church-spiritual. These differences between religious men such as Wise and Noyes signify the greater battle waging in Boston between giants like the Mathers and the Brattles."

Facing forward, he increased the volume of his voice, "A small parish, like yours or mine or Beverly's, becomes as treacherous as the edge of a whirlpool which may suck us under. Each issue, no matter how trivial, must be squarely faced and resolved, no less than that between Goodmen Bishop and Herrick, or Satan will again gain the upper hand."

"What part should I play in today's meeting?"

Nearing Ipswich, he replied, "Follow the dictates of your conscience, provided it's under *God's* command and not your own!"

'Counsel I might have expected from your daughter,' I reflected as we beached our craft. 'Lord, help me keep my silence unless what I have to say advances the cause of peace.'

John Wise's reputation, buttressed by his fame as a wrestler, had not diminished from the time he had been sentenced to twenty-one days in prison for opposing Governor Andrus' tyrannical taxes. In later years, his protestation of John Proctor's innocence of witchcraft enhanced his stature, except with Nicholas Noyes. His dispute with the Salem minister, although not as much discussed, would crown his career.

"When you side with Solomon Stoddard's thesis, that admitting carnal men to communion will regenerate them, John," Nicholas continued the discussion where it had been dropped a month before, "I side against you—citing no less an authority than Increase Mather!"

"Theologically, the only Mather I respect," defended Wise, "is Richard. He believed, you will recall, that children *were* in covenant— regardless of their parents' fitness or unfitness for communion. In fact, he *urged* us to baptize children of unfit parents, thereby bringing them into our covenant."

While their argument raged, Father Gerrish and I showed only passive interest. Unfortunately, the dispute blocked Beverly from settling on a pastor, his appointment having to be approved by our council. Both contenders were adamant that the newcomer, whoever he might be, not be on the other's side of the Half-Way Covenant.

"I oppose the new approach," Nicholas iterated, "as I earlier opposed antinomianism . . ."

"Ann Hutchinson's heresy has long been a dead issue, Nicholas." John Wise brushed his opponent's objection aside like so much pipe-smoke. "The notion that faith alone brings salvation, such that a person may lead a sinless life after receiving the covenant, in no way relates to our present issue."

"Well, I associate the two," Noyes now raised his hand in objection. "As I see it, the Half-Way Covenant that you—and others not so vocal," he glared at my father-in-law and me, "espouse, is a diabolical wedge undermining our church and society."

"The Half-Way Covenant," our host countered quietly, "will democratize both church and society."

"De*moc*ratize! An unfortunate word," Nicholas taunted, "unless you mean it will make a *mockery* of our religion!"

"You know your Greek as well as I," Wise thundered. "I mean

both church *and* society must become more popular, less elitist, than our Papal and Anglican rivals. We dare not condemn innocents to Hell just because their parents were not baptized!''

"I suppose your next un*wise* move, John, will be to extend a voice in government to Quakers, Jews, and the like.''

"Brethren, I consider Man in a state of natural being, as a free-born subject under the crown of Heaven, and owing homage to none but God Himself.''

My father-in-law's startle matched my own at the direction in which the Chebacco pastor's logic was heading, but he was determined to elaborate on his thesis.

"It is very plain that the primitive constitution of the Churches was a democracy, a form of government which the light of Nature does highly value, erected when a number of free persons assemble together in order to enter into a covenant . . .''

"I gather you view our present Church government as a continuation of that 'primitive constitution?'' my Father Gerrish probed.

"Precisely! This plundering of the Churches falls within the second grand division of time, not within the first three hundred years.''

It became obvious to me, if not to my colleagues, that Reverend Wise had given considerable thought to the matters he was presenting to us, but so far had not circulated them for us to read.

"Under our covenant, modeled after the early Church, there is no lurking place for *symony*. There is no buying and selling of offices,'' his tone became more intense, "here is no backstairs for cousins and favorites to climb to high seats without desert; it is merit and intrinsic worth sets the value, and so it is the very democracy, Nicholas, of our Church government which keeps us from tyranny and slavery.''

None of us was prepared to counter or even question John's argument, nor did anyone show agreement with it, and so the meeting ended with Nicholas' prayer.

"The people of Beverly might be better off if they found a minister without counsel from our wise, if noisy brethern,'' my Father Gerrish quipped as he left me to complete my homeward journey.

"You see,'' I explained to my wife after thirty unexpected guests from Salem Town had finally vacated our parsonage, "this Church cannot grow in communicants unless people whose parents were never baptized become eligible to be admitted to communion. Moreover, without such growth, the mammon, 'Commerce,' will surely overwhelm us—as it threatens to do by following the outrageous thoughts of John Locke.''

"Nicholas faces the issue head-on," she undressed for bed. "He's watched his church members scatter, start new farms and businesses, and demand their own churches." She put her finger on my lips to complete her thought. "He's fought new congregations at every turn. He's made each vacated or new ministry a battleground."

Feigning sleep, I came to the conclusion that I would attend foremost to the needs of my own people rather than become embroiled in the larger issues of the day, in spite of William Brattle's counsel.

To implement my vow, I used my new *Cambridge Concordance* to sharpen my lectures against divination. To my dismay, Eli Porter's death at sea was taken as another sign of approaching doom.

"Goodman Porter, together with four others of the ship's company," Tabitha Deal babbled to the womenfolk after my lecture, "starved to death—or was murdered." She gloated in her listeners' gasp, "Their bodies were then eaten by the rest of the crew!"

The horror of her story spread across my parish, embellished as it passed from Farmer to Farmer, and forced me to sacrifice precious study time to seek the truth from the ship's master in Salem.

"The truth," I announced to Beth after returning Hutch's shallop, "is that Goodman Porter and others died of fever . . . The well-provisioned crew rightly threw their bodies overboard." I sighed, "The same fate befell three of my brothers . . ."

"Let *me* squelch Tabitha's latest gossip," at the time we did not know that Beth's brother, Joseph, would meet the same end, "you just go ahead with your sermon preparation."

Reluctantly, I agreed and began to sift through my escritoire in search of a suitable quotation with which to launch my next attack. Like an answer from Providence, the Church Record fell open to the perfect entry.

"I find in the Church Book," I concluded my sermon against divination the following Sabbath, "record of Martha Corey's excommunication for supposed witchcraft."

Amid the hush, I remembered Quaker Buffum's charge to me as we wrapped her body in linen, "Make her soul the first of thy concerns."

In reverence, I lowered my voice, "Since we all recognize the errors which prevailed ten years ago . . ."

'Did Ann Putnam shudder?' I wasn't sure, my attention focused on my proposition.

". . . I believe it our duty to *recall* that sentence in order that Goodwife Corey not be damned to everlasting Hell for a diabolical crime she did not commit!"

Joseph Putnam and Samuel Nurse brightened. I looked for Daniel Andrews' reaction before realizing he had died earlier that year, 'Would that he were here to advise me.'

Tabitha Deal's pock-marked face pursed and purpled, while in the men's pews, Ben Hutchinson stomped his feet to register his disapproval.

"Since I did not know her, and am ignorant of the specific crimes alleged to her," I prided myself in having found an issue of local importance, "I shall leave the matter entirely to your consideration, hoping that we will determine the matter by vote at the next convenient opportunity . . ."

"Dear Joseph," my wife protested as we crossed the road to the parsonage, "why can't you leave well-enough alone? I thought I'd settled Tabitha for awhile; I even thought you'd vowed to work on 'local' matters—instead, you've not only upset our parish but embroiled the entire patent!"

I attributed her distress to her pregnancy rather than to me and busied myself with the Scripture rather than upset her further.

6 The Queens Closet Opened

"I swear by all that's holy!" I stormed into the parsonage, frightening Anna and John such that their mother hurried them to bed before attending to my rage.

"I swear, I'll not attend another town meeting as long as I live!"

"Dispute over Martha Corey?" Beth filled my jack with ale, "you might have expected as much . . ."

"More like rebellion! Ben Hutchinson railed at me, joined by Tabitha Deal—I hardly knew who had been among the accusers or accused."

"Not so loud, you'll keep the children from their sleep."

"It was horrible, Christian adults ranting like a mob," I puffed too deeply and gasped, "believe me, I'll not attend another meeting . . ." I waved her objections aside, "Oh, the shabby way they treated me tonight!"

Elizabeth tended the fire in order to allow me to vent my anger at the Inhabitants.

"Even Deacon Putnam steadfastly refused to favor repeal of her excommunication, rising to shout, 'My conscience forces me to vote nay.' I feared Ann Putnam might add her voice against me but, even at the final vote, she showed no emotion."

My wife beckoned me to join her on the settle.

"What hurt me most," my wife rubbed my shoulders with her strong fingers, "was Ben's tirade."

"Against the motion?" I nodded as I pulled away.

"Obstinately! He said we ought not blame Goody Corey's excommunication on . . ."

The rhythmic tapping of a musket on our door distracted me. 'Hopefully Ben's come to apologize,' I scowled as I opened the door.

"Putt! So pleased you're here!" I lied. I did not want to see anyone before I had regained my composure.

"Welcome," my wife offered him canary to refresh him after his chilly ride.

"How did the meeting fare? Business kept me in Salem Town all day."

'I'll have to recount the events carefully,' I lamented. 'For all I know, Putt may side with Ben.'

Fortunately, John cried, probably awakened by our guest's arrival, and I excused myself, leaving my wife to report the night's events. Upstairs, I picked John from his crib, patted his back until he passed wind, and then re-covered Anna.

"Now that Putt knows about the dispute," Beth greeted me on my return, "what *was* the outcome of the vote?"

"After an interminable, disputatious, factious, free-for-all . . ."

"To be expected," he smiled, refilling my jack.

"*I* didn't expect it!"

Elizabeth grabbed my elbow, whispering loud enough for our guest to laugh, "The *vote*?"

"The motion passed," I mumbled, "six or seven dissenting."

My wife embarrassed me with a hug and kiss as Putt clapped his congratulations. I confessed I saw little victory in the meeting's proceedings, but my wife suggested that Putt tell me more about Goodwife Corey so that I might appreciate the Farmers' conduct.

"You remember that grisly night we met on Gallows Hill?"

"Too well—Martha Corey's dangling corpse . . . ."

"The last hangings," Putt frowned. "She was a devout woman, taught me my catechism."

"Goody Corey got in trouble with the accusers from the start," Beth took over. "She refused to attend the trials at which gals like Ann Putnam made their wild charges. Her husband, Giles, however, never missed a session. When asked about the 'afflicted girls,' she called them 'bitch witches' who only demonstrated their poor religious instruction and lack of faith. You can well imagine how the Thomas Putnam family reacted!"

"Sad to say," Putt was now in control of himself, "my niece, only twelve, complained to my half-brother, Edward, that Goody

Corey'd pinched her and showed him welts on her body. He took it as a duty of his deaconship to test Martha at her house in front of a witness, Goodman Cheever.''

"They demanded to know," my wife broke in to relieve our guest whose hands were so tightly clasped across his knees that his knuckles whitened, "what clothes Young Ann was wearing. When Goody Corey claimed she didn't know, for she hadn't seen the girl recently, the deacon decided she was lying."

"That's correct! My niece protested that Martha had blinded her. Edward took this as a clear sign of witchery, confirmed for him when Ann threw another of her feigned fits at the moment that Goody Corey entered Sergeant Putnam's house to answer the summons against her."

Goodwife Corey's fate sealed, the proceedings were perfunctory. Nicholas Noyes joined Sam Parris to examine her at the ordinary during which Ann screamed, "A man is whispering in Goody Corey's ear!' "

Martha, however, was so composed that her responses, fully recorded by the Sergeant, put her accusers to shame. Even when her aged husband, Giles, testified that her piety was Satan-bred, citing that she had hidden his saddle to prevent him from attending a hearing, Martha refused to refute him, which further condemned her. When she bit her lips to concentrate on an answer to her accusers, Young Ann bit her own lips until they bled.

"You've eased my mind, Putt," I thanked him while Elizabeth fetched his coat.

"With your wife's kind help," he waved as his horse trotted into the February snow.

"I'm deeper in your debt," I panted in Beth's ear as I lay atop her minutes after our guest had left.

"No more than I to you, my love," her laugh forced me out of her, her knees flipping me to my side.

"I don't mean just now . . . . I meant our earlier discussion."

"Regardless of the fight, the vote was a victory for you."

"No, not for me, I'm but an instrument of God and this parish. The defeat, however, was mine—defeating my own self-centeredness . . . ."

"Enough, Joseph, enough self-pity." She reached beside our bed and handed me a book. "Here, read before the candle burns out. What Anne Bradstreet had to say applies to you."

'Fire hath its force abated by water, not by wind,' I wished my antagonists had read the passage before the meeting, 'and anger must be allayed by cold words and not by blustering threats.'

The candle snuffed, my wife sound asleep, I lay awake. Until I prayed forgiveness for my earlier blasphemy, I could not chase images of Gallows Hill, Ann Putnam's accusations of Goody Corey, or the evening's acrimony from my mind.

*   *   *

During pregnancy, many women took a preparation to relieve their nausea upon waking in the morning. I decided to surprise Beth with one. I got a lock of our maid's hair, a virgin about half my wife's age, and powdered it. After drying a dozen ants' eggs, I mixed them with the powdered hair in a quarter pint of our strongest ale wort. Triumphantly, I offered it to my waking wife.

"What Devil's brew is *this*?" she sniffed the mixture and jerked her head away. "Get rid of it!" Holding her mouth with both hands, she bolted upright, "I'm going to vomit!"

"Beth! It *prevents* morning sickness . . ."

Toppling the concoction into the chamberpot, the violence of her action dispelled her need to vomit. Dejected, I rummaged through my escritoire, found my copy of *The Queens Closet Opened,* and scratched an 'X' through the recipe. 'If I don't try these remedies in my own family, how can I expect they'll be accepted by my superstitious parishioners?' Having secreted the book in its compartment, I joined my wife for bevers.

"Anna, have you noticed any toads about the yard?" My four-year-old grimaced her negative answer. "How about you, Beth?"

"No, thank . . ." she choked off a blasphemy. "Whatever do you need toads for?"

Ignoring her question, I left the table to choose an earthenware pot beside the hearth. Finding one of the right size, I set it atop the dyepot for safekeeping.

"Smallpox ravages the Farmers," I pinched an ample pipeful of tobacco.

"I fear for our children, too," my wife accepted the change of topic with a pensive movement of her hand across her pockfree cheek.

"Anna, you and John must always obey the constable whenever a funeral procession passes. He'll walk in front of everyone, including the casket, warning all of the danger of infection if death was from the pox." I knew my words registered on my daughter as she sought the safety of her mother's skirt.

"Dear husband," my wife hobbled toward my place at the hearth, dragging a reluctant Anna. "Why add so much wood to the fire. You know we're running short, and so much winter lies ahead—you'll have the Inhabitants on your neck again."

"Uh, uh . . . to keep the house warm for the children . . . against the pox."

"You're being devious." She pulled me to the settle, drew the pipe from my mouth, kissed me, and then drew away, her arms crossed above her ample bosom like a schoolmarm. "Answer me!"

"I read . . ."

"In the Scripture, I hope—some of your other books provide more heat than light."

". . . a remedy for relieving the pox." I spoke hastily, hoping if I finished the entire thought it would sit well with her. "You catch as many toads as possible, put them in that clay pot, cover it with an iron plate, upend it, and cover it with hot coals . . ."

"Not *my* pot! And not in *my* fireplace!"

"Calm down! Hear me! Now, that's better . . . After the fire is out . . ."

Anna clasped her hands over her ears and fled upstairs.

"Shame on you, Joseph!"

"How can you disapprove of the remedy when you haven't heard all of it?"

"I'll make some saffron tea for those sick people," she smiled with open arms, "if that fails, try some cider, ale, a stonewall, or a flip." She laughed as she hugged me, "So many of your complicated 'remedies' are saturated in one or another of those liquids . . ."

The matter temporarily laid aside, we discussed plans for the weeks ahead. She would take Anna to visit Wenham while I weaned John. I offered to help her dye some clothes before attending to my ministerial visits, but she only asked that I fetch the dyepot, careful not to spill its urine, so that she could dissolve the indigo. Carefully, I lifted John from his seat on the dyepot to the settle and carried its sloshing contents to the table.

The smallpox abated in the late spring, sparing our family. No sooner was that epidemic over than another began: a Negro revolt. A slave, found guilty of poisoning his owner's wife by putting ratsbane in her milk, was lashed thirty-nine times and humiliated in the pillory.

"His punishment's ignited an uprising of Negro, Mulatto, and Indian slaves across the patent," I commented to Elizabeth. "There's a nine P.M. curfew on them until this mania is over."

"Ratsbane in milk, hmmm?" Her murmur toyed with my mind and her hands with my body.

"That's the story," I squirmed, "though they're not sure the Black, Nicholas . . ."

"Nicholas?' An unusual name for a slave?"

"So named to spite Reverend Noyes," the conversation eluded me as I became engrossed in lovemaking.

"Amusing," Beth stretched, her belly rising high.

"Amusing? I deserve more approval than that . . ."

"Of course you do. I meant the slave's name was amusing."

"I fail to see anything amusing about using a noted preacher's name for spite!"

"Just consider, dear," she continued, drowsily, "you might have suffered the same fate." My quizzical frown pleased her. "Yes, you might have been similarly punished, whipped and pilloried, had you forced those terrible 'remedies' on me . . ."

My sleepless night was probably to blame for my lapse the following day, allowing my horse to escape, and forcing me to chase my hogs out of Ben Hutchinson's cornfield before I set out on foot to find my errant sorrel.

*   *   *

Providence had blessed my farm and enabled me to set aside money for furniture. New loom? Spinning wheel for Anna? Inslow Table? Carver chair? I chose to buy us a new bed. 'Something to share. I'll justify it in view of Anna's need for our old one.' When I casually mentioned my decision in a letter to Master Brattle, he offered me an extra bed he owned at a fair price.

"Now that we've settled the price for the bed and cost of shipping it to you this summer," his letter ended, "I compliment you on your recent sermons against divination, and enclose a copy of my brother Thomas' '92 treatise: *A Full And Candid Account Of The Delusion*

Called Witchcraft. It illuminates our earlier conversation and prepares you for the argument you'll soon have in your Ministers' Council.''

The privately-circulated treatise, parts of which I had heard mentioned, arrived just before the council meeting at my home. In spite of Father Gerrish's admonition, it encouraged me to take an active part in the debate over spectral evidence.

"Thomas Brattle forcibly condemns Nicholas Noyes' touch of his hand to return an afflicted girl to her senses," Father Gerrish shrugged as I practiced my argument on him. "He denounces this as 'sorcery' and 'superstitious.''

"Joseph, better let well enough alone.''

"His treatise also asserts that the twelve girls might not have been afflicted at all, in spite of Doctor Griggs' diagnosis. He says it was a 'very gross evil, a real abomination' to have consulted them . . .''

"I'd omit quoting *that* to Nicholas . . .''

". . . an error compounded by the fact that ministers actually *sought* the girls' advice.''

"Sam Parris and Nicholas, of course," my father became glum because of my enthusiasm.

"What caused our most famous astronomer to doubt the accused were witches was the selectivity of their 'poisoned' looks," I explained, "afflicting only the few gals, not others who also came under their stares.''

"Regardless of Thomas' eminence, (rumor has it he'll soon be elected to the Royal Academy of Science), you cannot fill his shoes in argument against Nicholas. Keep silent. Let others carry the debate.''

After we assembled, Joseph Capen set the tone for the discussion following my father-in-law's prayer for accord.

"None of us denies the presence of Satan . . .'' The Topsfield parson began.

"Nor his diabolical ability to invade all manners of life and convert them to his cause," Benjamin Rolfe of Haverhill added from his seat opposite Joe Capen.

"Why has this issue arisen?" Reverend Noyes emphasized his fury by banging the table so hard the trencher jumped and clattered. "We all agree upon the Devil's power to bewitch.''

"Brother Noyes," John Wise's tone was unusually calm, "we meet to draft an address to the General Court, a request that spectral evidence be rejected in cases of persons accused of this heinous crime. That is the sole purpose of today's meeting.''

"One, mind you, only *one* view I fail to share with you!'' Nicholas rose, gripping the sides of the trencher as if it were a pulpit. ''The cryptic 'S.G.' of Brattle's infamous manuscript, I suppose refers to me—for I was one of those 'Salem Gentlemen,' I am proud to say.''

"Brother Noyes,'' I saw my chance when he paused for a quaff of ale, ''why were *you* not afflicted when the accused stared at *you*?'' my Father Gerrish winced.

"As a minister of the Lord,'' he roared, ''I was amply protected from the Devil's curse!''

"But your namesake, Goodwife Hale, nee Noyes, of Beverly, was accused,'' I pressed, further dismaying my father-in-law. ''Was not this false accusation the straw that broke the camel's back and ended the blasphemous proceedings?''

"Blasphemous? *Blasphemous!*'' Nicholas shouted so loud I feared he would frighten the children upstairs. ''I remind you all, our host was too *green* to have witnessed the Devil's rampage . . .''

'Thank the Lord he doesn't know of *my* escapade on Gallows Hill— I pray he never does!'

". . . that John Hale was quite helpful to me in limiting the spread of witchcraft throughout this patent.''

"Aha!'' my emotion got the better of me and I regretted it. ''No sooner was Hale's wife falsely accused than he recanted his earlier statements. Perhaps that accusation helped him see through the lies of spectral evidence . . .''

Nicholas seemed to choke on his ale, some seeping from his lips. It reminded me of Sarah Good's defense against the Salem minister, when she not only called him a liar but promised, ''God will give you blood to drink,'' and I felt ashamed for having gone too far.

Fortunately, John Wise took up the cudgel against spectral evidence.

"You recall Matthew Hopkins' infamous test for witchery,'' he walked to the center of the room, ''the ordeal by water? He cross-bound the accused: right thumb to left big toe and vice versa.'' The wrestler-parson bent with ease to demonstrate, his voice as audible as before. ''Then, with the unscientific belief that pure water would not permit a witch to drown, the accused was flung in a pond, as often as three times, and declared 'Guilty!'' if the poor creature floated!''

"Thank Heaven people tested Hopkins!" Ben Rolfe interjected. "They finally hanged *him* for witchcraft after *he'd* floated three times!"

"In our enlightened times," I resumed after filling my guests' jacks, "spectral evidence is as diabolical a test as trying to find who is a witch by cutting off a pig's tail and ear, tossing them in yonder fire, and assuming the first passerby is a witch."

To my horror, Elizabeth flitted past the hearth on her way to the leanto as my speech ended.

"I hold no brief for 'Science,' Master Green." My wife's coincidental action went unnoticed by my colleagues, for which I thanked Providence. "I consider it blasphemous of that satanic Quaker, Edward Burroughs." Nicholas tried to pace but Father Gerrish restrained him, "to suggest testing, by laboratory analysis, whether bread and wine change into the body and blood of our Lord!"

"Blasphemous? Yes!" John Wise supported. "It is a misuse of the scientific method."

"Would all of you, then, replace the logic of our martyred Huguenot brother, Pierre de la Ramee, with the materialist 'scientific method' espoused by Francis Bacon?" Nicholas' anger was as fierce as it had been on Gallows Hill.

"You dare accuse *us* of being in league with that . . . that Leveller," John stammered.

"Richard Overton," I assisted.

"Yes, Overton, the fool who misunderstood Bacon when he proposed we use the method to test for the existence of the soul."

"I wouldn't put it past any of you," Nicholas accused, "though you do so out of folly. Your minds are clouded—if not deluded."

"You accuse us of being bewitched or of witchcraft?" My father-in-law's quiet tone disarmed the Salemite.

"We're letting our affections overcome our reason," I came to my father's defense. "As Reverend Mather might have put it."

"Which Mather?", the Salem pastor challenged.

"Richard, as I said before, the only sensible Mather, Nicholas," John Wise chided, but the Salem minister only sneered in return.

"*Increase* Mather," I corrected. "He states that mere physical evidence reduces the power of Providence in matters such as these. Science, he claims, applies to matters of the senses; reason and logic, including mathematics, to concepts and imagination." I felt strangely equal to my seniors and grateful to William Brattle for his warning to prepare myself for such a discussion. "Therefore, brethren, as ministers to and leaders of our people, we *must* address the Court against the use of spectral evidence: it denies us our God-given use of reason, plays into the Devil's hands, and threatens to perpetuate the frenzy that began here, by this very hearth."

Ominously, my wife re-entered on tiptoe and made her way to the kitchen. Her father's, "Amen," broke the silence.

"I propose this wording," John read from his notes, "that the accusing persons were under 'diabolical manifestations.' Further, that many innocents suffered because of the fallaciousness of accepting spectral evidence. I believe we ought to conclude our address with the admonition that God might have continued controversy with us and our land, because we supplanted Reason, with which He blessed us, with wildly affected accusations and superstitions."

"Have humility, brethren, I beseech you." Nicholas' voice sounded desperate as Beth presented him his hat and cloak. "We *could* be acting as giants in the Lord's behalf . . ." He slammed his hat almost over his ears, ". . . instead, we're behaving like *dwarfs!*"

"Reverend Noyes," my wife challenged, "was it not our departed brother, John Hale, who wrote, 'A dwarf, upon a giant's shoulders, sees farther than the giant?'"

Flushed and speechless, Nicholas flew out the door, leaving the rest of us to write the address to the Court and sign our names.

"Leave it to my daughter to have the last word," Joseph Gerrish remarked before leaving.

*　　*　　*

"Wake up!" my wife's heel dug into my shin.

"The baby's come?"

"No, not yet . . ."

"Then what . . . why?"

"I told you I'd wake you when the moon eclipse began."

Without dressing, we crouched at the window to watch the event. Beth, heavy with child and sleepy after our vigil, needed my help to rise and return to bed.

"I pray no one will seize this eclipse as an omen, Joseph," I fell quickly into a dreamless sleep, but it seemed I had just dropped off when I was nudged, "JOSEPH!"

"What's the matter now?" I grumbled, "haven't you seen enough for one night?"

"The baby . . . it's coming!"

I catapulted from bed, stirred the fire, fetched wood from the shed, and held my poor wife's hand as our maid helped deliver our baby only minutes before the drum sounded calling us to meeting. Following my morning sermon, I baptized our son, Joseph, in fond memory of Beth's brother who had been killed at sea the past spring.

"Birth on the Sabbath?" I heard Goodwife Deal remark to Ben Hutchinson as they made their way to his house between meetings. "It means, of course, the child was shamelessly conceived on the Sabbath some nine months ago!"

"An evil omen," he agreed, "coming on the heels of last night's eerie sky."

Too joyous about our new baby, I let their comments pass to concentrate on improving my afternoon sermon.

"Again, I urge your ardent support of our army," I exhorted. "Its reputation has been ignominiously maligned for having failed to locate our Taranteen tormentors. Take heart in our preparedness as witnessed by Brother Joseph Putnam's red ribbon, won for marksmanship on Training Day."

"Reverend," Captain Putnam caught me as I hastened to comfort my wife. The night having fallen, I invited him for a tankard of hot metheglin, fermented honey and water.

"It's a *pitaugan*, Master Green," the captain handed me a small leather bag. "Please open it."

Inside, I found a blackened rawhide strung with white fishteeth interspersed with black seashells.

"On my last, fruitless trek with our militia, I found this in the waste of an Abenaki campsite. Save it for young Joseph—a token of my esteem for his father's support of our army."

As I fumbled with the string, I noticed one end was stained. Holding the section toward him, the captain's grin became dour.

"That caught my eye, too. You see, when the Indians make peace, as the Iroquois and Abenaki did a few years ago, thus relieving Mohawk pressure on the Taranteens, they exchange wampum painted white . . .''

"But, Captain, this wampum . . .''

"Stained with dried blood! Meaning war's been declared between the Indians and ourselves."

"This wampum confirms Queen Anne's War?''

"Precisely. Is it too grim a gift for the baby?'' My guest's gruff manner melted.

"On the contrary. It will remind him we live in a hostile land. Hopefully, it will encourage him to join the militia when he comes of age."

Visibly pleased, the captain paused long enough to warm his hands and then left in the December cold.

During the winter of '04, I took it upon myself to learn more about the Indians and concentrated on my military training as never before. Although my wife joked about my horsemanship, she was always ready to help me understand Indian ways.

"Remember,'' she nursed Joseph in spite of John's envious eyes, "Father served with the army and received a considerable grant for his duty. What I know about Indians, I learned at his knee.

I placed Joseph in the cradle, too close to the fire for my wife's comfort, and so she moved it farther away.

"*Must* you light your junk just now? It could annoy little Joseph.''

"There's more smoke from the fire than from my new pipe . . . besides, it comforts me. Have a puff?'' She declined, saying it might affect her milk.

"Captain Putnam's right, the danger we face is greater now than ever,'' Beth rocked in tempo with my puffs. "For years, the Taranteens have warred against the Mohawks,'' sheepishly, she reached for my pipe and took a few puffs, "and that kept the tribes from focusing on us.

"About ten years ago, Mohawks raided a Taranteen village. Before the Abenaki hunting party returned, most of the unarmed villagers had been massacred. The survivors set out to track the raiders but found no trace of them—they'd taken refuge at Skull Place.''

"Like our own army's failure . . .''

"Then, an Abenaki shaman, using squirrels as his helpers . . .''

"Elizabeth!" she knew her willingness to credit pagan superstitions distressed me.

"Their great shaman, Gluskabe, used animals too, changing moose into squirrels . . ."

"I pray Goodwife Deal hasn't heard these tales!"

Our laughter woke the baby and so Beth held and rocked him as she continued.

"As I was saying, the shaman sent squirrels to find the Mohawks. Changing a nearby rock into a canoe," she awaited my reaction and I obliged with a snort, "he slashed the enemies' canoes to block their escape. The Taranteens slaughtered all but one, whose ears they lopped off, and sent him home to teach his tribe a lesson."

Baby Joseph sound asleep, I tucked him in his cradle, careful not to blow smoke on him. "Fascinating, whether or not true. We face a formidable enemy with papist French commanders."

The wintry night was peaceful for us and our fellow villagers— but a horror for our Deerfield neighbors! The deep snow allowed more than a hundred Indians, guiding two-hundred French to mobilize near Three Rivers. Trekking on snowshoes, their dogteams tugging sledges, they reached the heights above Deerfield. At dawn, running atop the crusted snow, they overwhelmed the village before the alarm was sounded.

Only three days earlier, Captain Putnam's troops had chased hunting parties near Pigwacket. Diabolically, the Indians tricked our troops into believing that nothing serious was in the offing. Desperately, Brother Williams of Deerfield had warned Governor Dudley that the village was ripe for an attack and almost defenseless. His call for aid went unheeded.

"An Englishman who escaped, only one among the hundred-sixty or more souls captured by the devils, and forced to march three-hundred miles to Quebec, detailed the massacre," Captain Putnam told the crowd at Ingersoll's later that March. "Williams' life was spared because the pistol he held against the breast of a painted savage misfired— otherwise, he might have been scalped!"

He paused to encourage the crowd's anger to flare.

"After pillaging and torching the village," he choked, "boiling some of our people alive, it's said," again he waited for the shock to register on us, "they split into parties and began the march to Canada."

Along their freezing trek, those who tired or became ill were likely to be tomahawked, as happened to John Williams' wife, Eunice.

"When they camped at night," the captain thumped his tankard on the table, "all stood in fear of death. The Demon Rum intoxicated the savages. Only intervention by their papist French masters saved the hostages from butchery, rape, or mutilation . . ."

Putt swore, as did others. I chose to ignore their blasphemy—I felt like doing the same.

"Even so, in spite of the Frenchmen's attempts, the parson's faithful Negro slave was murdered by the pagan devils!" The captain spilled the remainder of his flip on the floor in disgust.

I quieted the milling Farmers with a prayer for our Deerfield brethern, dead, alive, or in captivity, and closed with another exhortation in favor of military training.

*   *   *

As might be expected, Training Day was taken more seriously than before the Deerfield Raid. Putt again established himself as our leading horseman, racing across the training field with brandished sword and musket to my wife's vocal admiration.

The captain chose the day to punish our sentinel, caught napping on watch. Anna and John joined other children, taunting the miscreant as he rode the wooden horse, Putt's having tied a musket to each of the sentinel's feet. That the punishment sobered him was evident, the sentinel was the most avid listener to my lecture that concluded the day.

The following Sabbath I lectured against drunkenness, too many Inhabitants having used Training Day as an excuse for misconduct. That my words did not register evinced itself on Election Day—'Nigger Election'—when so many Farmers were cited for drunkenness there was a queue awaiting the stocks after my Thursday's lecture. Among them was Ben Hutchinson, a red 'D' placard hanging around his neck.

"Why do we call it, 'Nigger Election?'" Anna asked from her perch on my shoulders. We had watched the boys play stool ball, disgraced somewhat because John had been banished for impeding the ball's roll to the post.

"Because Negroes are allowed to attend events on this occasion," her mother answered, Joseph tucked under one arm.

"At Artillery Election," I added, "Negroes may not be present, under threat of severe punishment."

"Don't you feel that's unfair?" my wife probed while we enjoyed our pipes and ale after the children were in bed.

"Not at all! Anyone who fails his military duty *deserves* to ride the wooden horse—maybe run the gauntlet as well!"

"I wasn't questioning *that*. Of course we must be alert to attack by land or water. I wondered whether you agreed with Judge Sewall's treatise against slavery?"

'Will she *never* cease to adopt unpopular causes?' I had skimmed *The Selling Of Joseph* but was of two minds about it. On the one hand, I had set aside some money to buy a slave to assist my wife so that she could better attend to rearing our children. On the other, I felt that Negroes were as much in league with the Devil as were Indians, the darkness of their skins attesting to the sign of Cain.

"Until I've convinced myself to the contrary, Beth, I'll continue to support our practices."

In truth, the havoc raised in our parsonage by Parris's Negro and Indian slaves raised questions in my mind as to the safety of my family should we own one.

"Alright, dear, I'll drop the subject, for now . . ." Beth stretched a scrap of white linen over a dried corncob and tied a ball of wool to one end as a doll for Anna.

"Give it to her on your way to your study," she instructed as she prepared the loom.

My wife's work was never-ending. By midsummer, I became so involved in farming we were both too fatigued to be interested in lovemaking. To make matters worse, the drought forced us to leave the parsonage open and so mosquitoes tormented us night after night.

"Still awake?" my wife poked me. "The skeeters are terrible! Light your junk—maybe we'll get some sleep."

As she sat on the edge of the bed, puffing gently on my pipe, I felt a heat inside me which had nothing to do with the sweltering weather.

"Joseph, dear Joseph," she fell backward, "we'll only sweat more . . ."

Pulling her on top of me after we had enjoyed ourselves, her eyes showed weariness mixed with love. I wiped her face with the bear and moved her beside me.

"Except for your sperm, sweat's our only moisture tonight."

"Your father, Nicholas, and I hold a fast for rain tomorrow," I whispered to her snores.

Riding the parched road to Beverly, I decided to buy a slave but wasn't sure why. 'To relieve Elizabeth's exhaustion?' I preferred to believe so. 'Or because you can't control your lust?' I argued with myself. 'Both reasons hold, except that 'lust' does not apply to loving feelings in a marriage.' I recalled supporting passages from Cotton Mather's essays on Christian love which took my mind off the thirst of my trip.

"Before they call to me," Brother Noyes' black cloak soaked with perspiration, "I will answer." We were now in our tenth day of fast for rain. "And while they are still speaking," he read from 65 Isaiah, Verse 24, "I *will* listen."

Listen we did! Not to Nicholas but to a clap of thunder more intense than had been heard earlier in the week and then to a cloudburst crashing on the roof. Our fast had been answered, the drought was over!

"Nicholas has a way with the Lord," I wondered to my wife as I dried my clothes by the fire upon my return from Beverly.

"If only the Lord would bless your way with horses," Beth handed me a jack into which I plunged a poker for my flip.

"I couldn't help it. The thunder and lightning frightened him as we crossed the Horse Bridge . . ."

"We imagined as much when he galloped into the leanto without you. Next Training Day—take some lessons riding the wooden horse . . ."

"Didn't I see a woman ride away from here?"

"Ann Putnam just left."

"Did she come to see me?"

"No, to visit me and the children," my wife relieved me of my tankard as I raked the fire for the night.

"Remember," she continued after prayers, "I've known Ann a long time. Now, lonely and still unmarried, she tends to her orphaned brothers and sisters and visits me occasionally."

Knowledge that Young Ann had visited the parsonage in my absence distressed me. 'Only the Lord knows what deviltry she may be up to—pray, protect my stubborn wife and innocent children.'

The thunder and lightning which accompanied the rain kept me wakeful. 'Superstitious Farmers may take this storm, as they did the drought, as a sign of God's wrath or the Devil's doing.' Goodwife Deal's scowling face crossed my mind. 'Joyful as we should be about the answer to our prayers, rumors will spread about the fury that accompanies it.'

Immediately after I had dispelled Tabitha's visage, a flash of lightning replaced it with that of Ann Putnam—not the frail orphan for whom my wife felt pity, but the cart-driving pissabed of Gallows Hill.

7   I Desire to Lie in the Dust . . .

'Horses, horses, horses!' No sooner had I chased Ben Hutchinson's jades from my apple trees than I found another horse tethered to my hitching post. 'Oh, no, don't tell me . . .!''

My wife waddled to greet me, careful not to bump her stomach against my musket. "Ann's here to talk to you," tears welled in her eyes. "Be kind to her, as you are with me. She's been sleepless these past nights—nightmares about a stubby man in a winding-sheet. She'll tell you more.''

Dressed in faded plain baize, Ann had seated herself beside my escritoire. I could hardly see her deep-set grey eyes in their black sockets. 'Beth's right, she *does* look worse than before. Let's pray she doesn't resume her antics.' I seated myself opposite the former member of Putt's 'Devil's Brood' without any sign of greeting from her.

"Giles Corey's ghost haunts me nightly," her squeaky voice quavered. "Wearing only a winding-sheet, he stomps, stomps, stomps . . . Then he groans, 'More weight, MORE WEIGHT,' and gasps for breath." Her eyes closed to dispel the image, her hands clasped across her ears to block the sound of her words.

Unfortunately, my wife's curiosity had got the better of her and so she slipped into my study, seating herself behind Ann. 'Beth's curiosity could be her undoing if she insists on witnessing this bit . . .' I caught myself, 'this hag's testimony.'

The picture Ann painted matched that which her late father, Thomas, had described in a letter to Judge Sewall before Goodman Corey's torture. Cotton Mather used its contents to prove Corey's guilt of witchcraft, insisting that Young Ann could not have known of an incident which occurred five years before her birth.

"When I'm awake," Ann droned, "I'm able to chase the apparition away."

'Well enough,' I meant to comment, but my wife's head-wagging silenced me.

"Even during prayer, my thoughts are filled with memory of that naked old man, his back flat on the earth, planks across his chest . . ." she shuddered, "as Sheriff Curwin heaps stones on them to Goodman Corey's demands, 'More weight, MORE WEIGHT!''

Ann tugged a tuft from her hair, vainly trying to rid her brain of the ghastly memory. Beth rose to knead Ann's frail shoulders.

"With the Lord's mercy," my wife's action relaxed Ann's grimace and brought a feeble smile, "relating your tale may be a step toward removing its haunting memory."

Anna entered, carrying a tray of hoe cakes and cider, which Ann refused. When I scowled at her as a father might a reluctant child, she took a bite and finished the cakes without our help.

Giles Corey's punishment arose from his refusal to plead 'Guilty' or 'Not Guilty' to the charge of witchcraft. Had he pled either way, his property would have been confiscated. So, when he remained silent, he suffered the *peine forte et dure*. His will left his considerable estate to his two loyal sons-in-law.

"I can finish now, Reverend," fortified by food, Ann reverted to moroseness. "Each time his shoulders moved, mine twitched; each time his head turned, mine jerked; each time he groaned for more weight, I silently screamed the same." Her tears flushed down her wizened face as she rejected Elizabeth's consolation. "It was much the same as had happened in the ordinary," her voice fell to a whisper, "when I mimicked each gesture he made. The difference was that during his trial I could control my actions, while later, when . . . when he was being pressed to death, I lost control! I fought—I prayed not to copy him—but I had no control!"

It was hard to imagine a girl of twelve able to identify with a gruff, eighty-one-year-old scoundrel. Well before the frenzy, he had been accused of stealing wood from a neighbor; charged with having beaten Goodman Goodell; prosecuted for having cheated John Gloyd of his well-earned wages; and suspected for having torched the Proctor's home. But there she sat, tormented, unable to restrain herself from feeling his suffering and admitting *she* had been Satan's tool.

Suddenly, she stuck out her tongue, I thought to mock me, and beckoned Elizabeth to examine it. We both complied, but it made no sense to us.

"See the dark spot at its tip?" she lisped.

'Spectral evidence!' The thought frightened me for my wife's safety.

"No, dear, I see no mark," Beth soothed.

"I know, I've searched for it in the mirror, but the pressure's so strong I gag."

Elizabeth and I flopped into our chairs, strained by Ann's histrionics, but prepared to hear her out. She composed herself by vigorously scratching her lice-ridden hair and then cleared her throat with a gulp of cider.

"I first felt the pressure when the weights on Goodman Corey's chest . . ." she gagged.

"Squeezed his tongue from his mouth," Ann controlled herself when my wife interjected, "and so Sheriff Curwin used his cane to force Giles' tongue inside . . ."

"I feel the very place on my own tongue! This instant!"

'A terrible ordeal for anyone to suffer, whether the falsely accused Corey or this once-frenzied waif who has yet to ripen into womanhood. Dear Lord,' I prayed silently and then aloud, "Dear Lord, may Your own suffering and death atone for sinners such as we." I suggested we pray together for His mercy and forgiveness and continue at another time.

Anna accompanied Ann to her horse while my wife stayed with me to pray. "Dear Lord, forgive me for my enmity toward this forlorn child and pray she's taken the first step toward a full confession."

*   *   *

Pregnancy again disabled Elizabeth. Even with Ann's help, the chores piled up. Rather than buy a slave, I chose to add seven-and-a-half acres to our estate. This meant, of course, I must oversee the workmen who cleared the glebe of trees and built a wall around it. 'That'll stop Hutch's horses from eating my apples,' I gloated.

From early May through the end of June, '06, I put Commerce before Religion, supervising three or four teams of workers, sometimes numbering as many as twenty-two, all of whom my wife graciously fed. Sam Nurse, whose drinking water was the best in the village, let me haul it from his farm across the Crane River, over Haddock's Bridge to the parsonage. At day's end, I treated my workers to ale at Ingersoll's before they left for their homes.

"Rumor has it," Goodman Nurse commented casually as I worked at his well-sweep, "Ann Putnam's visited you quite often this summer."

Feeling it unnecessary to confirm or deny the story, I pumped all the harder, hoping he would let the matter drop.

"Putt tells me her health is poor," the son of the martyred Rebecca Nurse insisted, "I've noticed as much at meeting."

"We pray together," I obliged, cinching my saddle.

"I wonder . . ." he knew he was close to compromising the confidence between my parishioner and myself, "I wonder, has she mentioned my poor mother?"

In response, I held out my hand to thank him. Angrily, he spun away, feigning a shot at a bounding hare that was well beyond his musket's range.

'There are no secrets in this isolated hamlet,' I mounted to haul another load of water. 'Better scotch rumors about Young Ann before they bloom—or Beth may suffer their consequences!'

Providentially, the parish remained calm through the summer. Ann chose to talk with me while I worked in our fields, only once dismounting to help Elizabeth cultivate our flax patch.

As a result of Goodman Nurse's rebuff, Putt also avoided me, although he came by in my absence with some pork as part-payment of his rate and stored it in the powdering tub at my wife's request. About to leave, he mentioned testily that Goody Deal's butter had refused to churn. According to her husband, she had jammed a hot needle into it to rid it of imps.

"A common practice hereabouts," my wife had tried to placate him, but he spurned her as Sam Nurse had me.

"We've so many apples," Beth bubbled after she saw my distress over Putt's conduct, "I can make a good number of barrels of cider this fall."

Taking her cue, I had the sawyer come by to repair the press. He installed a new lever and checked the screw. When I paid him, he agreed to sell me some hay for squeezing the pomace, and so we were ready for more work.

'Worms in the peas,' I wrote in my diary, followed a few days later by another entry, 'BUGS!' The plethora of such pets led me to declare a fast day. Unfortunately, it brought a cloudburst that damaged more crops, albeit relieving our infestation. 'Another ill omen?' I scribbled.

"How many bushels of grain did you send to the gristmill?" Elizabeth shouted as she sifted the coarse flour.

"Six," I called from the shed where I was currying my horse.

"We got only five-and-a-half in return . . ."

'Another annoyance! If only she'd leave commerce to me.' I filled the Indian Barrel with cider in case any Taranteen might want to slake his thirst after helping other farmers tend their fields.

When the Winslow Table arrived from Boston, Anna helped me set its drop leaves. Beth delighted in its circular shape because it broke the monotony of our otherwise rectangular furnishings. We celebrated with cider brandy from the same shipment.

"Just a drop, Joseph, enough to get the juices flowing," my wife admonished before we made love, clumsily, because of the advanced stage of her pregnancy.

"It's November Fifth," I announced. "Time for me to take John to Salem."

"Oh no, no, he's only four . . ."

"Sorry, I promised we'd witness the centennial of Guy Fawkes' Day."

"John, hold tight to your father as you sit on my pillion. Joseph," she stretched to reach me, "wouldn't the shallop be safer . . . your horsemanship?"

"I'll protect father," my son added to my humiliation.

John's eyes gaped at the ox-drawn cart, filled with its figures of the Pope, his monks, and Satan as it lumbered down the Salem street. He paid even more attention to the older boys who begged, "Hear my little bell go chink, chink, chink," a refrain he yowled, making it difficult for me to acknowledge Reverend Noyes' invitation to his parsonage, "Please give me a little money to buy my Pope some drink."

The parade over, Nicholas accompanied us to his home. Fortified by a tankard of meglathin, John napped on the hearth.

"Have you read this?" My host pushed a manuscript across the table. "No? It shows no author, although it's circulated throughout the Bay area."

"Hmm, *Questions And Proposals*," I thumbed through it without studying its contents.

"You'll find it worth your while. Read it carefully. We'll discuss the issue at a council meeting." John stirred, and my host covered him with my cloak. "I trust you will agree with me: the clergy *must* take a leading position in the governance of men's affairs—even if it means less influence for the congregation."

Noise from Pope's Day celebrants woke John, and so I thanked Nicholas, who lashed my son to his pillion and retreated to his parsonage without my having a chance to comment on his statement.

> "The Fifth of November,
> As you will remember,
> Was gunpowder, treason and plot . . ."

Drunken revelers deafened us as we rode past the pillory, a white man being punished for having married a mulatto, then beyond the meeting house to the pyre on which burned the hay-stuffed figures we had seen in the parade. When John screamed that the figures were headless, I slowed our gait to explain that the heads were saved from year to year, the latest head being that of the Pretender.

"Chink, chink, chink," he chorused. My horse responded to the cadence all of the seven miles home to John's mother's anxious arms.

"Ann visited," she reported after the children were safe in bed, having lulled them to sleep to the tune of Guy Fawke's ballad. "She confided to me, I expect she knew I'd tell you, she's never developed as a woman—she's never passed blood. Lord have mercy on her, Joseph. Pray, be most tender when she calls on you."

"I pray for *your* safety, Beth, as much as for *her* forgiveness."

"The Lord is *my* protector," her tone was unusually gruff, "*you* must be hers . . ."

She left me to rake the fire after which I treated myself to canary and fell asleep on the settle, only to be startled awake at midnight by her scream. Upstairs, I found my wife in labor. Our maid joined us moments later and served as midwife to our son whom we nicknamed, 'Nedd.'

"I hereby baptize you, Edward," I proudly announced to the congregation, "in memory of my mother's father and my dear brother, without whose legacy I might not have been able to purchase my library."

In spite of her painful recovery from the birth of our fifth child, Providence helped Beth regain her strength. Ann Putnam dropped by to help with household chores, but neither Goodman Nurse nor Joseph Putnam offered me his congratulations.

*   *   *

"You tidied my desk again," I accused from the stairwell. "Where'd you hide my book?"

"Which book?" Her delay and tone reflected my wife's mood.

"Not my diary—the notebook with my sermon ideas."

Suckling Nedde, Beth strode into my study to search my escritoire, its fall locked in place. Within moments, she tossed my battered notebook at my feet. Never able to locate items I had misplaced, I moved sheepishly to kiss her but she evaded me. 'She'll soon get over it,' I rationalized, 'at least she'll leave Ann alone with me.'

"Thank you, Anna," I bent to kiss my daughter, but she rebuffed me after she had ushered Ann into my room. I sat my guest in the Carver chair from our Boston shipment, pleased that she showed no sign of fatigue, although she appeared to have lost another tooth due to poor diet. 'I'll suggest to Putt that he provide better for her family in exchange for his payment to me.' I felt Ann was ready when she stopped fidgeting with the arms of her chair.

"Let us pray." I followed the same approach I had taken with my Roxbury boys. "We have already broken the law: to love the Lord, whole-heartedly, and our neighbors as ourselves. We are, therefore, powerless to obey God's law. Hence, we have broken His commands." I opened my eyes to find hers shut. "I shall leave it to your conscience to judge whether you have broken each commandment." My tone was as harsh with her as it had been with my wife.

"Have you kept the First Commandment?" She remained silent.

"It means to know, worship, and glorify the Lord, asking His pardon and mercy."

"Must I answer?"

'If she can't reply to this first question, what more can she do?' I ought to have expected disappointment.

"I . . . I suppose I have . . . have not kept it."

'The Lord would consider a 'supposition' insufficient,' I wrote in my notebook. 'I'll probe her later on this issue; hopefully others will be easier for her.'

"Second, have you always prayed, worshipped, and studied the Scripture with diligence and regularity?" I forced myself to be more gentle. "Private prayer is vitally important, followed by public worship."

"No, not always, Reverend," her voice steadied, "shall I explain?"

"You *must* elaborate. A 'yes' or 'no' does not suffice."

"Since my parents died, I've been unable to read much Scripture— even when they were alive, they were both too busy to teach me to read well."

'Sermon on the need for a village school' I underlined 'school'. It's been five years since the vote was taken, and Putt's yet to act.'

"If you attend to my sermons and lectures," I leaned toward Ann, "you know the Scripture warns against spectral evidence, superstition, divination . . ."

"I . . . I confess—I *have* broken the Second Command. As recently as my last visit here, I had nightmares about Goodman Corey. And," she clasped her hands to control her nervousness, "years ago, when I was half as old, I was raptured by the tales of Tituba, Sam Parris' slave. I went so far as to let her—that's not true—to *beg* her to show us magic she'd learned in the Indies. Have I said enough?"

"Is your conscience clear on this commandment?"

She reported that among the tricks Tituba had performed was mixing the gals' urine with corn meal, forming it into a pone, and feeding it to the Parris' dog. Watching the animal devour the mixture thrilled the twelve-year-old, but she had since rued her folly and was ashamed.

"Third," Ann's reply satisfied me, "did you ever take the Lord's name in vain?"

"I did. I did! Once, to test His power—the fear that swept over me prevented me from ever doing it again."

'Better, much better,' my confidence grew with hers. "This commandment may be broken if you've ever despised any fellow-creature, each of them is made in God's image.''

Ann hitched her hips in the chair, leaning her head against its high back, her eyes closed. 'Surely, she's loathed someone, sometime,' I fought my impatience.

"I . . . I hated Pastor Parris," she murmured. "Hated him for spiriting his daughter away," she twisted her head to show she meant the parsonage, "leaving me as almost the youngest of the girls. I resented being treated as a baby—I was the oldest in my family." Her lips pursed with bitterness. "To show how I felt toward him, I decided I'd outdo the others. Ooh, how I hated that man!"

"You claim the parson caused your actions?" It seemed inconceivable that Ann despised the man who had prevented her horsecart from disaster on Gallows Hill.

"It was so long ago. I don't know. I'm confused."

"Hatred willfully violates God's law. It disables us from forgiving and forgetting well after the feeling has passed. While we burn in Hell with hatred, it prevents us from facing our shortcomings."

"I never thought about it that way. All these years, whenever I've recalled those days. I've seen Reverend Parris as the cause for my distress. Talking with you, I have trouble remembering the loathing I felt for him." She wiped her tears, "Will I be free of hatred—now I've confessed it?"

"An explanation is no excuse. You've explained how you used hatred of your lowly status among your friends to impel your actions. Whether you'll be forgiven is in God's hands."

Without pause, I challenged her as to whether she had also broken the Fourth Commandment. I knew she had upset Deodat Lawson's sermon. Unfortunately, he was so enthralled by her Sabbath-breaking, he essayed about it, further abetting the frenzy.

Ann retold her folly and begged forgiveness for her willfulness.

Anna's arrival with a trayful of hoe-cakes and cider reduced our tension. I prayed the Lord bless our food and silently pled for His protection of my family against accusations which might arise from Ann's presence in our parsonage.

"Five: honor your parents."

"I have, while both were living, and now by sacrificing myself on behalf of my eight orphaned brothers and sisters . . ."

"Sacrificing?"

"I . . . I've carried out my parents' dying wishes."

"And when both were alive?"

"I obeyed them!"

"During the frenzy?" I slapped my knee.

"Especially then!" Ann claimed she had obeyed her mother's every wish, taking each as a command. When I insisted that this contradicted her prior assertion about her fury of being treated as the baby among her friends, she became sullen.

"You ask God to believe your conduct was merely that of an obedient daughter? Absurd! You seek refuge behind this command!"

Her knuckles whitened as she gouged her eyes to block my meaning: that God expects us to do our parents' bidding—in all matters, without second thoughts—unless their requests are sinful.

"I . . . I was often more willful than mother wished. I had to prove myself. I felt jealous. She always doted on her youngest child. For a brief moment that dreadful year," she sobbed, "I regained my mother's favor." She opened her eyes without wiping her tears, "I *dis*honored my parents, didn't I?"

"You dishonored the Lord, your parents, and yourself . . ."

'I'm drained, utterly drained, as Ann must also be.' I rose, lit my junk, and without a word went outside to relieve myself, guilty for having been so harsh in my interrogation. 'It's your duty—to the Lord, your parish, and to Ann,' I consoled myself. 'Besides, your inquisition was gentler than her Uncle Joseph, let alone Sam Nurse, might wish.'

"Ann wants to continue," my wife greeted me on my return, "have a swig of canary, dear—and *do* be understanding with her."

"The Sixth Commandment forbids anger without cause—including revenge toward someone who's wronged you," I drew deeply on my pipe. "Anger can also damage your health."

"I have often broken this command," she burst, "and beg God's forgiveness."

"Your mother was disposed to hold grudges, was she not?"

"Oh, yes! Her brother was so mad when a widow spurned his marriage proposal, he died soon after. Her sister, Aunt Mary *never* forgave the Inhabitants for the way they hounded her husband, William Bayley. Her hatred led her, too, to an early grave. Mother could be vengeful, yes, and I've been vengeful, too."

The Seventh Commandment, forbidding adultery, seemed least relevant for this immature woman. While I tried to hide my indecision by relighting my pipe, Ann took the initiative.

"I have *not* committed adultery. I'm sure your wife has told you about me. I . . . I used to have unchaste thoughts, when . . . when the older girls told me about their escapades. It made me so resentful that I determined I'd prove I was as much a female as they." She shifted in her chair to gain full control of herself as she continued.

"The solution came to me in a dream. It was no apparition—I'd listened to my parents berate the minister who followed Pastor Bayley. The man was so strong! He picked up a barrel by putting his thumb in the bunghole. He shouldered a barrel of cider from his shallop to his house. On Training Day, he held a musket perfectly level at arm's length. My head swam with his image, and so I asked my parents more about him before bedtime. They told me two of his wives had died and suspected he'd been responsible. I . . . . I dreamt more about him, especially after Mary Warren and Sarah Churchill told us what they'd overheard going on in their masters' bedrooms. My dreams got more confused. When I shared them with Parris' niece, Abigail, I found she only dreamt of *horses!*"

"Are you saying that resentment toward your friends led you to accuse George Burroughs of bewitching you?"

"I testified I'd been frightened by the ghosts of the two wives he'd murdered: stabbing one beneath her left arm and covering the wound with sealing wax; drowning the other from his shallop." She wrung her hands. "See how evil I was! I felt nothing would happen, he was living in Wells, Maine, and hadn't been to the village since his wife's funeral, when he went into debt to pay for the canary . . ."

She paused to smooth her tattered skirt.

"I vomited when George Burroughs arrived in chains—I'd dreamt of him as a giant, but he was so *small.* The only way I could stay in the good graces of my friends was to claim he'd . . . he'd tried to rape me."

A grimace, perhaps a smile, bared her wretched teeth. I pretended not to notice, for I had no intention of diverting her.

"I made the gals swear not to tell anyone, entrancing them with how George Burroughs, after killing his wives, attacked me while I slept. *That* ended their giggling about me!" Her voice dropped. "Even at his gallows speech, when he might have been freed, my dream protected me from admitting my lie . . . If it hadn't been for that Boston minister . . .''

"Cotton Mather?"

"Beside his great white horse, he mocked Reverend Burroughs, and so he was hanged—as the man who'd wronged me. If my words sound prideful,'' she apologized, "I don't mean them to be. I've lived with this lie fourteen years—over half my lifetime.''

Ann's confessions humbled me. Now *I* wanted to rush through the last commandments, coupling the Eighth and Ninth. The Eighth, I explained, required one be just to one's neighbors, not wrong them, for stealing was only one manner of doing wrong. Ann tried to speak, but I hushed her until I had recited the Ninth Command.

"I've broken both,'' she quavered. "The Ninth by lying about my neighbor, Goodwife Nurse; the Eighth by stealing her dear life . . .''

Ann confessed to concealing pins in her clothes, making sure the examiners found them, and accusing Goody Nurse of having pricked her. The seventy-year-old, so respected in the community that she shared a pew with Ann's grandmother, was awed at the gal's testimony, if her deafness had allowed her to hear it. As if Young Ann's lies were not enough, (she judged from her friends' actions they were not), she then bore false witness against Rebecca's sisters, Mary Easty and Sarah Cloyse.

"I stole Goody Nurse's life as suredly as Mercy Lewis stole Goody Easty's—Mercy's tantrums forced Mary's return to prison.'' The image of Goodwife Easty's linen-wrapped corpse lying in the shallop below Gallows Hill restrained me. 'Ann must purge herself before she's accepted to communion.'

"It scared me when Rebecca was declared, 'Not Guilty,' especially because Uncle Joseph was soliciting thirty-eight people to petition Governor Phipps in her behalf. Everything was about to collapse about my head! Unless I acted, I'd again be the laughing stock of my friends.''

Ann testified that Goody Nurse had whipped her, but the frail woman had been nowhere near her. To prove her claim, Ann showed red welts on her arm resembling blows inflicted by a chain. She admitted to me she had sobbed when she whipped herself but the false evidence impressed others.

"When Deliverance Hobbs confessed to witchcraft and joined us, I knew I'd won—no one would call me a liar.'' Ann concluded, "You see, Reverend, I was sure that Deliverance's false confession, causing Goody Nurse to mumble, 'She is one of *us,*' meaning 'Innocent,' would be accepted by the Farmers. So I threw a fit, making sure Rebecca's words would be taken to mean that Deliverance was *also* a witch,'' she sighed with relief for having finally told the truth. "That act made me guilty of stealing Goody Nurse's life . . .''

'Lord, pray help me when I repeat Ann's tale to Sam Nurse. I implore you, have him accept it as a full confession of her guilt in his dear mother's death.' Not knowing Goodman Nurse too well, I resolved to discuss the confession with Putt first.

"Did you ever covet your neighbor's goods?'' the question seemed trite but had to be asked. "Or were you always content?''

"I coveted the Nurses' standing in our village. Although Father was parish clerk and the eldest son, his younger half-brother, Uncle Joseph, inherited Grandfather's estate. I hated that! Had Father been heir, *our* family would have been the richest!''

"Surely you were too young to be involved in such commercial matters . . .''

"It was table talk. I still remember my parents' anger at the Nurses' winning the Bishop Farm. Mother always reminded us of the hardship she had suffered from the age of sixteen at the hands of the Nurses and their Topsfield friends. She was most furious when Uncle Joseph married Israel Porter's daughter, making *him* so wealthy. But now, now I don't blame my parents—I blame myself for using their covetousness for my own desires.''

Elizabeth entered quietly, offered each of us a glass of canary, and seated herself beside me. I would rather have been alone at this critical juncture in Ann's private confession, but I appreciated that my wife wanted to hear the end of it. 'Her being here will implicate her in this sordid affair. Like Pandora, I've opened the box—only the Lord knows what evils lie ahead for all of us.'

"Back to the beginning, Ann. How do you now answer, have you broken the First Commandment?''

"I confess—I've often *played* God rather than obeyed Him. I played into Satan's hands—a sin I deeply regret.'' She gazed so fixedly at us I marveled at the power she could wield.

"Dear Ann,'' I approached her with open arms, "insofar as I am the Lord's instrument, I accept your confession on His behalf.'' She sank to her knees as I blessed her, my right hand on her scraggly hair. The rustle of Beth's skirt broke the silence as she swished to my side.

"It is now incumbent upon your neighbors, many of whom, fourteen years ago, were among the accusers like yourself, and equally incumbent upon those whom you and others accused, to unite with God, accept your confession, and admit you to our communion."

As I helped the wisp to her feet, with the full realization that my greater challenge lay ahead, Elizabeth handed her a glass of canary which she finished without pausing.

"Delicious. I haven't tasted the likes of it since my dear mother's funeral seven years ago . . ."

"That reminds me, Ann, have we ever thanked you for the lovely scarf?"

"I'm only sorry I couldn't afford a funeral ring for you, Pastor."

My wife whisked Ann away, leaving me to compose a confession Ann could sign; a confession suitable to read to the congregation; a confession first to be endorsed by Samuel Nurse.

*   *   *

"I desire to be humbled before God for that sad and humbling Providence that befell my Father's family in the year about '92."

I began reading Ann's confession to the church meeting. She stood near the Seat of Gloom, facing the Inhabitants, a place usually reserved for miscreants but also used for occasions such as this. Although I agreed with William Brattle that confession should be private, between the individual and the minister, the congregation's acknowledging its acceptance by a silent vote, Putt warned me the Farmers would reject such a practice, especially in his niece's case. Beth confirmed his view, and so I placed Young Ann's situation ahead of my preference, praying that her confession might show sufficient humiliation to admit her to communion without further ado.

"That I, then being in my childhood," I winced at how childlike she remained, "should by such a providence of God, be made an instrument for the accusing of several persons of a grievous crime whereby their lives were taken away from them . . ."

This passage had caused me considerable distress. Initially I had written, 'by such a providence of *Satan*.' Rereading it, I decided not to roil the Inhabitants, particularly Hutch and the Deals, and substituted reference to our Lord.

Some days prior to the public meeting, when I had showed Samuel Nurse my draft of Ann's confession and bade him read it aloud to Putt and my wife, he became infuriated.

"That shittabed claims innocence! She calls herself an 'instrument'—she was the prime mover against my Mother."

"Read further, Samuel," Beth advised, scotching an outburst from me.

". . . whom now I have just grounds and good reason to believe they were innocent persons,"

Goodman Nurse nodded vigorous approval of the line,

"and that it was a great delusion of Satan that deceived me in that sad time, whereby I justly fear I have been instrumental, with others, though ignorantly and unwittingly, to bring upon myself and this land the guilt of innocent blood."

Having read that far, Sam handed me the manuscript. Putt argued for both of them. Elizabeth and I listened with restraint. Again, the notion that Ann had only been an instrument was unacceptable, as were the terms, 'ignorantly and unwittingly.' Putt insisted Young Ann acted of her own volition, goading the other gals, her venom increasing whenever the momentum seemed to wane.

"My niece was fully knowledgeable of village gossip about the Nurse-Putnam feud. She had her wits about her at all times!"

I feared he might cite Ann's horsemanship on Gallows Hill but he kept our secret. Taking my wife's cue, not to dispute with my guests, I shoved the manuscript back to Sam.

"Though what was said or done by me against any person I can truly and uprightly say, before God and man, I did it not out of anger,"

Both men grimaced at the private reading as did Tabitha Deal from her pew during my public reading,

"malice, or ill will to any person . . ."

I had grabbed the manuscript from Goodman Nurse, afraid he might destroy it. When Beth seized the moment to serve canary, I whispered to her to fetch my notes on the confession from my escritoire. On her return, Sam and Putt seemed refreshed enough to talk reasonably. My wife used the pretext of refilling their glasses to mention she had witnessed the end of Ann's confession, my notes on which she laid on the table. I then explained my manner of preparing would-be communicants, reviewing with them their sins against God and man in view of the Commandments.

"Before God and man," I had reread to the two Farmers, "I did it *not* out of anger, malice, or ill will to *any* person," and finished aloud the part at which Goodman Nurse had balked,

"for I had not such thing against one of them; but what I did was ignorantly, being deluded by Satan."

Underlining with my pipestem the passages in my notes I wanted them to read, never taking my eyes from theirs, I insisted Ann's girlhood accusations *were* made in ignorance.

"My notes confirm it was only during our conversation that Ann came to realize the 'anger, malice, and ill will' she'd so violently expressed were directed against her pitiful self, and only secondarily, yes, 'ignorantly,' against others."

I could not tell if my argument was convincing, my guests' eyes never followed my pipe's path across the page but impaled me.

"God alone, neither you nor I, can judge whether Young Ann was satanically deluded or acted out of girlish vanity."

"And particularly," I read her confession to the congregation in the same tone with which I had resumed reading it to Goodmen Nurse and Putnam,

"as I was a chief instrument of accusing Goodwife Nurse and her two sisters . . ."

Tears had flooded Sam's eyes when he first heard the passage; as I now intoned it publicly, his eyes were clear,

"I desire to lie in the dust and to be humbled for it . . ."

Without wiping his eyes, Sam Nurse had risen, I thought to leave, and reached his hand to me. Clasping my hand, he covered his grasp with his left, not shaking his arm until Putt and Beth had added theirs.

Thus we stood through the prayer I offered for God's mercy, the prayer with which I had concluded my conversation with Ann.

"In that I was a cause, with others, of so sad a calamity to them and their families; for which cause I desire to lie in the dust, and earnestly beg forgiveness of God . . ."

My voice boomed as I neared the end of Ann's confession, my eyes no longer searching the meeting house for signs of disapproval. As I finished, Ann's mouthings became almost audible, her stare focused on the pews which held the survivors of those she had accused.

". . . and from all those unto whom I have given just cause of sorrow and offense, whose relations were taken away or accused."

The congregation's silence was eerier than that which had overcome the four of us in the parsonage. When we had broken our grasp, I asked if either man wished to read my notes on Ann's confession. Too shaken to respond, Sam slid them to Putt, who fed them, page by page, to the flames.

"I must inform you, *I* insisted Ann not take full blame for all accusations in '92," both men recoiled, "or for all the diabolical actions which took place." I silenced them with my hand. "Had I allowed her to do so it might inhibit or absolve others in our village, Salem Town, even Boston, from confessing their guilt."

"Understood, Pastor," Putt spoke for his companion.

"I acknowledge this as my confession," Ann summoned her strength to bellow, "and have signed my name to it."

Fearful that some Inhabitants would deny Ann from our communion, I chose my closing prayer from Edward Taylor's 26th Meditation, based upon Hebrews 9:13–14:

> "Thou wilt have all that enter to thy fold
>> Pure, clean, and bright,
>> Whiter than the whitest Snow
> Better refin'd than most refined Gold:
>> I am not so: but foul: What shall I do?
>> Shall thy Church doors be shut,
>> and shut out me?
> Shall not Church fellowship my portion be?"

Although Elizabeth and I were humbly grateful about Ann's admission to our covenant, I felt disquieted about the effects her confession might have outside our parish.

*   *   *

Glorious though August 25, '06, had been, my neglected glebe called me to mundane activities. While repairing the wall between my orchard and the Hutchinson's, to keep my hogs from his corn, Providence prevented me from another nasty fall.

"Buy a new saddle before winter," Beth demanded as I limped beside her to the shed, "Father has one for sale."

Our funds committed for wages to our field hands, I gave him a note for forty-five shillings and suffered the soreness of a new saddle throughout the autumn.

Although Ann continued to visit my wife, try as I might, I heard few comments critical of her confession, all of which came from my neighbor, Ben Hutchinson.

"Beth," I wondered aloud as I prepared for a Salem council meeting, "should I approach Nicholas about the possibility of his marrying Ann?"

"Outrageous! Absurd!" She inspected my saddle straps. "Ann's not idle with that household to care for. Nicholas, that crusty bachelor, is equally occupied—too often with affairs other than his own."

She handed me some jugs of cider, drawn from one of the eight barrels we had made that fall, as a gift to my host and slapped my horse gently. The sloshing liquid accompanied my horse's gait.

It bothered me that Ann, unlike Mary Walcott, Elizabeth Booth, and Margaret Jacobs, her former conspirators, had not found a husband. 'Surely Ann suffered no more than Margaret,' I began a gallop past Gallows Hill, 'so instrumental in her own father's death. Yet, Margaret's been married to Goodman Foster almost seven years . . . Why not Ann?' I would raise the question with Nicholas, regardless of my wife's admonition.

"Many thanks for the cider, I'll store it for a warmer day." Upon his return to the fireside, Nicholas carried a tray offering me ale, a new clay pipe, and some of his precious tobacco.

Before I could discuss Ann's plight, he confessed concern about my own, doubting that I believed in the Devil's presence.

"Satan plies his evil in various ways, Brother Noyes, one of which is capturing the loyalties of God-fearing people and converting them into witches—of this I have not the slightest doubt." Having me on the defensive, we sat across the table, I nearer the fire's warmth, engrossed in our separate thoughts. 'This is *not* the moment to ask about a match between him and Ann,' my wife's intuition might be correct.

"What prompts me to challenge you is that so-called 'confession' you deviously extracted from Ann Putnam." He then lambasted its contents and rhetoric, line by line, as if he had spent the autumn preparing for our confrontation.

The euphoria I had experienced since Ann's acceptance to communion inspired me with a serenity which I attributed to having served God's will. So I let him rant, ignored his invective, and laughed to myself at his puns and witticisms.

"Why, Green? Tell me *why?*" His frustration at my silence gave me the advantage. "Nearly fourteen years after the incident was closed, why did *you* reopen it? Had you some satanly whim to satisfy—or was it just another example of your greenness?"

In a tone calmer than I thought I could muster, I replied, "To use our Lord's words, *Young* Ann's faith was no greater than a mustard seed, but during our conversation it grew to a mature plant as she begged to join our covenant."

"You should have referred her to *me*—perhaps to Cotton Mather. After all, *we* are far less green in such matters . . ."

"It never entered my mind," I startled him. "To tell the truth, I considered accepting her private confession in lieu of a public humiliation . . ."

"That implies," his reddened face confirmed I had gained the upper hand, "you *oppose* the Proposals I gave you to read?" His anger made him dribble ale down his front as I slid his manuscript, my notes scribbled in the margins, across to him.

"As a pastor, I serve God first; my flock second; myself last—in keeping with the two Great Commandments. I did my duty in the Lord's service, helping Ann understand her relations with Him, her neighbors, and herself." I was not about to share my fears with him of all people. "As you will read, my notes reject the Bay ministers' notions about church governance. I prefer the factious obstinacy of my Inhabitants to a church filled with synods, bishops, and other Papist trappings.''

Abruptly, he strode to his cupboard, retrieved the cider jugs, and pointed to my coat and musket beside the door. A fiery log's plunge to the parsonage floor gave him the excuse to replace it and so I left without further salutation.

'If you meant what you said, you're better off with Putt's friendship than that of a crusty old bachelor like Nicholas. The idea warmed me during the December snowfall, although I stopped to leave the cider jugs by the roadside, 'No need to hurt Beth's feelings.'

Putt was leaving my house as I approached. He had come to settle his rate before the new year, for which I thanked him.

''Putt,'' I held his stirrup for him, ''it's been five years since you were charged to see about a school.

''Surely you know how rough farming's been . . .''

''The school?'' I tightened my grip.

''The Devil take the school!'' He yanked his leg but I held fast.

''I'll forgive your blasphemy—this once. But, my friend, if the Farmers had had a school, perhaps those gals you called the 'Devil's Brood' might have occupied themselves with the Scripture rather than become preoccupied with Tituba's heathen magic.''

I released my hold, hoping the guilt I stirred in him would provoke the action I wanted.

''*I* get no special rate, only my own hard labor keeps famine from my door,'' he wheeled and rode off with no more salutation than I had received in Salem.

''Must you forever provoke people?'' Beth carped, ignoring my snowy clothes. ''Putt's as close a friend as you have in this parish—why must you bait him?''

''It's been a long, long day,'' I put Nicholas and Putt out of my mind.

''Agreed,'' she moaned and then brightened. ''We'll eat, read our Scripture,'' her arms engulfed me, ''and snuggle into a loving bed.''

8 Have You No Faith?

The sexton, having swept the pews the day before, rapped on the parsonage door which Anna opened. When she broke into a trot to join the line of women and girls marching toward the meeting house, the tithingman scolded her for profaning the Sabbath. John and Joseph found their places across the road from the women and we proceeded to services.

"May the Lord have mercy on the soul of Doctor James Bayley," I closed my opening prayer with the admonition that all contemplate death and eternal life.

"I understand Uncle James died at Roxbury where you once taught school," Ann Putnam caught me after the service, careful not to draw the tithingman's notice. "But you referred to him as 'Doctor' not 'Reverend.'"

"After your Aunt Mary died, and the furor abated over the false charge that he failed to hold family prayers, he rode with a doctor, earned his license, and practiced there until this year."

Following my prayer, I bade the congregation be seated. "Quietly! Quietly, Goodwife Deal! Don't kick your cricket lest you find yourself in the stocks come Thursday."

My wife always made sure that our boys stocked the firewood high late in the week so that we could have a roaring fire on Saturday. We were thus assured of sufficient coals for our menfolk to replenish their women's crickets between my sermons. Deacon Ingersoll and Ben Hutchinson did the same, but our fire seemed more popular with the Farmers.

My admonition to the women was not lost on the men, they seated themselves without ado. The trouble lay with the boys who scuffled for the best seat on the pulpit stairs. Thus the tithingman's knobbed pole bonked one lad's head after another, causing more commotion than it reduced. Finally, I interrupted my sermon to yank one imp from the rest and stash him inside the pulpit closet beneath me, careful not to slam the door. 'Hutch's son, again. I'll expect my neighbor to give him a sound thrashing after nightfall.'

"You profane the Sabbath with satanic clamor in God's house," I exhorted. "You profane it by not preparing your fires so you'll have coals to fill your crickets before sundown Saturday. You gals, you profane the Sabbath by passing herbs and notes through your pews—twisting their newels 'til they squeak like the Devil's imps." Ann Putnam's youngest sister withdrew her scrawny fingers from their grasp.

"You profane the Lord's Day by late arrival, Tabitha Deal," the congregation's buzz added to her humiliation, "and you, Goodwife Porter—by your hasty departure after services."

Sam Porter claimed his wife had horsewhipped him for having spilled some peas from his trencher. Judah countered that he came home so late from the fields that his food was stone cold. When I castigated them for their late arrivals to meeting, they blamed each other, contending their tardiness was due to the distance of their farm from the meeting house.

"Keep the Lord's Day holy. Spend it in prayer. Read the Scripture. No matter how distant you might live, allow ample time for your ride. Should the weather be foul, that is Providential, a test of your obedience. I welcome the forthcoming Sabbath when all of you will be in line at yonder door before the sexton summons me to preach . . ."

Mentioning the bloodied door, stained from the heads of wolves and bears which had been nailed to it, reminded me I must repair the parsonage door. 'Blasphemy! You harangue others about their sinfulness, yet consider work on the Sabbath.' I vowed to spend more time in prayer as penance.

"Sabbath' means 'the ceasing." It pleased me to see my literate parishioners scribble my words in their notebooks. "It refers to the Lord's ceasing from His six days' labor. The Sabbath is for *praying*—never, never *playing* . . ."

Rumor had it some children had played hubbub in Ingersoll's leanto the week before while their parents refreshed themselves between services. One of them, of course, was the tad hidden in my communion closet. I tapped the door with my toe to be sure he knew I had him in mind.

"Gambling is the Devil's doing. Gambling on the Sabbath compounds the sin. This game of hubbub you learned from your Indian slaves plays into the hands of Satan and his Papist allies." My conscience twinged when I recalled my own skill at rolling the five dice on a wooden plate, my friends and I in a circle, chanting, "Hub, hub, hub," with each roll.

"Stay and have another glass," the sand had almost drained from the hourglass, and so I upended it to complete my sermon against Sabbath-breaking. The sound of scuffling from the Strangers' Pew comforted rather than annoyed me, the Farmers having voted all strangers' donations would come to me. 'Thoughts of commerce on the Sabbath?' My shame added fuel to my sermon.

"Pray! Fast! Thank God for His favors. Never violate the day with industry or commerce. Be industrious in contemplation of the Scripture. Have commerce with the divine word—not with one another." I cited Nehemiah 10:31, which warned against barters or sales on the Lord's Day, pointing at Goodman Bishop, whom the tithingman had overheard talking with Hutch about his sawmill the previous week.

"You dare not allow your slaves or servants to substitute their labor for yours on this day." I reminded my flock of the slavery suffered by the Israelites in Egypt and warned that the same fate might befall us should we be captured by the French as had happened to those at Dunstable the year before.

"The vilest, most ungodly activity with which some of you preoccupy yourselves," I used both hands to accuse Goodman Bishop and Goodwife Deal, "is drunkenness! Drunkenness is intolerable—on the Sabbath, a venal sin! You claim alcohol warms you against the cold," the windblown sleet pelted the roof to accentuate my anger. "You claim ale cools you in the heat of summer. There is, however, no excuse for drunkenness."

Eyeing Putt, I wondered if he believed my sincerity in view of his earlier experience with my inebriation. The blank earnestness of his ruddy face forced me to feel more contrite.

The sand again exhausted from its glass, I felt satisfied with my sermon however often I might have to repeat it. Imagine, then, my distress the moment after my final prayer and blessing when the pews slammed back, the crickets clanked, the men scrambled for their stacked muskets, and even the sentinel ran out the door.

"It's due to my sinfulness, Beth," noise from the ordinary dejected me so much I refused to eat or drink.

Letting me sulk, she calmly nursed and burped Nedde. "What happened shortly after Jesus delivered his message to the crowd near Galilee?"

"He joined his disciples for a sail on the lake," the question seemed trivial.

"And then?"

"A sudden storm arose . . . ." I disliked her catechizing me.

"Like the storm during your sermon," she opened the Scripture to Mark 4:35, "the storm threatened to capsize their boat." Laying the Bible in front of me, she pointed to the fortieth verse. "Imagine, after their attentiveness to the most glorious sermon ever preached— they panicked! Read the passage aloud, Joseph."

"Why are you such cowards? Have you no faith even now?"

"If the Lord Himself found His most trusted friends faithless, why can't *you* be more humble?"

*   *   *

As I lay beside Elizabeth, who tossed fitfully, I appreciated how hard she had been working. The winter's rigors, cooped up with our sickly children while I travelled the parish, had taken their toll on her. With spring planting ahead I would be out in our fields and orchards in addition to ministering to my flock's needs. 'Regardless of the expense,' I dressed for Salem, 'I'll hire someone to help around the house.'

"My advice, my son," Elizabeth's father suggested as we downed flips at Gedney's Ship Tavern across from the Salem Parsonage, "is buy a slave—don't hire another farm girl."

We argued the pros and cons of a hired servant or slave, especially the money I would lose if the slave did not live long enough to recoup my investment. Furthermore, I might be stuck with an idle, if healthy slave, but could always rid myself of a slothful servant.

"Buy a slave. House her in the garret above your study. A servant-girl may prefer to live with her own family—a slave will live with you."

My reluctance about a live-in slave, I confessed, had to do with the ugly history of John Indian and Tituba, Sam Parris's Barbadoes slaves, and the mischief they had wreaked on his daughter.

"Easily resolved—buy an Indian."

"A Taranteen?" I had rejected that before. "You know of my support for our army. How would it look if I had a French lackey in my home?"

"Abenaki women are skilled herbalists. With all the sickness in your family, you'd do well to have one serve you."

"Wouldn't you fear for your daughter's safety?"

"Why should I? Unlike the Mohawks, the Abenaki are docile, their hospitality rivals your own."

His view conflicted with what I had heard of the Taranteens' ferociousness that same morning. No matter how fierce they were as warriors, he insisted, they were also fiercely loyal to whomever they befriended.

"It would compromise me with the Farmers," my defense was weakening. "I'm intent they vote for a school—John and Joseph are nearly ready. The thought of having an ignorant, illiterate . . . ."

"Hold on! Where did you learn that rot? The Abenaki's written language predates our own, probably by centuries! They inscribe their characters on birchbark: recipes, medications, instructions for planting and harvesting, tactics for hunting and fishing, and so on. And, I might add, they learn English faster than their French masters . . . ."

Reluctantly, I let him negotiate for a female Taranteen. I paid twenty pounds outright, gave bond for ten more, and promised the final two if she lived a month. The totem with which she inscribed the document resembled a flower.

"It's not her personal sign, Joseph, it's her family's."

"All right, I'll call you, 'Flora,'" I announced to the deerskin clad, supple young woman, perhaps Ann Putnam's age, unaware that 'F' and 'R' were consonants foreign to her language. She mimicked my pronunciation a few times, with a French accent, until she was satisfied.

"*Po ba tam win no?*" she quizzed my companion while pointing at me.

"Yes," Father Gerrish repeated her phrase without explaining its meaning, which made me regret I would have someone in my home whom I couldn't possibly understand.

"Wi la wig win no?" her toothy smile made me revise my estimate of her age downward.

"No, by no means!" Beth's father laughed so hard he spilled his flip. When Flora reached for his tankard, pleading, *"Ka dos ma wa gan,"* he quickly recovered and offered her cider instead.

"She's thirsty . . ."

"That goes without saying," he tantalized me as his daughter often did. "What did she mean by pointing at me that caused you to laugh?"

"Noticing you were dressed in black, she first asked if you were a religious man—like one of her tribe's shamans. I said you were. Then she asked if you were *rich*—I said no!"

Flora became surly as I loaded her in the cart which Hutch had loaned me. Again I had second thoughts, but my wife's father assured me Beth understood enough Abenaki to speak with the Indian. As I prepared to drive, he confided to me that my slave was probably fluent in English but might not speak it until she felt comfortable in new surroundings.

We rumbled to the parsonage, chilled by the leontine March wind. Anna raced her brothers to greet me only to stop short with awe as she spotted Flora. Their mother shepherded our children toward me as I feebly justified my purchase. Beth's delight, however, allayed my reservations.

"Wlag zi. Wlag zi!" Flora shrieked when I helped her from the cart. No sooner did her bare feet hit the icy ground than she vomited over the wheel.

'There goes my investment!'

"Her bowels ache, Joseph," my wife shooed the children indoors.

"I need no translation for *that*," I snapped, comforted that I would at least save two pounds if her ailment were fatal within the allotted period.

Unfortunately, Flora's illness added to my wife's chores. I was no help to her, having to prepare for the ministers' council which would replace Pastor Symes who had deserted his post in Boxford against our wishes, but I was both distracted and maddened by our slave's stubborn ailment. In desperation, I boiled some of our precious castile soap in the strongest ale we owned and fed it to her while Anna fetched Doctor Hale.

"*A kwan!*" Flora exploded, vomiting the medicine on the garret floor, "Too bitter!"

"Aha! You *do* speak English!" Her intense pride increased my apprehension about my purchase.

When the day's chores were past, the children fed and bedded, Doctor Hale paid, and Flora recovered from my medication, I queried my wife about the Taranteens.

"Flora comes from a unique people." Elizabeth undressed while I lay on our bed, hoping we could recapture the passion so long buried under pressures of work. "Her people have always lived in Nolumbeka, 'the land of quiet water between the rapids.' They believe 'The Great Spirit' created them in His own image and so they recognize no ancestors." Beth always delighted in lecturing me, and now was no exception, except that I had requested it. "This belief imbues them with such confidence that they maintain their traditions in spite of our occupying their fishing grounds and deforesting their winter hunting places."

My kisses quieted her as she opened her mouth to receive them and we lost ourselves in separate yet joint ecstacy.

"*Ma wia,*" Beth purred, repeating herself for me to imitate.

"*Ma wia?*"

"Better, dear, *much* better . . ."

Falling asleep with total satisfaction, I felt if Flora's presence lightened my wife's burden, my purchase might be a good investment after all. To be on the safe side, I prayed, 'May our Indian's presence not arouse my factious flock against my beloved wife and family. Amen.'

*   *   *

Beth's taunts about my poor horsemanship came to mind as I followed my errant horse's trail from Reading through Woburn to Cambridge Farms where the groom insulted me by charging four shillings for the beast. Now, in '08, the impish animal had added Mistick to its itinerary—and the groom another shilling. 'If the Devil can possess any creature, my jade's a prime candidate,' I jerked my reins in anger as the rain soaked me on my ride to the Deals.

"Lightning is the Devil's toy," Tabitha groaned, her warty hands across her eyes. "Never, never look toward lightning, Pastor—it will dry the humor in your eyes and blind you, your face will swell and erupt in witch's teats!"

John had called at the parsonage while I was hunting for my horse, Tabitha's having grown wilder with each spring storm.

"Our Father, who art in heaven . . ." I instructed her to repeat after me, "hallowed be Thy name . . ."

I thought she said, 'hollowed,' but dismissed it as my imagination. When I distinctly heard her say, '. . . and deliver us from *all* evil,' I could not ignore the blasphemy but was unprepared to confront her. Using the pretense that I had others to visit that day, I demanded she remain kneeling in prayer until she felt better.

'Were her errors careless or sinister?' Consumed by my thoughts, my horse exploited my distraction and headed us toward Reading.

"Your favorite haunts? Not this time," I reined the stubborn animal back to the main road, disturbed by my choice of words, and trotted toward the Goodle's.

"Sam, I want to hire you to build a clockcase," I shouted from the fencerail to the farmer. We negotiated a price and he reminded me to buy some coloring in town.

Riding past the meeting house, I was ashamed for George Martin, seated in the stocks, soaked by the downpour, his clothes stained from the red dye of the 'D' he wore about his neck. 'I'll preach more firmly against drunkenness,' I added to my list.

Spring's rains turned to summer's drought. The crop damage which worms failed to accomplish was more than compensated for by the pigeons' ravenous appetites. My only satisfaction came from my improved musketry, which Beth attributed to Putt's tutoring, when I killed eighteen birds with one shot, the flock so dense it eclipsed the sun.

"That's more than ten dozen you've shot this year, Father," seven-year-old John bragged.

"Your patience with fowling contrasts with your impatience with your flock," my wife remarked as she dressed our sons.

"The boys' schooling can't wait on the Farmers' indecision," I snapped when she mounted them behind me.

Leaving my sons at the room I had rented from James Houlton, I prayed the Lord forgive my temper.

Beth had either forgiven or forgotten my anger for she showed surprise when I apologized to her that evening.

"Have patience?" I repeated forlornly. "I *have* patience—seven years' worth."

"It's only been a few days since the meeting agreed to build a school," she squeezed my hand as we walked from the well-sweep, Flora laden with buckets.

"I count time differently. Putt disappointed me by not moving faster about the school . . ."

"What more can you expect? The Farmers haven't been blessed with our education. Why not reason instead of rail at them?"

As usual, her advice paid off. When I answered each question, no matter how silly it seemed, they commended the school's design without objection. 'Thank you, Lord, for giving me such an understanding spouse and deliver her safely of our child.'

I baptized our sixth child in Elizabeth's name. I then plunged into supervising the school's construction while Flora helped her recover.

"Sir Andrew will teach the boys—Dame Deland the girls," I boasted while my wife nursed Liz.

"*Sir? Dame?* Pretentious titles for the Inhabitants."

"I gave it careful thought. I suffered under one idle teacher and later as the teacher of unruly boys. 'Sir' and 'Dame' will impress parents and children alike."

"Your reasoning is faulty," she handed me the sated baby whose half-digested milk dribbled down the rear of my coat. "Lord help the teacher when Nedde reaches school age—he seems to have received all your peevishness."

I was delighted that my wife had snapped back from childbirth so quickly, an event I attributed to Flora's aid. The Indian's lithe, willowy frame belied her strength. My delight, however, became dread when I found the cradle empty the next morning.

"The Taranteen's stolen Liz!" I was horrified.

"Joseph," my wife called from the bedroom as I armed myself, "Flora's taken the baby outdoors for the Sun God's blessing . . ."

Musket in hand, I scolded our slave for her foolishness, assuring her that baptism was a sufficient blessing.

"*Ki no ho ma sin,*" Flora sneered, tucking cloth around the sleeping baby.

"Instruct her to speak English," I chastised, "she jabbers in Abenaki to confound me!"

"Preaching," my wife chuckled the translation. "Admit it, dear, that's what you were doing," Elizabeth lit my pipe, took a puff, passed it to our slave for a puff, and then handed it to me. "As a minister's daughter, now a minister's wife, I'm used to being preached at. Why can't you pastors find other means of persuasion?"

'Father Gerrish warned me about the mixed blessing of having an educated wife. Now I'm further cursed with a pretentious slave.'

"Joseph, you've been around Nicholas so much, you're starting to talk like him" she taunted.

On the defensive, I blew a gust of smoke around the cradle to ward off the mosquitoes and studied until early candlelight. The August evening was so warm, Beth and I sat up until dark. I felt so relaxed I actually enjoyed overhearing Flora tell the children a bedtime story: how the shaman, Gluskabe, pursued by a woman who wanted to marry him, became invisible to elude her. 'Perhaps I should have done the same' I mused, 'but I was the pursuer, Beth the pursued.'

"It's so peaceful, Joseph, lying here beside you," she turned to kiss me again. "It's unbelievable that anything—the summer's sweltering heat, the winter's penetrating cold, the school's slow construction—can disturb this heavenly calm."

Hopefully, Reverend Rolfe in nearby Haverhill shared our bliss, unaware it would be his last night on earth.

*   *   *

Hagar, the Rolfe's Negro slave, cowered in the parsonage basement. In front of her were two empty upended barrels, one of which sheltered Mary, the other, Elizabeth, two of the Rolfe children. Only Hagar could hear the other family members' screams of terror or smell the acrid smoke.

Benjamin Rolfe lay shot and tomahawked beside the front door. His wife's tomahawked body lay near the well-sweep toward which she had run. Their baby, Mehitabel, lay dead on the hearth, her head having been smashed against the stone fireplace. A similar scene was repeated more than forty times throughout Haverhill, but few scalps had been taken—a sign the army took to mean the Taranteens would return.

In fear of her life and the lives of her wards, Hagar hid in the cellar until the marauders had quieted. Soothing the girls, she warned them to stay hidden and crept up the stone stairs to the hideous scene. Stepping across her owner's body, she cradled Mehitabel in her arms only to be stunned by the sound of footsteps descending from the garret. Frightened, the black slid beneath the dining table.

Her joyful relief to see two soldiers, rather than rapacious savages, tiptoe across the hearth, turned to fury as she realized they had secreted themselves during the raid, making no attempt to defend the parsonage. As Mehitabel's blood etched itself into the slave's clothes, the soldiers' faces etched themselves into her memory.

Allowing time for the men to clear the glebe, Hagar stole to the cellar, rescued her wards, and led them to the ordinary, making sure they did not see the slaughtered bodies of their parents and sister. To her surprise, the cowardly soldiers were boasting of their bravery to the attentive ears of the heavy-drinking survivors of the massacre . . .

Blissfully asleep, my wife nestled spoon-fashion against my back. I startled when Flora's fingers bit into my naked shoulder, an index finger to her lips. 'Lord, what's this Indian up to now?' I dressed and went downstairs to find Captain Putnam, in full regalia, removing my musket from above the mantle.

"Haverhill's been raided—we're to join Major Turner in pursuit of the savages."

"Where to now?" Beth's shout startled me. "What's happened, Captain?"

"An attack on Haverhill," I answered as Flora helped me into my gear.

The captain refused the food my wife offered, instructing me to hurry to the training field. After thanking our slave for waking me, I hugged Elizabeth, promised to protect myself, and warned her to do the same.

We rode hastily, in spite of the sultry August weather, Putt and Hutch on my flanks. 'Our village is now defenseless, pray the devils don't attack it in our absence.'

"Notice these different arrows?" Putt held one in each hand, having retrieved them from beside Goodwife's Rolfe's corpse. "One's got a point made from a bird's claw—the other uses a spur off a wild turkey. Diabolical, eh?"

Captain Putnam summoned me to the task of blessing the corpses and sent others in our party in pursuit of the murderers. The Indians, however, had divided into their traditional five-man parties to infiltrate the forest, confusing our army by avoiding a pitched battle.

"Thank you for the funeral ring," I wrung the Haverhill deacon's hand and bent to hug the Rolfe's orphaned daughters, reluctantly entrusting them to Hagar. Aware that an Indian raiding party might attack us, we rode home warily in deep gloom.

Father Gerrish had stayed with my family during my day's absence, but my midnight arrival caused us to postpone discussion of the raid until the next day.

"We ought to have expected the attack," he fumed. "The French-led Indians were piloted down the Merrimac, probably seven hundred strong, by Taranteens paddling twenty-foot birch canoes, the bark seamed with branches and sealed with pitch. As early as the eleventh we had forewarning of their maneuvers . . . ."

"But they didn't strike 'til the twenty-ninth," Beth interjected.

"I *said* we had fair warning! Beware, Joseph, the trouble's not yet over. Assacumbuit's a wily sachem. He's just returned from France, honored by our Papist enemies—so he'll want to prove his loyalty. Carry your musket at all times or prepare to lose your scalp." Heeding his own advice, he checked his firearm and rode cautiously toward Wenham.

True to his prediction, rumors reached us in late September that three hundred or more Indians were massing for a second attack on poor Haverhill. Major Turner rallied us for another forced march in the town's defense.

"Look at this, Pastor," Ben Hutchinson handed me a piece of birchbark etched with characters. "What do you make of it?"

From Father Gerrish's report, I recognized it as an Abenaki inscription. I could not, however, decipher it nor did I understand why it lay in the clearing.

"I can't read it either, Reverend," Captain Putnam scowled as he examined the bark, "I suspect it's a message from an Indian commander, maybe the *bashaba* himself, to a raiding party in the field."

It awed me that our savage foes sent written messages to their scattered raiders. 'Lord, we face a formidable, satanic enemy.' My admiration for the Indians' tactics conflicted with my hatred of their murderous ways.

The rumored three hundred enemy turned out to be no more than twenty or thirty, some of whom we located in the nearby forest. As we flushed a party, I fired my musket at a fleeing, painted marauder. Whether my shot hit him, I could not tell, but a leg wound slowed him enough for our troops to capture him.

"*Wha gakw!*" he screeched, hand clamped to his pate, "*WHA GAKW!*"

The fear in his voice matched the fearsomeness of his red-and-white-painted face. Stunned by his shriek, our guards relaxed their hold and the wounded savage bounded into the woods. Our captain warned us not to shoot, he wanted to interrogate the Indian, and so Putt and Hutch teamed up to waylay and recapture him. They then dragged him to the Haverhill ordinary, ignoring his repeated screams.

"He's afraid we'll scalp him" the captain explained. "Considering the many scalps he's taken—I'm of a mind to oblige him—but he's worth more as a captive than a corpse."

The interrogation was conducted in French, the Indian unable or unwilling to speak English, and none of us fluent in Abenaki.

"He refuses to betray his 'French brothers.' He claims," the translator explained, "they share prayers, the same wigwam, one fire to each man. Moreover, should we raise a hand against his beloved French brother, he threatens to tomahawk us . . ."

'Brave words from a lame captive,' my thoughts differed from the boisterous shouts from two loudmouthed drunks in the ordinary, the pair who had been quartered with the Rolfes. As they crowded closer to our captive, threatening to scalp him, I climbed on top of a table to offer a prayer for the safety of our troops who foraged the forest in pursuit of the enemy. Captain Putnam's nod was all the approval I needed to know my action had been correct, members of the crowd content with hearing the two militiamen retell their acts of bravery during the raid. Putt, meanwhile, threatened the innkeeper with a whipping unless he stopped serving alcohol.

We waited in the ordinary until our troops reported that the Indians had fled, after which the captain gave our captive to Major Turner and led us back to our village.

In late October, the captain and I made a last journey to Haverhill where I preached from the late Reverend Rolfe's pulpit. I stressed support for the army with trust in Providence. I excused the captain from my sermon so that he could examine a deserted Taranteen encampment at which I later joined him.

"Notice how neat and orderly these wigwams are. Each tepee's poles are covered with birchbark—the entire place laid out in a manner that puts our towns to shame. But that's not the half of it . . ." he beckoned me to crawl behind him into a wigwam more distinguished than the rest.

"A library!" I gasped.

"Right, Pastor, this housed their shaman. Look," he handed me three tomes: prayers, a catechism, and a mass. Then he gestured to the many birchbark scrolls containing the shaman's medications.

"You didn't summon me for the sole purpose of exploring this '*wji gon*,' as you call it?"

"No," he chuckled, "I wanted to add, shall I say, to your schooling?"

'At least my sermons on the need for a school have registered on our captain,' his scowl broke my train of thought.

"Confidentially, Master Green, I need your witness when I accuse two Haverhill militiamen of treason—gross cowardice during the massacre."

On our return to the ordinary, I recognized the accused as the pair of drunks who had wanted to scalp our captive the previous month.

"My accusation of your treachery," the captain boomed, "although you've tried to confound innocent Haverhillites with boasts of bravery, has the support of an eyewitness . . ."

The crowd was no more stunned than I as Hagar, escorted by two deacons, came forward to testify. 'The Lord spared her namesake's child, although conceived by her master, Abraham, and now He sees fit to invest this slave with the burden of a horrible truth.'

Listening attentively to every detail of her story, the Inhabitants were convinced—their trusted sentinels had indeed betrayed them. The two, of course, protested their story be taken before that of a black slave, but Captain Putnam condemned them for their onerous treachery. The deacons then asked him to dispose of the pair as he saw fit.

With one miscreant tethered to each of our horses, we dragged them behind us, never stopping on the trek through Topsfield, until we reached the stocks in Salem Village.

*   *   *

On Training Day, the captain divided our militia into two facing columns. The rest of the Farmers crowded as close to the lines as possible. The first culprit was stripped to the waist and forced to follow the backstepping sergeant whose rapierpoint pressed on the man's chest to prevent him from running too swiftly. Along the gantlope, soldiers whipped at him with a lash or switch. The punishment awed my older boys, who stood with Hutch's son among the first rank of onlookers.

As the second coward approached the gantlope, he sprang from his guards and charged directly toward the boys. His move enabled his bleeding partner to break away and join him. The crowd was too dense for me to slip through but, just as the three children would have been trampled by the fleeing pair, Flora threw herself at the runners' legs, her hips catapaulting them over the lads and into the screaming mob. Before I could reach her, she had melted into the bystanders.

Needless to say, John, Joseph, and Young Ben were given the front row when the sergeant's sword lopped off each criminal's right ear and the constable branded a 'C' for cowardice on their left cheeks. The boys then led the chase behind the cart hauling them to Salem Town to serve their time aboard a ship of our fleet . . .

"*In*justice, gross injustice, Master Green," Reverend Noyes challenged me vexatiously at the following minsters' council in Salem. When I feigned ignorance, he elaborated. "That you, a minister of the Gospel, stood idly by while that black, she-devil—what's her name—fabricated a tale about our own soldiers. *In*credible!"

"Thoroughly credible, Nicholas. Would you rather the cowards had gone unpunished?"

"Not if they'd been truly witnessed in their crime—but for you to take the word of the Black Man's black agent over that of one of your own kind . . ."

"Hagar's no more Satan's child than . . ." I was about to say, 'you are,' but said, "I am."

"Perhaps you are, Greenie." He invited the other pastors' support, finding none, he attacked again. "You seem to have the key to the Devil's closet in your hands and use it to unleash his imps. For example, that High-Flyer, Philip English, had the audacity to petition the Court for damages he supposedly incurred in '92—a venal act I doubt he'd have pulled were it not for the likes of you."

I searched Father Gerrish's face for signs of agreement with my tormentor. His blank expression encouraged me to keep silent until Nicholas waned.

"Not only have you bought a French-loving Taranteen," I remembered Flora's proud suppression of the pain her bravery had brought her, never showing the slightest trace of a limp throughout the weeks it had taken her cuts and bruises to heal, "you've added insult to injury, accepting the false witness of that Haverhill black over the honorable word of our noble soldiers . . ."

"If I'm not mistaken, *you* were among the first to seize upon the so-called testimony of Tituba and John Indian, Parris' slaves, when it suited your purpose. *Their* evidence was spectral—Hagar's visual. Therefore, Brother, perhaps the time has come for you to confess *your* grievous errors during those unfortunate times. I suggest you begin by seeking your congregation's revocation of Giles Corey's unfair excommunication . . ."

"Enough! Enough!" he burst. "Let's turn to this Boxford mess."

After the stormy session, others scolded me for being too harsh but complimented me for keeping my temper. 'Our host has a long road to travel before he can humble himself before God or man,' I reflected.

We made no progress on Symes' successor. True to his allegiance to Cotton Mather, Nicholas remained adamant that we ministers had the first and final say.

"My Chebago Parish agrees with me," John Wise argued. "The 'Proposals' you've signed amount to episcopacy—only a step away from Papistry . . ."

"Little wonder that Cotton called you a 'hot-headed, crack-brained Furioso!" Noyes' defamation adjourned our futile talks and we went our separate ways home.

"We had good issue about Boxford," I refused to embroil my wife in Nicholas' tirade at me, she disliked the man so intensely.

"Don't undress, Joseph—Putt's wife suffered a fall."

I galloped across the fields of ripening corn, past Whipple Hill and Beaver Dam Brook, not pausing to acknowledge Goodman Osburn's wave, to what had been the homestead of Thomas Putnam, a village founder. The enormous house sat amid a blooming orchard behind which was the family crypt in which Ann's parents were buried.

Equipped with Flora's medicine for relieving bruises, (a mixture of herbs and simples I had accepted without question), I prayed with his Elizabeth for a speedy recovery.

A few weeks later, our dry weather having been broken by a series of devastating thunderstorms which further threatened our harvest, Tabitha Deal took a turn for the worse.

Deacons Ingersoll, Putnam, and I were haggling over how to distribute the thanksgiving offering among our poor, agreed that the late Sarah Good's husband was deserving but divided about the others, when my wife's frantic signals disturbed my concentration.

"*Must* you interrupt?" I hissed, "I'm about to have my way about the dole."

"Goodman Deal dropped by," she overlooked my peeve, "his wife's in torment—something about lightning."

I resumed my place at the table, fortified with a fresh jack of ale, and supported Deacon Ingersoll's concern for the Carrells' plight in exchange for his agreeing with me about the Reas'. After my prayer, we left together, I underway to the Deals.

"My wife won't sleep," the distraught farmer hung my coat to dry. "She's upstairs. She . . . she doesn't know I sent for you."

"Goody Deal," I greeted her solemnly, "let's close our eyes in prayer for your health."

Unlike our first session, her recitation was flawless. Her sunken eyes and timorous voice suggested she had exhausted herself before my visit and would sleep whether she wished to or not.

"I daren't sleep—I just daren't." Tabitha groaned at the end of our prayers. Rather than probe her reasons, I slowly shut my eyes as if in prayer.

"Don't you dare!" she panicked, her scream bringing John upstairs. "*Never* close your eyes when lightning's about."

Downcast at her outburst, her husband shuffled from the bedroom.

"If lightning strikes you in your sleep, you'll die with your eyes open—and so they will remain until the Day of Judgment!"

I stepped to her bedside, slowly lowered my palm to her forehead, as if in blessing, and deliberately slid it across her wild eyebrows and blackened lids. Startled, she tried to stay my hand with an icy index finger but was too feeble. I held my ground until her heavy breathing signalled she had lost consciousness. 'Thank the Lord, this poor soul will have a good night's rest—and her husband, too.'

Shortly after I left the Deals, a cloudburst soaked me. I fancied a cozy scene at home where I could dry out, but a shock awaited me.

Our house was freezing cold, the fire barely strong enough to heat our food, my unhappy family huddled near the hearth.

"Flora says we're out of firewood," my wife answered the question I was about to ask.

"That does it! That's the last straw! After all I've done for these ungrateful Farmers, the least they can do is provide the firewood they promised."

"Careful," Elizabeth reminded, "firewood's been the bane of more than one village preacher."

I slogged to the ordinary to play my hand. Without removing my wet coat, I ordered a flip, downed most of it, and pushed my way toward the roaring fire which was every bit as large as those in the Salem, Cambridge, and Boxford parishes where I had preached while each searched for a full time minister.

"Brrr," I spotted Joseph Putnam, "how long's it been since we first met? Ten years, maybe?" I toasted him with my tankard, "sometimes it seems only ten days," he frowned quizzically, "and then, on cold, wet nights like this—ten millenia.

"And you," I spun toward Hutch, my second target, "how long have we been neighbors? I'll tell you—ever since my shivering wife and I moved into that freezing parsonage in '98."

Nonplussed by my behavior, they shuffled nervously.

"Ah yes, my friends," I offered my jack for a refill and again drowned most of it. "Ten years' service seems like a millenium with one flock," I let my comment register. "Now, with Salem's Reverend Higginson laid to rest, Boxford still without a pastor—even my beloved Cambridge preacherless," I sipped as if it were communion wine, "one *must* consider the *warmth* with which those congregations received my sermons . . . .

I clanked my empty tankard on the table and pushed past my friends to the door, Putt a half-step behind me.

"Hold on, Pastor!"

"Putt? *Do* accompany me home, you're always welcome. I'm sure Beth and the children would welcome another warm body . . . ."

"Firewood!" He twisted my shoulder with such force I almost fell in a puddle. "You threaten to leave us . . . ."

"For want of firewood." I insisted I held no hard feelings toward him or Hutch, who had caught up with us, but that my yearly battle

over firewood was more painful than amusing. 'Heed Beth's advice—
no need to remind them how poorly they treated Sam Parris when he
complained about the lack of fuel.'

Our home's bitter cold abbreviated my prayers and Scripture reading.
The older boys bundled under a featherbed on one side of the hearth.
Anna slept beside Nedde across from her brothers. My wife and I,
warmed after lovemaking, placed Liz between us. 'Pray Flora doesn't
freeze in her unheated garret,' was my last thought for the night . . .

CRASH!

'Thunder? An Indian attack?' The clamor that woke me before dawn
froze me more than the cold. Flora entered before I could stumble
out of bed, cradling half-a-dozen logs.

The boys first fed the fire, then joyfully stacked pile after pile of
logs beside our leanto. Beth, Flora, and Anna hummed as they prepared
bevers, while I rummaged through my escritoire for my diary.

'Some talk of my leaving the place for want of wood,' I read my
last entry and thawed my ink at the roaring fire, I gleefully inscribed,
'WOOD CAME!'

9 In the Tradition of Melchizadek

'*You* are a witch!' Nicholas' accusation haunted me as I listened to the General Court debate damages to Widower Good, 'and you *know* you are a witch!'

'*You* are a liar!' the soon-to-be-hanged Sarah snapped. 'I am no more a witch than you are a wizard; and, if you take my life, God will give you blood to drink!'

Now, eighteen years after Sarah's death, the impoverished Farmer was suing on behalf of his demented daughter. Accused of witchcraft when she was five, Dorcas suffered through the summer and fall of '92 chained to a prison wall. At twenty-two she still showed what her father called, 'No reason.'

'Good Lord! What a contrast between this poor waif and Sam Parris' daughter, happily married to Goodman Barnes of Concord. Pray, have mercy on her.'

"You're to blame for loosing twenty-one undeserving claimants against their neighbors, Green," Nicholas admonished. "You serve Commerce not Religion. Just look at that smirking French Papist, 'Angleterre,' who calls himself, 'English.' Yes, Green, you've unleashed a pack of snarling wolves against us."

"My advice, Brother, is to have your congregation rescind the excommunications of Rebecca Nurse and Giles Corey."

"Rubbish! That would only fan the dying embers of an almost forgotten fire." He strode from the Salem meeting house leaving me free to paddle home.

Gliding under the Crane River Bridge, I wondered how he might react when members of my village petitioned for their own church, mid-way between Salem Village and Salem Town.

"Don't tease him!" Elizabeth took his part while our boys saddled my horse. "Absorb yourself in preaching. Minister to the sick. Let the past be past." She embraced me. "I worry so about losing you, Joseph—moreso when you set out on horseback than when you canoe . . ."

"I'll return before candlelight. First, I'll ride toward Wills Hill, then past Deacon Putnam's, and leave the Northside for another day."

Sickness had spared my family but laid many low. Whenever I fingered the black-enameled gold ring from Captain Putnam's family, I felt sad at the loss of his wisdom. But that day called for me to relieve the Wilkins and Baileys with prayer and Flora's medications.

When illness abated, madness replaced it.

Goodmen Balch and Blowers squabbled over repairing their fence. When my words of comfort failed, I grabbed the ten-foot-long palisadoes from them and fixed it myself, warning that further childishness would bring both a public whipping.

Next, Edward Bishop passed out beside Goodman Proctor's Tavern having become disorderly after drinking at three other inns along the Ipswich Road. I threw him across my horse, dumped him at his door, and watched him pilloried on Lecture Day after his suspension from communion.

The final straw, which forced me to sermon the Inhabitants against their troublesome ways, was Goody Tallie's thrashing of her husband. I stayed the brethren after my sermon to hear his complaint. They agreed she would be chained to a post, her back stripped, and publicly whipped following my Thursday lecture.

"Look, Joseph," Beth nudged, "Tabitha giggles each time the rawhide bites her neighbor's flesh. She's over her insomnia, but I suspect more trouble brews within her."

"You *suspect* trouble, do you? Well, I've enough real trouble, day in, day out, without hearing your suspicions." I felt bad about hurting my wife's feelings, but I had fallen so far behind in my plans for a new barn that her comment upset me. She, however, ignored my pique for she never mentioned it that night.

"Why can't others be as loving as you, Beth? Why must these Farmers seize every opportunity to fight?"

"Without disputes, there'd be little need for your services. Without ignorance, little need for your wisdom." Her caresses aroused me. "Without hatreds, little need for your love."

"With the Lord's help, love sometimes soothes them," I nibbled her ear as I entered her moist body, "and fills you with child."

* * *

William was born in mid-August, an event ignored by his older brothers who alternated between helping me with the crops and sneaking off to play with Young Ben Hutchinson. Flora was a mixed blessing. No sooner had the baby's cord been cut than she grabbed him and plunged him into a tub of cold rainwater. Before I could punish her for such a pagan act, she had made a paste of hickory nuts and began to feed him before Beth's milk came in. But when I caught her fashioning a cradleboard, I put my foot down.

"No! I'll not have my son swaddled and strapped to that device!"

"My *tkinogan* will keep his legs straight, like our people . . ."

"Not while I'm alive," I snatched William from her arms and delivered him to his mother so that I could study in peace.

Our army's ineptness in pursuit of the French and Indians, coming on the heels of our captain's death, left me alone to confront the increasing hostility against military service. The crisis came in mid-September when nine of our men were pressed into service aboard the *Flying Horse* for an attack on Port Royal. Postponing my studies, I chased from inn to inn to calm the riotous Farmers.

"You shall not seek revenge or cherish anger towards your kinfolk," I exhorted from Leviticus 19:17. "You shall love your neighbor as a man like yourself." I explained this meant forgetting quarrels, especially differences about support for the fleet. My logic was confounded, unfortunately, by Goodman Hutchinson's outburst which caused Nedde to slide from the pulpit stairs accompanied by cat-calls from his brothers and friends. I had no recourse but to haul him by an ear and shove him into my communion closet where I found him fast asleep at my sermon's end.

"I know it bothers you, Joseph, having to drop your studies to settle these disputes, but they're bound to happen among strong-willed people, in such atrocious weather, under everlasting fear of invasion by land or sea." My wife consoled and then criticized me. "Truly, you add to your grief by over-concern for your farms."

"You forget, I *know* poverty. Were it not for my brother Percival's friends, this tailor's son would never have finished HC. And were it not for Brother Edward—a sailor in whose memory I sermoned today—I'd not have a library. Congregations make no provision for parsons' widows. Providence willing, I shall provide for you and the children."

"No need to defend yourself with me. Your charity is legend: a donation to the meeting house, another to the school. But chasing about for more land, more trees, more corn, more livestock, consumes the energy you need for your parish."

I watched her weaken as she knew she had failed to sway me, William's nursing interrupted by her whimpers, until Flora relieved her of him and we went to bed.

"Pastor," our slave's whisper woke me, "noise outside."

Careful not to disturb my wife, I warned Flora to stay indoors, grabbed my musket, and stepped into the autumn chill. The source of the commotion was evident: three of Hutchinson's horses were feasting on my apples. Sleepily, I chased them to the fence, which they jumped with ease, and tumbled back to bed.

"I pray you, neighbor," I shouted to Ben the next morning, "keep your animals out of my orchard."

"The snow's begun," he returned, "if your apples aren't soon eaten, they'll be ruined. Don't bother me, Reverend, I've work to do."

Night after night, Hutch's horses woke me, and so I sent John to fetch his friend's father to my study.

"Again I pray you, Brother," I opened after offering him some rum, "mend your fence near my well-sweep and keep your animals inside."

He reacted by slamming my favorite tankard on the table and stomping downstairs and homeward.

'My first good night's sleep in a week,' I luxuriated the following morning, proud of the Christian manner in which I had resolved my problem, and devoted the rest of the day to my sermon.

"Joseph," Beth shook me that midnight, "there's a disturbance outside . . ."

"Ben's cursed jades!"

"Don't blaspheme. Flora will help you chase them."

"No need—I may just shoot one!"

'Easier said than done. These animals have such a hankering for my apples, they only leave after they're sated.' For more than two hours I chased one horse after another across the fence only to have it sneak back to my orchard.

Deadtired the next morning, I agreed to Flora's help, and so she added leather leggings to her deerskin smock and chased the first marauder across the fence. I was less fortunate with the others.

"How the Devil did my jade get killed?" Ben pointed at the dead animal.

"My Indian and I drove the first safely home—the other two tried to leap the fence together and one got bumped into my well."

"The Devil take you!" Goodman Hutchinson drew his blade from its scabbard.

'Superstitious people will see this event as Devil-caused. Keep quiet and let it pass.' I stood, humiliated by his curses, as the sleet pelted us unmercifully. Wordlessly, he dragged the carcass behind his horse while I checked my well for any debris.

"Be cautious with Ben," my wife warned as I raked the fire. "He's what the Taranteen's call '*mingo!*'"

"Treacherous," Flora translated, burping William before she tucked him in his harthside cradle. "Our name for what you call Mohicans."

"I'll have you know," I dismissed our slave, "I'm cautious with everyone."

"You may not know it, Joseph, but during George Burroughs's trial, Hutch testified he threw a pitchfork at the pastor's apparition, tearing its coat—or so Abigail Williams reported." Her hand waved me quiet. "When Abigail said Burroughs had changed into a cat, your neighbor decapitated it with his rapier."

"A violent man," I conceded, "a generation ago."

"Treacherous, especially toward his pastor—*and* neighbor. Don't anger him. I pray the Lord will guide you."

The incident seemed over. My sons enjoyed Young Ben's company as before and I the quiet time to study and catechize, until John burst into my room.

"Father, Goodman Hutchinson sent us home to summon you."

"I demand you pay me half the price of my colt, Pastor," we shivered outside the door to his house. "I consider myself neighborly for not charging you full price."

"I am in no way, no way, to blame for the death of your jade!"
My stubbornness flushed my neighbor and frightened my boys home.
"Its death was a Providential rebuke for allowing your animals to
rob my orchard."

"Providence may side with you, Pastor, but I have my sidearm to
speak for me," he slapped his scabbard. "I remind you, it is our
custom to let our horses forage where they choose."

"A proper custom when farms were few and far between," I refused
to budge, "fencing and fettering are now the rule." I wheeled away,
hoping to hold my tongue, but added, "So, stop your stupid saberrat-
tling and let me get back to my studies."

"Please, Dear, please," my wife's horror at my report showed by
the way her hand shook as she lit my pipe. "Please accept his offer."

"He stands on custom—*I'll* give him custom. The custom is to
make a counteroffer: twenty shillings for the dead colt, in view of the
damages to my orchard, which I also value at twenty shillings!"

"I'm scared to death," Beth's words were little comfort to me as
I presented my proposal across the fence to my angry neighbor.

"The law does not oblige me to pay you anything for a horse that
leapt a lawful fence and fell in my well."

"I accept your paltry offer," his tone icier than the weather.

"See here," I rapped the fence with my musket, "if you feel
cheated, no matter what the amount, we've settled nothing—even worsened matters between us."

"Don't preach to me! I told you I'd take what you offered. What
more do you want?" He kicked my musket from my hand and disappeared before I could retrieve it.

Elizabeth's worry intensified throughout the winter. Our sons no
longer saw Young Ben, and Hutch was strangely quiet in meeting.
Adding to my wife's distress were rumors, spread by Goodwife Deal,
that my dispute with my neighbor was another omen that the world
would end in 1710.

"Have you heard what some Farmers call Hutch?" my wife taunted
as we lay in bed one February night, "Ben-oni!"

"Son-of-my-ill-fortune? How cruel! Word-play only adds heat and
hides the light . . ."

"But I worry so!"

"Alright, stop worrying and *do* something about this name-calling."

"You're right," she cuddled under my arm, "the children and I will try our best to end it. But," she murmured as she dropped off, "*do* be careful of him—he *is mingo* . . .''

Cold steel pricked my earlobe as I lay in bed. 'A dream? Perhaps an apparition? No!' The blood that trickled down my neck was real, the sword that caused it held by Hutch.

"Out!" The slap of the weapon into its sheath frightened my wife awake.

"Ben! Don't harm my husband."

"Hush, Beth, you'll rouse the children," I warned as I dressed.

Armed with a prayer, I vaulted the icecoated fence and scrunched across the crusted snow, not even pausing to wipe my boots before I climbed my neighbor's stairs.

"Young Ben," my neighbor sobbed and closed the door silently behind me. Delirious with fever and gasping for breath, my sons' friend tossed and moaned, cooled only by the melting snow that dripped off my cloak onto his forehead as if in baptism.

'I pray, Dear Lord, Young Ben's fever will break with the dawn.' To no avail, his fever worsened and the boy died.

Accustomed though I was to death, yet aware of the glory that awaited him in Eternity, I felt guilty for the months of estrangement from my sons caused by my spat with his father. Thus consumed by remorse, my back to the door, my lungs almost burst beneath Hutch's sudden bearhug. My prayer and my wife's warning of Ben's treachery gave me strength to free myself.

Gasping for breath, I almost overlooked his outstretched hand, his eyes as filled with tears as mine . . .

"Ben's handshake was so firm, I plunged my hand into a snowbank coming home, just to relieve the pain", I reported to my wife who seemed unusually calm after her fright during the night. "You were panic-stricken when I was taken away, my dear, yet so calm when I returned?"

"I found this meditation on Psalm 105 among your letters from Edward Taylor. Read it aloud to me before bevers."

> "Joseph constrains his brethren till their sins
> > Do gall their souls. Repentance babbles fresh.
> Thou treatest sinners till repentance springs

Then with him sendst a Benjamin like messe.
Joseph doth cheer his humble brethren. Thou
Dost stud with joy the mourning Saints that bow.''

*   *   *

Anna completed her birchbroom as she watched Flora bathe in a huge mud puddle behind our leanto. When the two entered the house, I felt both wonder and anger at the way my slave had braided wampum through her walnut-oiled hair, although it had the effect of restraining her from scratching so often.

'Add a lice comb,' I wrote on my list. 'Ginger, starch, wine, rum, molasses . . . what else?'

''Buy a hat for Nedde while you're in Salem,'' his mother instructed.

''He just got a new one!''

''He threw it at a pigeon he was trying to net and lost it among the swine.'' I added, 'Portugal Cap.'

The aroma of brewing ale made me thirsty but Beth ignored my request for a tankard.

'Five pounds set aside to buy three acres of woodland from Hutch, ten more to be paid within the year,' the noisy flutter of our caged pigeon made my writing poorer than usual.

''Isn't it about time we released our flutterer or killed it, Joseph?''

''When I get back—maybe Nedde will have 'capped' another by then.'' She bit me gently on the cheek and cautioned me against sharpening my wits on the family before confronting Nicholas.

To my horse's consternation, the March gusts tore at me, forcing me to squirm, and increasing my discomfort. Aside from that, the trip was without incident, probably because I chose not to visit with Nicholas but return as soon as my shopping was completed.

I expected Flora to be pleased with her turtleback comb and she did not disappoint me. Nedde, however, grabbed the cap and was well out of earshot before I could warn him about losing it. Anna, too, dismayed me when she wastefully lit a bayberry candle for the sole purpose of snuffing it with the snite I had bought. I only refrained from lecturing her because I wanted to hear my wife's reaction to the hooked rug.

''There goes the budget,'' she sighed, although she caressed it as she would a child.

"Well, you've had a pipeful and a flip since your return, but you've yet to sit down."

My grimace was all the response she needed.

"Flora, pulverize our turtle head and mix in some egg white as an elixir," she smiled at my agony.

Rather than take the concoction, I dropped to the settle with a groan, my exasperation thoroughly enjoyed by our Indian.

'If I ever needed a good reason to travel by water,' I washed the mixture down with a gulp of flip followed by a deep draught of tobacco. My displeasure satisfied both women who went back to their work, allowing me to toss the rest of the dose into the fire and giving me an idea for my sermon.

"See here, Pastor," Captain Gardner criticized between sermons, "you dwell too heavily on death."

I had chosen Revelations 20:12–15. The passage, 'Death and Hades were flung into the lake of fire,' fit my feelings about Flora's medication.

"We have trouble enough recruiting for the army and finding men to impress into the navy let alone listening to your diatribes on death and dying."

"He's right, you know," Beth offered no consolation, "it's obvious your choice of Scripture was ill-chosen."

"With May in the offing, I'll lecture against any frivolity," she nodded assent. "For all I know, some fool may try to set up a maypole in the village."

Imagine how I felt when our Indian traipsed downstairs that day, her hair braided with wampum, her face painted in gaudy red and blue . . .

To make matters worse, John Deal chose the day to complain to me about his wife.

"It happens every spring. As soon as the flowers poke through, Tabitha goes into her act. Oh, she listened to your lecture, but last night she doused our bedroom fire and pulled the featherbed from me. I nearly caught a chill!"

'What can I say? He's surely seen Flora's display. If I can't control my own household, what can I do for his?'

"Wouldn't an hour or so in the stocks humble her, Reverend? It's done wonders for others."

"It may yet come to that, John. At present, I suggest we not make her private misdeeds public." A family spat could easily grow from a molehill to a mountain. I prayed that Providence would allow me to keep this strife between the Deals.

"One thing does disturb me," I don't know why I pressed the issue, "your wife sometimes misses Thursday lectures, and when she's there, her squirming distracts me."

"She claims, she claims she's sorely bothered . . . ." He fumbled with his cap in search of words, "Her . . . it's her bottom . . ."

"Ah! She suffers from . . ." It was my turn to grope for the right term.

"Yes, that's it. I know how it hurts. I have the same problem. Even riding on a pillow doesn't help. She complains to and from the meeting house, especially after sitting there three hours."

"I'll tell you what," I put my arm around his shoulders and guided him to Flora in the kitchen. "My slave has *just* the medicine for Tabitha."

Flora prepared the mixture as she had for me.

"Thank the Lord for you, Pastor," he pumped my hand, "this will do the trick."

"It's no trick, merely a remedy. With the Lord's help, it may relieve your wife."

Smugly, I closed the door behind him and turned to face Beth and Flora, their lips pursed to keep from laughing.

"I asked Flora to make a little extra—take it with you to your study," my wife held her sides as our slave presented me an even larger dose.

"No thanks!" I trudged upstairs, unlatched the fall of my escritoire, and pounded my fist on it as I shouted to my tormentors, "I shall *stand* to study!"

Brilliant sunshine greeted me when I prepared for Salem Town, and so I borrowed Hutch's white-pine canoe.

"I know it's twenty feet long," my wife comforted me, "but you'll manage it better than a horse."

A gentle push from Flora and I was underway, down Beaver Dam Creek to the Crane and Woolston Rivers, then starboard to dock at Salem's North River. The trip was so pleasant I had no time to worry about strategy for the council meeting.

As host, Nicholas sat at the head of the table with John Wise at the far end, a foreboding of the quarrel they would have.

"Welcome, Green, sit across from your Father Gerrish," our host instructed, prayed, and bade us remain standing. "I toast our green colleague for his text and sermon at our *Botch*-ford fast!"

'Two puns in his first sentence—that sets the stage.' I silently acknowledged their approval but wondered if he had got the meaning of my message from John 13:7. 'You do not understand now what I am doing, but one day you will.'

"Let us pray," we were gestured to sit, "that today we will be blessed to understand what Green meant by selecting such a text."

My brethren's mumblings confirmed my suspicion that Nicholas was off to a fast, if faulty, start. No longer the youngest preacher, and with greater tenure than some, I wondered why I had become the butt of his remarks.

"Let's stop this ridiculous word play," John Wise began, "you'd do well, Nicholas, to be as generous as your namesake from Antioch, chosen by the disciples to be charitable."

Ignoring the comment, Nicholas plunged into what he considered the 'botching' of Boxford and bemoaned that Rogers' ordination had been delayed four months due to the congregation's demand that it select it's own minister.

"That issue's two years dead," Beth's father tried to shift us from past to present issues.

"History dominates what we discuss and decide, however 'garish' that might be!" Nicholas persisted. "In spite of Rogers' presence among us as an ordained preacher—the issue burns alive as ever."

"Pray, Nicholas, leave it to Providence and get on with today's topic," my father-in-law plcd.

"I will *not* drop the matter," John Wise insisted, "as I reminded you before, our Church government keeps us from tyranny and slavery."

'Too bad we haven't a tithingman to keep order,' I rued, as Nathaniel excused himself to stoke the fire. Prescott then bolted to the outhouse, complaining of stomach gripings, and was gone almost an hour. 'Oh, for a tithingman' There'd be some sore noggins today!'

"We, around this table, and we alone," our host aimed to recapture our attention when Prescott finally returned, "are the Lord's emissaries.

As such, we alone have the right, the duty, come what may . . .''

'Amazing how he sustains a speech, qualifying each phrase, hardly breathing, adding parenthetical comments, interspersing puns, to keep conversational dominance . . .' I quit imitating his style and offered a prayer in apology.

"Since you never end a sentence," Wise ejaculated, "I'll commence a speech of my own." And so he did, his mimicry putting my imagined one to shame.

At what seemed a prearranged signal, Rogers and Prescott stood, the latter paler than before, and begged our leave.

"So much for your emissariate," John derided, "there go two of your so-called 'stalwart' preachers, for whose appointments and ordinations you fought—neither seems to have the stomach for strong discussion."

"Debate," I blurted, "debate, not discussion." A faint smile from Father Gerrish cancelled the animosity toward me from both ends of the table and stimulated a contribution of his own.

Reciting the Ninetieth Psalm, which we had sung at Rogers' ordination, he paused at the end of the first line to allow us to respond with the next. At the seventh verse he enunciated slower and louder, "We are brought to an end by Your anger and *silenced* by Your wrath."

Oblivious of the verse's implication, Reverends Noyes and Wise plunged into the following verse without a pause.

At verse Fifteen my Father tried again, "Repay us days of gladness for our days of suffering, for the years You have *humbled* us." His tactic having failed, he whispered the final verse and slumped to his chair.

Both debaters spoke at once. Possibly in deference to Nicholas, John quit first while our host droned on. I confess I lost track of the argument until stimulated by his mention of Cotton Mather, which reminded me of my meeting with him at a Reading funeral two years earlier.

I had chosen my text from the Second Book of Samuel 1:26, because it expressed the deep love I felt for my departed friend. Cotton then preached from Revelations 2:19, how our colleague's love, faithfulness, good service, and courage had grown throughout his ministry.

"A good selection, Joseph," the Bay minister shook my hand on parting, pressing the funeral ring he had received into my palm. Surprised at his behavior, I had only enough presence of mind to give him the funeral gloves I had received in exchange . . .

"*Tobacco?*" Reverend Noyes' slur ended my reverie, "so you're headed home this early, John?"

"The trip to *Chebacco* Parish is better made in daylight," were John Wise's parting words.

"I'll accompany you as far as Wenham, John," my father-in-law's departure took me by surprise.

"That leaves us two to complete the council's business," Nicholas commented as we studied the complaint against Deacon Fitch.

"The parishioners' petition favors singing the Psalms by following a tune-master rather than the deacon," I read.

"A severe blow to Fitch's pride. I'd dismiss it as trivial—I'm sure you agree?"

"No, I favor a congregation's doing away with *a capella* singing. Cotton Mather has written . . ."

"He's forever writing, writing, writing. The tract to which you refer is trivia unworthy of even his usual blather."

'I might have expected that from you. The question is: how long will we be at an impasse before they hear of our decision?'

"Logical and reasonable as I am," he pushed paper and pen to me, "never 'victory-minded,' as the Greek meaning of my name implies . . ."

My knowledge of Greek having been damaged by illness and frivolity at Harvard, I accepted his comment without question and wrote our opinion to the parish, phrasing it as a theological rather than political decision so as to protect the deacon from embarrassment.

I was especially proud to cite Cotton Mather's preference for 'regular singing' as more pleasing to the Lord than sounds which often 'made a jar in the ears.' Nicholas snorted when he read the answer but signed the note in the space above my signature.

'The day was not entirely wasted,' I argued during my upstream paddle homeward. 'When we meet in Salem Village, there'll be more peaceful, reasonable progress on the issues.'

Worn-out from disputing and canoeing, I struggled to report the day's events to Elizabeth. Flora was unusually reserved and courteous as she heard me out, listened to my prayer, and nodded as I read the Scripture.

When she reached the ladder to her garret, however, she spat, "*Piz wat,*" before she disappeared.

I was astonished when Beth laughed so heartily. 'Such irreverence after prayers and Scripture!' Too tired to ask what Flora meant and disturbed by my wife's complicity, I sank on the bed.

"Good-for-nothing!' Hearing your story, that's how she felt about Nicholas."

"Shameful! Blasphemous! Profane!" I wasn't sure my voice was loud enough for Beth to hear. 'I'll punish that Indian tomorrow for her disrespect.'

Try as I might that night, whenever my dreams reviewed the day's events, they were irreverently punctuated by '*piz wat.*'

*   *   *

Beth prevailed on me to accept an invitation to preach at East Hampton on the Long Island. Anxious as I was to get away from the Farmers for awhile, I was reluctant to absent myself from her for two weeks.

"Check into a Narragansett Pacer in New London," she suggested, "it's supposed to have an excellent, easy stride."

"Just promise you'll accompany me to Boston the next chance we get," I hugged her and began my trek.

Lodging in Providence with Mister Wight, we witnessed a sailor seated on the gallows, a rope about his neck, in punishment for an unnatural crime, the 'U' branded on his cheek as an eternal reminder.

"I'm proud to say there's no such villainy in my parish," I thanked my host who directed me toward Canterbury, my last stop before Captain Prentiss's place in New London.

"What news have you of Admiral Walker's fleet?" he greeted me, concerned as we all were about its venture against the French at Port Royal.

"None, none at all. But there's a rumor of the French marauding our fishermen and blocking supplies from Old England and the Indies."

The captain shoved the shallop I had borrowed from Mister Coit and launched me across the Sound toward Gardiner's Island. Before it met the shore, two husky Mingos hoisted me and deposited me on the sand at Fire Place.

'Gluskabe could've carried me alone,' I smiled as I paid my bearers, 'without ever wetting his feet.'

The East Hampton deacons complimented me on my sermons from Luke. Then, the Sabbath having ended, I visited first with Mister White at Sag Harbor and later with Mister Whiting of South Hampton, thoroughly enjoying the island and its quaint people.

I took a whaleboat back to New London, decided I couldn't afford a Pacer, and bought a less expensive horse for my journey through Canterbury and home.

"Welcome," Elizabeth's charge almost knocked me over, aided by Nedde's jumping on my back.

"Fetch my saddlebags, Anna."

"Father has a new horse!" Her shout brought John and Joseph racing from the leanto while Anna let Liz carry my bags.

"A Japan case—the loveliest I've ever seen," my wife showed it to Flora who opened it at my request to find a string of beads.

"In gratitude for the care you've given my family these past years, Flora."

"My *natick*," she whisked toward her garret, "this is *my* home, too."

"Have I hurt her pride, Beth?"

"Mother, a pewter porringer," Anna interrupted, handing the dish to her mother.

Nedde, peevish for having been left out, grabbed the saddlebags from Anna and found the Monmouth Cap I had used to protect the porringer, which he declared was *his* gift.

"He lost the last one," my wife apologized. "Polish the porringer, Anna, and set it on the mantle."

Beth and I sat on the settle, my weary back appreciating its support although its oaken seat hurt my sore bottom. She asked how my new horse handled and I answered in glowing terms, without telling her I had lost it during my Canterbury sermon and had to wait two hours until Mister Easton found it.

"That reminds me, Goodwife Howard will be by before candlelight. Her maid left a complaint for you—about a beating."

'Better than an unnatural act. One dispute in two weeks bodes well for this parish.'

"I repent, Reverend, if I *have* done something remiss, as my servant claims. I did not smite her, only gave her a sound whipping for her surly manner and disobedience."

"You may have been cruel, Goody Howard," her spirits sank, "but have repented and confessed."

With the Sabbath only minutes away, I fairly pushed her out the door. "I see no reason for you or your husband to mourn to the grave for supposed cruelty to a naughty servant."

"If only all quarrels could be resolved so easily," my wife's comments reminded me I must prepare for the next ministers' council. 'With the help of Providence, I'll find some way to mollify them,' I prayed during my last-minute thoughts on my coming sermon.

The commotion that disturbed my congregation did not occur at the end of the service, but later that evening in Ingersoll's.

"A fleet! A strange fleet's been sighted off the Maine coast!" The roar greeted my entrance. "It's the French—come to attack Salem Town or Boston."

"Putt," the Inhabitants had elected Joseph a Salem Selectman by pricking a pinhole beside his name on the ballot, "this crowd won't listen to me. Find the truth about this matter as soon as you can. Hutch, help Putt and me chase this bunch home."

It took a good half-hour to clear the ordinary, but longer than a week for Putt to squelch the rumor: the sighted fleet was part of ours, no French ships were found at all.

"I bear worse news than those diabolical rumors spread here last month," Goodman Putnam, wet through from rain and sweat, stood on a table, his anger hushing the crowd. "Our fleet lost eight-hundred-and-eighty-four men. Poor piloting ran the ships aground, well short of Quebec, on the rocks of Egg Island near the mouth of the St. Lawrence . . ."

Hutch asked me to say a prayer to the stunned audience, and so I prayed for the safe return of our impressed friends and brothers, receiving a grateful nod from Captain Gardiner who took it upon his own authority to close the ordinary for the night.

"Flora, let me give you a hand with that Dutch oven," I arrived home just in time for supper.

Following prayers, Anna brought a pitcher of milk, John and Joseph spoons, and Liz and Nedde cider. My wife then poured milk into the center of the hot, seeded pumpkin, stirred it vigorously, and motioned us to scoop as much as we wished.

"Place the pumpkinshell beside the hearth, Flora," she directed, "when it's dry, we'll use it to store the tinder rags."

Liz insisted she was old enough to rake the fire; *I* insisted Joseph supervise the operation. Nedde, however, wailed that he should have a turn banking it the next night, which he did—refusing anyone's supervision.

"Smoke!" Beth's elbow bruised me near midnight. "I smell smoke!"

Groping my way downstairs, I found the lintel charred and belching smoke, the wood from the once-roaring fire almost embers. Rescuing my musket from above the mantle, I checked to be sure its stock was undamaged, raked the fire, and dragged myself back to bed.

"Well?" Beth mumbled.

"Nedde will draw *all* the cider tomorrow . . ."

"That's a girl's job—it's Liz's turn."

"*Nedde* will draw the cider tomorrow, and the next day, and the next—all week."

Draw cider he did! Not enough for the first day's needs; later in the week, too much, the leftover filling the vinegar barrel. At Flora's pleading, I changed his punishment to that of accompanying me each morning to relight the fire before the others were awake.

"You know, dear, Nedde *enjoys* being the first awake," my wife reflected, tired from salting eight-hundred pounds of pork that day.

"Don't remind me—he's wakened *me* the past few days. You should see his eyes sparkle as I strike the flint and steel. He even claps when the charred tinder rags catch fire and set the logs ablaze."

"Careful, Joseph. He could be learning a skill that'll burn us all to death."

I told her not to worry, it was I who lit the kindling. Nevertheless, I added a silent prayer, just in case.

The sooty stubble of a broom, pressed against my ear as had Hutch's rapier, startled me no less that December morning. Wordlessly, Flora prodded me down the fire-lit stairs.

'Beth'll never let me hear the end of this,' I ruefully searched for the miscreant, Nedde, while Flora scampered to check up on the children.

"Found him!" my slave returned, the charred broomstick now firmly tucked in the nape of Nedde's neck. "He pretended to sleep, but he reeks of smoke . . ."

'Dear Lord, what can a father do when a child turns punishment into play? In Heaven's name, how can I, Your humble pastor, succeed in parish duties yet fail so miserably with my own son?'

My well-calculated twist of his charcoaled ear brought tears to his eyes, but not as much as a peep from his mouth, as his mother arrived. Pulling out of my grasp, he ducked below her intended swat, and fled back to bed.

Flora swept the hearth of ashes and threw away the remains of the pumpkinshell. After I brought the fire under reasonable control, Beth and I nestled on the settle where we slept until Nedde gently kissed us awake at daybreak.

*   *   *

"Beth, only cider's to be served to the council today, and no tobacco."

Lined along a crack in the floor, as if being catechized, my children awaited my orders.

"When we complete our agenda, we'll come downstairs."

"Marching?" I pretended not to hear my wife's jest.

"That twenty-five-pound lobster Putt brought must be ready for us by then. Flora, soap and sand my study floor and then sweep up the droppings down here. And, while you're at it, rake the upstairs fire— I want it a bit chilly." She snatched a new broom from the hearth and left.

"John, Joseph, carry our dropleaf table to my study with chairs for six and take over my chores for the day. Anna, tend to Liz and William and do your mother's bidding."

I let Nedde stew while others plunged into their assignments.

"Since fire's become your specialty, Edward, build it according to Mother's instructions, tend the lobster while it broils, and perhaps I'll let you rake the fire tonight."

"Dis-missed!' He roared before he ran to the woodshed at his mother's command.

"I know it seems odd, Beth, to hold the session in a cold study . . ."

"You must have good reason, *Sangman*—I'll see to the troops."

"*Napiui*—scurry off. There's work to be done before they get here."

I felt a bit ashamed for countering her calling me 'Captain' with one of the few words of Abenaki I had learned, but quickly returned to my plan for the council meeting, priding myself on the idea of using our dropleaf table because its small size and circular shape would crowd us without anyone's having the advantage of sitting at the head.

Father Gerrish, the first to arrive, sat across from me, flanked by Nathaniel Rogers on his left and Benjamin Prescott on his right. I left a seat for John Wise, always late, to my left, next to Prescott. Nicholas Noyes, somewhat grudgingly, crammed into the space between me and Pastor Rogers.

"Nathaniel," I ordered after we had settled down, "please begin."

He recited the verse I had chosen from Isaiah 65:25. "The wolf and the lamb shall feed together," his resonance quieted us, "they shall not hurt or destroy."

"Benjamin?" my call caught John about to sit. "Let us hear verse twelve from Isaiah 28."

"You will build once more on ancestral foundations, you shall be called rebuilder of broken walls, restorers . . ."

Before the echo of his words had left the chilling room, I signalled my father-in-law to conclude the Scripture by returning to Isaiah 65:24.

"Before they call to me, I will answer, and while they are still speaking I will listen."

'Pray, Lord, our recommendations will be worthy.' I warned myself against mind-wandering and proposed a new procedure for our council.

"The vote of silence having become more accepted in many parishes, replacing the outdated show of hands, we'll use this to decide on the four topics before us."

Aware that discussion might bog down on this issue, I ignored objections from the brethren flanking me, apprehensive that either might consider silent agreement a Quaker heresy.

"First: how old a man must be before being allowed to preach or become ordained . . ."

Nicholas cleared his throat. Rather than allow him the floor, I raised my voice.

"Second: the new parishes expected or arising . . ."

John Wise dropped his pen to speak on the issue and so I hastily added, "Third: schools for our people."

'Not even a murmur, I expected as much.' The fourth topic would elicit the greatest controversy and so I almost whispered, "Fourth: the question of church consociation."

I paused to await the vote of silence that would confirm the sequence of issues.

"My Brethren, we're agreed," I announced. "Father Gerrish will take notes so that you can concentrate your energies on these vital matters."

The frantic refilling of cider jacks showed my friends' uneasiness as I hastened to ask Nathaniel, whose Boxford congregation had suffered because of the problem, to present the case for and against youthful clergy.

"Master Green," Nicholas broke in, "about the proliferation of parishes . . ."

"Yes indeed," John seconded.

"Brethren," my father stopped notetaking, "we have silently agreed to the order of business . . . Proceed, Nathaniel."

As I expected, the topic evoked little issue. One speaker after another bemoaned the shortage of qualified ministers, a crisis that forced us to seek ever younger, less prepared men for our pulpits. The last to comment was Wise.

"Under the Gospel, we have no precise time when to begin and enter the ministry. Therefore, I think it is not how long men have lived, but," he could suppress a smile, "how *wise* they have grown. Please hear me out! Considering Theology is a long study, and life is very short, why may they not begin young, considering that our Churches are no ways overcluttered with candidates . . ."

"If we accept your proposition, and I quickly add that I do *not*," Nicholas acknowledged my nod permitting him to continue the discussion, "how do you suggest we determine whether a candidate is *wise* enough to become a minister?"

"Academical learning we profess to be a very essential accomplishment in the Gospel Ministry," John Wise, the first son of an indentured servant to have been graduated from Harvard, again proved how much attention he had been privately giving to the issue. "Our Academy is the storehouse of learning, and of all men living, the best and most infallible standard for the philosophical accomplishments of our candidates, is the judgment of the Honorable President and noble fellows of our famous college.''

Although the matter was far from settled throughout New England, no one of us was then prepared to challenge John.

''Are we agreed? Preparation, rather than age, is what we seek in prospects for the ministry?'' I waited, heard no dissent, and directed my Father Gerrish to record our vote.

''Nicholas, would you care to open our discussion about new parishes?'' The shortest, roundest among us, his obesity prevented him from moving closer to the table.

''I oppose, without malice toward anyone here,'' he meant Prescott, Rogers, and myself, ''the senseless, blasphemous, proliferation of parishes across . . .''

He went on to cite the confusion which had reigned since the landing of the Mayflower, compounded by the Stuarts' unwillingness to clarify titles to the land and thus sowing the seeds of New England's destruction.

''Thank you,'' I interjected as he paused to wipe sweat from his face despite the increasing iciness of the room and turned to John Wise.

''As I'm sure you're all aware—I disagree. Not with your history, Nicholas, for Englishmen hate an arbitrary power as they hate the Devil! But, I remind you, neither Increase Mather's 'Happy Revolution' of King William, nor Cotton's calling us 'Our New English Israel' has done anything to relieve our plight.''

I expected these old foes to vent themselves and loosened my rein on the meeting, all the while staring at Pastor Wise.

'Petitioner against the use of spectral evidence in the case of John Proctor, whose poor widow still favors the child for which he gave his life in substitute for hers . . . Attend to the meeting!' I reprimanded myself.

''Benjamin?'' I broke in when John paused. Prescott and my father-in-law spoke in support of Nicholas, but Rogers favored his opponent. The discussion had reached a stalemate.

''As I interpret your position, Nathaniel,'' I spoke after John Wise had nodded his vigorous approval, ''we are not likely to cultivate further land although our people grow in number, their farms are becoming smaller as they are divided among the children, and now we find ourselves forced to carve new parishes from established ones.''

"Such as the pulpits you and I now occupy," added Prescott.

"And the one about to form" interjected Reverend Gerrish, "that'll put two churches between her and Salem Town."

"Sadly, sadly," Nicholas conceded.

'Consider how the late Daniel Andrews might have searched for a word to end this quarrel in compromise,' I prayed.

"As our population expands," I forced myself to attend to Nathaniel's argument, "we must expect our churches to proliferate."

'Speak simply,' that would have been Daniel's advice. 'So far we've heard 'proliferate,' 'expand,' and 'burgeon,' why not 'grow!'

"Only the Church stands between Mankind and Hell!" None could deny the truth of Nicholas's remark nor John's which quickly followed.

"By 'Church,' we mean a particular Church; which consists of a society of Christians, meeting together in one place, under their proper pastors, for the performance of religious worship, and the exercising of Christian Discipline."

As my colleagues reflected on the statement, I felt the moment for agreement was near.

"Brethren, I propose this council go on record in favor of church *growth*, ever wary against the *needless* multiplication of parishes. I await your verdict."

Silence answered my prayer.

"Now, schooling . . ."

My father read aloud a statement addressed to the Bay Ministers which deplored the colony's inadequate opportunities for education and implored them to establish schools, because education was God's way to prevent the Devil from capturing the ignorant for his mean purposes.

Shivers, which I did not take as dissent, answered my call for a vote. At John's suggestion, we commended my father-in-law and let the statement stand as he had read it.

Adding to our discomfort was the aroma of food which fumed through cracks in the floor and churned our empty stomachs. I resisted temptation to ease our plight, not wanting to lose the momentum we had established, but willing to accept defeat on our final issue.

"John, please lead off on the consociation of churches." All of us had read his manuscript, *The Churches' Quarrel Espoused,* written in the form of a mock trial in opposition to the Mathers' proposal for *A Cambridge Association.*

"The power of the clergy gradually increasing, they daily draw more new rights to themselves, which they take from the people." Eloquent, perhaps, but it would not convince others among us. "They snatch or take the whole business into their own hands," he clutched his fists for emphasis. "Let them spend the time in catching flies rather than contrive how to subvert the Churches by such despotic measures."

"Thanks be to God and the King!" Nicholas, having tolerated as much as he could, repeated part of his Election Sermon, "Our houses and our lands are our own, and yet we have the liberty of our religion, and the free exercise of it, if we have wisdom and grace to improve it rightly."

"Why, Gentlemen!", the Chebacco pastor pled, "Have you forgot it? Out comes these Proposals, like Aaron's golden calf, the Fifth Day of November! It is the day of the Gunpowder Treason, and a fatal day to traitors! *I* dare not join with you in this conspiracy."

"Conspiracy is a harsh accusation," my father-in-law looked up from his notes, "perhaps you could tone down your rhetoric before what you have said appears in print."

"Who is it Englishmen are thus afraid of?" John was undaunted in his attack, "It is neither France nor the Great Turk, therefore it must needs be somebody or another nearer home . . ."

Benjamin and Nathaniel squirmed at Reverend Wise's reference to the Bay Ministers, especially the Mathers, but I felt unusually peaceful as he finished his thesis.

"Usurpers in *Churches* affront the world, with the assumption that the best of the brotherhood are a company of fools. They take upon themselves the boldness to assume a prerogative of trampling underfoot the natural original equality of their fellows."

"We will not reach consensus on this issue today, Brethren," I declared, "dinner awaits us downstairs."

We ate gluttonously, washing the lobster and pone down with so much ale I prayed no Inhabitants would witness our depravity.

"Gentlemen," Nicholas refilled his tankard and rose from the table, "Goodwife Green," he summoned, as Flora cleared the table, and Beth came to my side. "I toast our gracious host with words from Psalm 110: 'You are a preacher forever, Joseph," my wife joined them, "in the tradition of Melchizadek!"

10 Scoring above the Breath

"Our *ka oz!*" Flora announced from the bedroom doorway.

"*Ka oz, ka oz,*" Nedde echoed his brothers' chant.

"Mulberry's ailing," Beth mumbled, "better see to her."

Our cow had been sickly since her calving, probably due to the weather, our barn roof having collapsed under the first snowfall, and so I sent the boys to fetch Doctor Twiss. The brewing ale's aroma of sage and tansey greeted his orders to Flora.

"Make some flip of this wort, add ginger, rum, sugar, and a touch of rhubarb." Fascinated by the recipe, Flora stirred it vigorously. "Now, tansey, sage, hysop, and catnip to the best of it and we're ready."

For two days, Mulberry dined on mulled cider, wort, and rendered hog fat. Twiss, whom Beth invited to stay with us, gorged himself on our best roast pork, but not before he had added a pint of boiled flax seed to Mulberry's fare.

"Look at the bright side," I pled with my wife who lay beside me, highly critical of both cow and doctor for depleting our larder. "If Mulberry doesn't make it—she'll die in comfort." Beth hugged me and turned aside to sleep.

Three days after her first treatment, Mulberry wobbled to her feet, eager for flip, but settling for corn. Twiss then blooded her tail, gave her a pailful of flax-wort brew and brought her calf to be suckled.

"Eight shillings? You paid him *eight* shillings! He ate and drank twice that amount!" It was unlike Beth to be miserly, something else was on her mind. I promised myself to ask her at day's end and attended to my farming.

"Help me!" she wailed as I finished catechizing the children, Beth's arms shaking with a load of pine coals.

Flora reached her first, relieved her of the peel, and took over the week's baking while Anna swept the hearth with her hemlock broom.

"It's a mixed blessing, having half-a-dozen men working on the meeting house, another ten hurrying about the parsonage, two more working on the leanto, and you in the cellar repairing the chimney!" Beth wept uncontrollably as she fell into my arms beside the fireplace.

'Don't lecture! Pay more attention to her needs than your own. Your chores can wait.'

I failed in my resolve. I shot and trapped pigeons, gathered winter apples, and husked thirty bushels of corn. I rode to Roxbury to buy some land, lost my horse and recaptured him, and bought two oxen at Wenham before I came home. Except for illness, my parish was peaceful, but I still averaged two funerals a week, interspersed among my commercial activities.

"Beth," I struggled to find comfort after slaughtering and selling Mulberry for five pounds and five shillings, Flora and my wife having salted seven hogs that same day, "how about our taking a trip to Boston?"

She lay on her side, her back toward me, without stirring.

"I rummaged through my escritoire, and what do you think I found?" I slid toward her to nuzzle her hair. "Since I've been ordained, I've been under or overbearer to dozens of people . . ."

'An odd way to open a conversation, no wonder she's unresponsive,' I ran one hand beneath her shoulders and fondled her breasts with the other.

"Over the past fourteen years," she backed against me, arousing me with her bottom, "I've accumulated funeral rings, scarves, gloves . . ."

Her hand ran down my belly, groped for my yard, and moved it gently up and down.

"Oh, Joseph," she flipped so quickly I just caught her before we rolled out of bed. Giggling apologies, we gave our bodies full rein, thoroughly enjoying the ecstasy we had denied ourselves so long.

"Come to the point," she panted, lying playfully on top of me.

"What about Boston? What's it got to do with the funeral gifts? When do we leave?"

"My brother Benjamin could sell them for us."

"I'll dress and we'll go . . ."

"Now, Beth."

"Unless you'd like to try again?" she teased.

"I'll settle for a promise: I won't let my duties get in the way of our trip."

"Agreed, I'll ask Nanna to watch over the children while father takes your pulpit."

*   *   *

Joyously, like young lovers about to embark on life together, we began packing for our journey the following Monday. True to my resolve, I even postponed quizzing our children on my Sabbath lecture, a sermon I had used before. My text was from Paul's letter to the Romans 8:28, to the effect that if God were for us, who could be against us. Little did I know when I chose it how great a part Providence played in my choice of that passage.

"You know," my wife paused from packing, "a week ago I felt you might need a dose of valerian."

"Why valerian? My heart feels fine."

"Valerian arouses lust!"

"The Scripture tells us that married love . . ."

"No need to sermonize! Just the same, a little lust sets things in motion," she kissed me so boldly I almost tumbled on the bed.

"I've changed my mind," she pulled away. "I'll ask Flora to prepare some waterlily roots instead."

"Whatever for?"

"They deter lust," she tittered, continuing to pack, "I'd better take some, too."

A fist's furious pounding, followed by a hand's sharp slap on the parsonage door shocked my wife and stifled my laughter. Waving me to continue packing, Beth left to welcome the intruder. Moments later she returned, closed her satchel, and nodded Flora into our room.

"Who was it?"

"Tabitha Deal," my wife returned her valise to its place behind our bedroom table. "I've never seen her so distraught."

"She'll get over it," I moved to continue packing but Flora blocked me. "Remember, Beth, we promised . . ."

"Our promise will keep," she reached her hands toward me as Flora discretely stored my satchel beside hers and tiptoed out. "You've more than satisfied me these past few days."

"Our trip?"

"Work before play! Tabitha needs you." She dropped my hands to tidy the clothes from the bed. "Get a move on. I'll have Flora fix some waterlily root . . ."

Her good humor overcame my disappointment enough that I queried her about Goody Deal's condition and complaint.

"It puzzles me. When Flora said you weren't available, the gamar blurted, 'The Devil take him,' jerked her reins, and raced off."

"Her *wskat qua*," Flora's interjection distracted me.

"Something about 'forehead,'" my quizzical expression encouraged our slave to repeat herself. "I don't know what she means. I didn't get a close look at Tabitha."

"*Wskat qua*," Flora startled me as she took a dead coal from the hearth and marked a line above her nose.

I shrugged to disguise my horror and not further alarm my wife and slave. My gesture had the desired effect for they shrugged in imitation of me.

'Lord,' I prayed as I trotted northward to the Deal's, 'if the sign my Indian reported is true, I need Your guidance as never before.'

The superstitious practice was to scratch or slash oneself above or below the nose to scourge the Devil's familiar by providing it with a vent. 'Scoring above the breath,' as the nonsense was called, signified that Goody Deal's miseries had become macabre.

Her husband confirmed my fears when he intercepted me at his fence.

"Punish her, Pastor, I beg you. She makes such weird noises in her sleep I've had to sleep on the settle. Even so, she creeps downstairs before dawn and splashes cold water on me. The only peace I get is when I row out on Nichols Brook and nap."

"Forced idleness is not sloth, John." I hitched my horse beside the door, "Why not take your shallop out while I see to your wife."

Entering their gloomy bedroom, I looked for a chair, hoping not to disturb the sleeping figure on the bed. Finding none, I edged closer. Above her sunken eyes were the telltale scratches my Indian had described.

"The Black Man comes to me each night," she choked, feigning sleep, "he tries to make me sign his evil book."

In order to hear her better and comfort her, I sat on the bed, taking as little space as possible.

"He makes me feel like a virgin fighting off a rapist."

Silence, which I considered my best tactic, only aggravated her and made my perch more precarious.

"Pastor!" she tore open her frock, "His imp! See, it tries to suckle me!"

Shocked by the suddenness of her action, I lost my balance and fell toward her, my hands across her breasts. Grabbing each in a vise-like grip, she pulled me on top of her.

"Gone! The imp's gone!" She rotated my palms across her gnarled nipples before I could break away and regain my balance.

'You fool!' I wiped her sweat from my hands while her fore-fingers and thumbs played with her teats. 'You can't cope with this deluded woman any better than with your Roxbury boys!'

"I'll . . . I'll send Doctor Hale with a physik for you . . ."

"The sabat, ugh," her eyes closed, she drew the carpet over her bosom and hitched herself upright. "Satan demands I share his tasteless meal."

"I'll fetch the doctor now," I groped cautiously for my hat, which lay beside her pillow, making sure she could not trap me again.

"The Black Man has other companions," she opened her eyes and stared through me. "He changes himself into an animal to torment me."

I would have liked to have responded but her gaze silenced me.

"A turtle! A turtle such as you've never seen. It outruns the fastest hare. It even scales my wall. I feel its presence now . . . beside you!"

Reflexively, I turned toward the window.

"Aha! *You* see it, too!"

"I only see a hazy sun filtering through a," I almost said, 'filthy,' "broken window pane."

"Sometimes," she ignored my denial, "sometimes he sends his

other helper.'' She slid to the far side of the bed, covered herself, almost demurely, with a long robe, and faced me.

"His *real* companion is a woman,'' she taunted me with a description that might fit any of many women, "tall, slender, lithe, swift . . .'' I thought she would never end until she added, "*dark.*''

"Dark?''

"Like the Devil himself,'' she sneered. "Her lice-filled hair, braided with strings of black shells and white fishteeth . . .''

'Flora!' I feared she might read my lips.

Entranced by her own fantasy, she let her robe slip from her shoulders, caressed the underside of her breasts, and threw herself, spread-eagle on the bed.

"Your slave torments me, Pastor,'' she pressed her eyelids with her fists, "Your Indian's a *witch!* Fetch your slave. I beg you. Make her touch my bewitched body before witnesses and heal me . . .''

Satisfied with having confronted me, she appeared to fall asleep. Concerned that her husband might suddenly return and find us in such a compromising condition, I make sure she had lost consciousness before I covered her with the carpet and left.

'Her spectral evidence damns Flora,' I put my own embarrassment aside to review Tabitha's report, my sorrel retracing our trail without my help. 'The hag describes my Indian exactly, even to her turtleshell lice comb, the elixir from a turtlehead, and that nonsense about a turtle's outrunning a hare—another myth about Gluskabe!'

I vowed to keep my experience to myself, certainly not to share it with my wife or slave, and to seek help from my Boston brethren before my next session with Goody Deal. After evening services, I waited until our family was asleep before I crept into bed, drained by the day's events.

'Eight firebrands of Hell.' Again I crawled up the ladder toward the whirling corpse. But when I reached for her feet, they were dark-skinned.

'Flora!' The ladder spun at my shock and I was face-to-face with a second dangling body.

'Beth!' No, Dear God! No!'

And so on down the gruesome line . . .

'Anna, Joseph, John, Nedde, Liz, William.'

*   *   *

"Lord save me! Mercy! Mercy!" Elizabeth trembled as she clung to me at the ship's railing.

"Oh, Lord Jesus, save me!"

"Come now, it's only your imagination."

"I'm sure I heard the wail of the Shrieking Woman as we rounded Marblehead."

"Just watch the whales at play," I was not about to have our trip to Boston spoiled by *her* apparitions such as my dreams had been filled by Goody Deal's.

"Spanish pirates murdered her. Can't you hear her cry?"

It was difficult to keep a secret from my wife. As far as she knew, our hastily rescheduled trip was primarily to shop for the year's provisions, although my purpose was to seek counsel from the Mathers and Brattles. Once out of sight of Marblehead, she settled down and enjoyed the voyage to Boston Harbor.

My mother came from Cambridge to tour my wife through the area with the money Benjamin got from my funeral gifts. I left them to shop together so that I could visit Thomas Brattle alone.

"Please play more music, Brother," the organ filled the room as we sang the Ninetieth Psalm, punctuated by my host's fit of coughing.

"My will leaves the organ to the church, Joseph. I hope the congregation accepts it."

"My Farmers would have none of it. It's too radical an invention."

"Speaking of inventions, fetch that box for me."

Lifting the device carefully from its case, he placed it on the table, adjusted the knobs, and peered into the eyepiece.

"Have a look." I stared into the gadget and saw all sorts of squirming beasts. "Van Leuwenhoek, A Dutchman, invented it."

"What am I looking at?"

"A single drop of ordinary drinking water."

"You mean to say the Lord created creatures as tiny as these and as large as the whales I saw the other day?"

"Indeed, Master Green. That's why I'm torn between Commerce and Science."

"Rumor has it you've been appointed to the Royal Society?" My gaze glued on what Cotton Mather had called the 'little eels' in a tract he had written to deny conflict between Science and the Scripture. I was flattered when my host complimented me on my account of the aurora borealis which I had sent him a few years earlier.

Another furious fit of coughing warned me I might be draining him, and so I never got around to asking his advice on how to treat Goody Deal's affliction but had to settle for Cotton Mather's.

"My father and I feel that the union of Theology and Medicine is an 'Angelical Conjunction,'" my white-wigged host got right down to business. "Your experience with Brattle's microscope is an example. Why, over twenty years ago, I made the analogy between a drop of water and New England. New England, a drop of water at which Satan has aimed all his sinful attention. Defeat him in our microcosm and we defeat him for Old England, too."

Although Cotton Mather's writings had been crucial in my rebirth, and his eloquence undeniably in the Lord's service, his many predictions were rarely correct. For instance, his study of earthquakes and the frenzy of '92 led him to assert that Jesus would descend to us before the end of the century. Undaunted when the Lord did not materialize, he predicted that William of Orange's proclamation against profanity would result in the Hebrews' returning to Christ, which also failed to happen. The Abenaki name for Salem, *Naumkeag,* he insisted, derived from the Hebrew words, *nahum keike,* 'comfort and safety,' and proved that the Indians were descended from the Lost Tribes of Israel. On this premise, he opened schools for their conversion, a sign the Millenium was at hand. With these errors of judgment in mind, I wondered how much I could rely on his analogy between a drop of water and my tormented Tabitha.

"I'll share a secret before you leave," he furtively closed the study door and beckoned me. "I've learned from Old England that there are experiments underway which may lead to preventing—guess what?"

Baffled, I might have blurted, 'Witchcraft,' had I not been awed by him.

"Smallpox! My colleagues write that they can see the beasties which cause it. With the Lord's help, and my own, we'll find a way to prevent the scourge!"

'Another worthless divination,' I smiled as we parted, having failed again to get the counsel which had brought me to Boston, albeit he became among the first in Boston to be vaccinated against the scourge, as did John Wise.

With Beth behind me on her pillion, we headed northwest to Woburn, stayed overnight at Reading, where she confided she was pregnant again, and so, very carefully, made our way to Salem Village.

"Good Lord!" she rapped my shoulder as we neared the meeting house, "Goodman Deal's in the pillory again!"

'What's Tabitha been up to now?' This latest action would make it more difficult for me to hide the truth from my wife.

After a joyous welcome, my father-in-law told me that Tabitha had complained her husband beat her without cause and proved her case by showing him huge welts across her buttocks.

"After consultation with the deacons, John was punished with an hour in the pillory."

"A just measure," I thanked him halfheartedly, afraid that public attention would further encourage Tabitha.

Following Nanna Gerrish's sumptuous meal of pork and beans, my in-laws left for Wenham. Flora packed the children off to bed, their many questions about our trip unanswered because my wife and I were too tired from our ride.

"Wake up! You're having a nightmare! You'll disturb the children," my wife shook me, my side of our bed soaked with sweat. "Now what's this nonsense about? 'Eels,' 'Deals,' you muttered as you tossed."

"I . . . I don't remember."

"Hmm! Well, *I* do! I remember a sermon you gave: evasion is as sinful as an outright lie . . ."

How could I forget? Try as I might to put the idea out of my mind, again and again the microscope magnified the Deals' distress until it spread like the pox throughout the parish, consuming my beloved wife and family and leaving me helpless and alone.

*　　*　　*

Ingersoll's ordinary could hardly contain the Farmers that unseasonably cold March night. I made it my business to warn against drunkenness, although most of my attention was focused on overhearing any rumors about the Deals. My wife had absented herself, her pregnancy causing so much trouble she felt able only to attend services, and so the burden of keeping the peace rested solely on me.

"I hear a rider," Putt called from his post near the door.

"He's headed this way."

The crowd quieted with anticipation: a vote of the Salem congregation could never be predicted. As a result, Samuel Nurse's arrival was met with silence rather than cheers.

Sam nodded his thanks to Hutch's treat, a jack of flip, but otherwise made straight for me, without any sign of the vote's outcome.

'Those icy eyelashes. Are they from tears of pain or joy?' I puzzled as I accepted the scrap of paper pressed into my hand.

"Read it to yourself, Pastor," he cautioned hoarsely, "take whatever action you deem necessary."

Like the Red Sea before Moses, the milling crowd opened a path for Goodman Nurse and closed behind him as he made his way toward Putt.

'Humbly requesting the merciful God would pardon whatsoever sin, error, or mistake was in the application of that censure,' my heart pounded with gratitude at the opening words and, with Hutch's help, I mounted a bench to call the Inhabitants to prayer.

"The First Church of Salem has voted to *erase* . . ." the roar drowned the remainder of my message. "Has voted to erase the excommunication of our late sister, Rebecca Nurse, mother to some of you, beloved aunt to others, friend to all."

When the outburst settled to a murmur, I completed my reading. "Our Merciful High Priest, who knows how to have compassion on the ignorant and those that are out of the way."

"What about Goodman Corey?" Putt boomed.

"After twenty years of delay, Giles Corey has also been restored to full communion." I watched Hutch wince at the news, and so climbed down unaided to pay my respects to Samuel Nurse.

"You've been God's instrument in this redress," Putt commented before I could catch Rebecca's son. "Those were Sam's words, Pastor."

"Let our friends enjoy themselves awhile then help the tithingman clear the ordinary. I must get back to Beth."

He smiled his agreement and helped me press through the celebrants.

"I was so humbled by Sam's words, I couldn't respond," I reported to my wife.

"You've suffered defeats in silence, now silence greets your triumph."

"Not *my* triumph. Like Nicholas and his congregation, I've only been the Lord's tool in righting this wrong.'' With our children around us I read from Romans 8:31, ''If God is on our side, who is against us?''

The unbounded joy which greeted the Salem decision became converted into a serene strength, arming us against the ravages of drought and illness through the Spring. It didn't even bother me that I would have to face Nicholas' wrath on my next visit to town.

''What vote are you speaking about, Joseph? We meet on the second Monday of each month, just as you, and so many, often trivial, votes are taken . . .''

''The vote which revoked the excommunications of . . .''

''Ah yes, I recall. After all, it was time our members took *some* action,'' he passed me a tankard of ale. ''Of course, as pastor, I broached the matter years ago, having repented whatever innocent part I might have played in that sorry affair.''

'Repented? Perhaps, but never confessed.' I knew better than to push him, 'though both Judge Sewall and Young Ann Putnam saw fit to do so.'

''Brother Green, you know how deeply I oppose this new parish on the Royal Side—yet another splinter from Salem.'' He plunged into the topic with his typical vehemence, citing our council's statement against the reckless growth of churches, and claiming this newest one would further 'splinter his Tree of God.'

''The Middle Parish seems firm under Prescott . . .''

''The Middling Parish?''

''I can't imagine the Royal Side's being worse.''

''The Riot Side *is* worse!'' he refilled my tankard before I could stop him.

''All parishes hereabouts fall under Salem Town's jurisdiction, Nicholas, none having been allowed to establish its own township. We support Salem Town with our taxes and men to serve watch, although they're needed to farm or guard our lands against marauders coming overland.''

''As it should be! In spite of the Mathers' attempts, the New Charter fails to clarify land titles—Salem Town is the only legitimate government.'' In my haste to block him from again refilling my tankard, he spilled ale on my coat. ''We protect you from French attacks by sea, but this diabolical proliferation . . .''

'Why did Cotton Mather grace Salem with his sermon, 'A Town In Its Truest Glory.' Did he know Nicholas would print and distribute it to support the status quo?'

Aware we were at our usual impasse and intent upon arriving home before candlelight, I told my host we had better continue our discussion later. No sooner had I crossed the Town Bridge, however, than my bowels began to ache. I galloped past Garner's Brook but the pace was my undoing and so I dismounted under a tree on Goody Osborne's land and rid my body of its unwanted contents, accompanied by a cloudburst. My horse took my indisposition and the downpour as a signal and left me to hike the rest of the way.

"Flora, punch a hole in that egg with this pin and drain the white," my wife instructed as I stood by the fire. "Add a pinch of salt and not too much rum."

Beth put the posset in the ashes until the egg was dry and passed it to me. Reluctantly, I gagged the mixture down, both women denying me even a drop of rum.

"Flora, watch the hourglass, that'll stop my husband from jostling the sand through it."

"What's this contraption on the mantle? It wasn't here when I left for Salem."

"Oh, that's a Needle-and-Bone game Flora made for the children. Why don't you try it? It'll help you pass the hour until your next dose."

What looked to me like four deer toebones had been hollowed and a thong strung through them at the end of which was a wooden needle.

"How does it work, Beth?"

"Simple. Just throw the thong and bones in the air and try to catch a bone by sticking the needle through one of its horizontal holes."

"I *did* it!" I cried after the hourglass was half-empty.

"Which bone did you catch?" my wife asked, Nedde's having burst into the room at my yell.

"The top one. See?"

"The lower the bone you catch, the higher your score, Father."

I had forgotten how ill I felt and had to be reminded to take my medicine.

"There! How about that!" I exulted. "Caught the second bone."

"But you missed on so many tries, Father."

Irritated more by my boy than my bowels, I threw the gadget at him, challenging him to do as well.

And so, until time for my last treatment of the evening, I watched Nedde consistently pierce the lowest bone, to the women's applause.

*   *   *

"I do believe Flora's partridge berry soothed me during Benjamin's birth, Dear."

Aware of our Indian's precarious situation, should Goodwife Deal spread gossip about her, I wished she had not become so important to our family. I even sampled the groaning beer she had prepared for Elizabeth and had to admit it wasn't the worst I'd ever tasted. But I put my foot down when I overheard her telling of Pemola, my children more attentive to her than they ever were to me.

"He can fly across the whole earth in less than a day, his spirit so evil its heat sets villages on fire . . ."

"Enough, Flora! Get on with your chores and stop filling my children's heads with your wild, heathen tales." I didn't have to warn them, they'd scattered at the first sound of my anger.

"The tale may be heathen, Joseph, but Flora was converted by the Jesuits long ago."

"How do you know?"

"She showed me a miniature wooden statue of Jesus' mother." My quizzical expression encouraged her to elaborate. "You see, the Abenakis sent a six-foot belt of wampum, with eleven rows, to the Canons of Chartres. When Father Bigot returned to St. Francis at Chaudiere, he brought a small silver statue of what they call the 'Holy Virgin' in exchange."

"Papist paganism!"

"Not so loud, I think someone's at our door . . ." Right as usual, she accepted the list of names of strangers who had settled in the village, and thanked Goodman Oliver for his trouble.

"Beth, that list comes at a propitious time. As our Selectman, Joseph Putnam, will see to it that all strangers are duly taxed."

"What's so timely . . ."

"Tomorrow I shall sermon on tithing, that's the tie in."

"If you insist," she attended to Benjamin, yet I could feel her disapproval before she added, ''but it seems to me there are troubles enough in the parish without your adding to them.''

''Put all your trust in the Lord,'' I intoned from the third chapter of Proverbs, my congregation apparently so transfixed by my sermon, the tithingman had nothing to do. ''Do not think how wise you are,'' I should have heeded that advice, ''but fear the Lord.''

Nedde, the snook had told my wife the day before, was suspected of swimming in the nearby pond, a serious violation of our law, but had so far eluded the tithingman. Thus, the words I read were directed at my son.

''Honor the Lord with your wealth as the first charge on all your earnings.'' This passage, the heart of my message, I read slower and louder, searching the impassive Farmers' faces for its effect. I purposely omitted reading the final verses, 'For those whom he loves the Lord reproves, and he punishes a favorite son,' believing they might reduce the impact I hoped to have.

I was thrilled by the quiet awe my people showed as they filed out, following Benjamin's baptism. Even the Deals rode away at a pace unusually slow for them.

Elizabeth's silence lasted through our light supper and confirmed my supposition about the success of my sermon, and so I solemnly reread the text to my family before bidding them a good night's sleep.

''Our *sog mo* is here!'' Flora announced outside my study the next morning. ''*Mos kwal dam wo gan,*'' she warned.

''Putt's downstairs,'' Beth interpreted. ''As Flora says, the Chief's furious with you . . .''

'The Putnam crest,' emblazoned with a red wolf's head, 'certainly matches his temperament,' I thought, then asked, ''What seems to be the matter?''

''Your sermon, Pastor Green! We barely survive, scratching a meager living from this miserable, infested soil, under threat of French invasion or Taranteen massacre . . .'' His fiery eyes shifted from me to my slave. ''Impressed into the navy, forced into the militia, made to stand watch for Salem Town . . .''

'Now I know how Sam Parris must have felt when you confronted him,' Goodman Putnam brushed my wife's offer of ale aside.

''The first charge on my slim earnings retires the debt on my land

and animals,'' he tugged at his shabby clothes, ''the second to support my family, albeit not in Boston finery . . .''

Embarrassed by his outburst, he reached for the jack he had refused and downed most of it in one draught, which gave me a chance to recover from the shock of having so grossly misread my parish's reaction to my sermon.

''You serve the people well, as spokesman and Selectman,'' with mischief brewing in Goodwife Deal, mischief directed toward my loved ones, I needed every ally, especially one as powerful as he, but not at the price of my conviction. ''As Selectman for the Lord, however, I only perform my duty . . .''

''Farmers better educated than I,'' he reached for the Scripture on the mantle, ''dispute your choice of text. Nowhere did it mention,'' he shook the Bible at me, ''tithing. You tricked us in a wordtrap, Master Green. You disappointed us. You acted more like that noisy 'Numb Keg' from Salem Town than the friend . . . than the pastor we've learned to respect.''

Dejected when he left without so much as a backward glance, I shuffled toward the stairs and the security of my study.

''For those whom He loves,'' my wife's voice caressed the passage I had omitted the day before, ''the Lord reproves.'' Replacing the Scripture, she walked toward me, reciting, ''and He punishes a favorite son.''

My tears poured down her cheek as I hugged her, lifted her to the step above me, and promised I would be more thoroughly prepared the next time I sermoned on tithing.

''The next time may be your last!''

11 That Afflicted Minister

"Could you spare Flora this morning?" I had to know more about the Indians to protect my slave and family from Goody Deal's accusations. "I've got to check on the Fuller boy's condition."

"If you'll snowshoe out there, yes."

Flora tucked her knee-high leggings inside her moccasins, her deerskin mantle almost trailing on the ground, and we set off toward the Log Bridge.

"By what name do your people call us?" I asked as we neared the Great River.

"We call you English the 'Yenguese,'" she strode ahead of me, stopping just beyond the Small's homestead.

I was not as adept as she on snowshoes and needed a moment's rest. "I imagine your people trap beaver in these many streams."

"We used to, but so many have been caught, their fur traded to the French, they have become quite scarce," she paused to adjust her leggings. "The beaver has other uses for us."

"As meat?" The thought did not please me.

"Yes, but you must obey two rules. First, you must remove the small bone from each hind foot; second, you must only prepare the meat by boiling it . . . or you will die insane! Be careful, Pastor!" she shouted. "I see a *podunk* before the bridge—your feet may sink!"

'Superstitious nonsense!' We skirted the soft ground and crossed the river. 'But no moreso than much of my flock believes.'

"And the other use you mentioned for the beaver?"

"Fat from its tail," for the first time since I had surprised her with my gift of a lice comb, she seemed embarrassed, "arouses one's passions."

'I have no need for an aphrodisiac,' her call distracted me from my musings.

"That furrow in the snow," she pointed to a half-mile-long path leading to the Fullers, probably made by someone's having dragged a log, "could be used to play our Snow-Snake game."

After forming a furrow, sometimes as long as a mile, she explained, an Indian would take his polished pole, its head carved like a snake's, dip it in freezing water, and slide it along the groove. "My brother, nicknamed, 'Our Sleeper,' could slide his snow-snake farther than that furrow."

"Nicknamed?"

"For our totem, *Ogawinno,* you call a bear, because he slept every chance he got."

"I named you 'Flora'," we unlaced our snowshoes and stood them beside the door, "but I'm curious about your Abenaki name."

"Women get their names from the earth," she waited for me to knock, "Flora will do . . ."

"But your true name?"

"Remains my secret. We call each other only by nicknames."

Doctor Hale ushered me to the boy's bedside. Unable to stop the youngster's bleeding, he left me alone to pray with the child until he died. Following my prayers with the Fullers, I found Flora waiting for me down the trail.

"Lord knows what disease struck him down," I reported.

"We see illness differently," she tightened our laces, "as a disturbance between the Human world and Nature. When the relationship, *ndo'dem,* becomes upset, one becomes ill and may die, just like failing to prepare beaver meat correctly."

'Will I ever understand these curious people?'

"See all these tracks? Rabbits are plentiful in these woods."

We bent saplings on either side of the tracks, fastened with a stick I slid into a notch, while she tied one end to each sapling. We then made horsehair nooses at the other ends, large enough to slip over a hare's head.

"Your sons will delight in tomorrow's catch," Flora laughed as she slid ahead of me across the bridge and home, leaving me with the sadness of the Fuller boy's death and the joy of my own sons' health.

"They'll freeze to death!" my wife reprimanded before the boys and I set out the next morning. "I won't have them outside in this miserable weather!"

"Have faith, Beth. John can take Joseph on one horse, and Nedde'll ride behind me."

"You're so stubborn! I see you've already told Flora to prepare some no-cake." Before either of us had risen, our Indian had parched yellow corn in hot ashes and pounded it into powder.

"Use no more than three teaspoons of *yokeag* for a meal," she warned. "The river's frozen, so melt some snow in your hands to mix with the meal."

The horses picked their cautious ways toward Wilkins Pond, the older boys' saddlebags packed with iceskates, mine empty, except with no-cake, in anticipation of our catch.

"A hare, Father, I found one!" John cried as we crossed the bridge. "Fetch it, Joseph, reset the trap, and put the hare in Nedde's saddle-bag."

"Ride on, Father!" my eight-year-old urged and my horse began to trot. "There's another!" Nedde's scream shattered my ear as he spotted a sapling down the path.

"Hold tight!" I warned when I felt his grip loosen, allowing my horse to slow his gait so his brothers could bag the hare and reset the trap. Nedde showed his displeasure by jabbing his heels into the horse's flanks.

"No more mischief or you'll not accompany us again," I fought to control the animal.

As soon as we got to the frozen pond, the older boys donned their skates while I fixed Nedde's.

"Looks different frozen than when you sneak off to swim, eh, Son?"

His blush confirmed the snook's report but I put punishment aside to teach him to skate. Once he gained confidence, he dropped my arm and slipped and slid his way to the far end of the pond. I lit my pipe and prepared the no-cake.

"Now see here, you two," I cautioned the older boys who were about to consume Nedde's share, "you've already had most of my portion—leave the rest for your brother."

They obeyed, finding it more amusing to have a snowball fight than to help me retrieve Nedde. He, of course, protested against my removing his skates, greedily gulped his food, and hugged me impulsively when I boosted him to the pillion.

"We'll race you home, Father," John challenged as their horse dashed out of sight beyond the Fullers'.

"To think, just yesterday, the Fullers buried their dear son.' I refused to race, my thoughts on the boy's last words, 'Father, help me . . .'

"Father, help me!" Nedde screamed as he lost his balance and fell, hitting the back of his head on the frozen river.

*   *   *

"Nedde's dead!" John ran toward me as I knelt beside my fallen son.

"He's still breathing!" Joseph bent over his prostrate brother, "See the frost from his mouth . . ."

A year before, I had been through the same tragedy when Joseph Prince's son fell from his horse near Putnam's Hill, went into a coma, and died. Then, I had time to pray; now, I had to act.

"Don't move him!" I pulled Joseph away. "I'll watch over him. You'll ride my horse . . ."

"But Father . . ."

"No 'buts,' Joseph!" I probed Nedde for broken bones, careful not to disturb him. "Ride my horse to . . ."

"He can't," John sided with his younger brother. "Your horse ran off!"

"Then *we'll* have to move him. He can't lie here." Running my nearly frozen hands beneath his limp body, I lifted Nedde to my knee and slowly across my chest. Ahead of me, the boys dug footholds in the river bank and took turns bracing me as I climbed, careful that Nedde's head did not bob.

"Don't wait for me," I panted. "Ride to Doctor Hale's and have him meet me at home. But don't alarm your mother."

They paused only long enough to be sure I could carry my burden, made heavier by the guilt I felt, and sped to fetch the doctor. 'If only I'd brought snowshoes in case of an emergency.' I rued as I retraced the tracks Flora and I had made the day before.

"*Wut tep!*" Hale cautioned our Indian, "Hold his head carefully."

"*Chi ba gi no guat,*" she commented, her supple fingers caressing his neck.

"Yes," he agreed, "it looks very bad indeed."

My wife's sob received a chorus of support from the children as I recited, "The Lord is my shepherd . . ."

Choking their tears, they responded with the next verse, joined by the doctor, while Flora gently massaged Nedde's bruise with honey brewed in ale.

Without warning, as we intoned, "My cup runneth over," Nedde vomited, his undigested no-cake soiling Flora's mocassins.

"*Wli!*" she clapped.

"Good! That's the spirit!" The doctor sighed and beckoned Beth to replace Flora beside the boy. "He'll recover, but he'll need to be watched."

As bad as I felt about the accident, I would have been relieved had my wife criticized me. Instead, she sent the children about their chores and ordered Flora to keep watch over Nedde, leaving me to repent my folly in silent prayer beside the hearth.

"He wants to see his *mat guas,*" barefoot, Flora almost bowled me over as she flitted across the snow to the leanto. Before I could ask the Lord's forgiveness, she bounded past me, a hare in each hand, "Your *mat guas!*" she dangled the carcasses at me.

"He can't stomach any food," Elizabeth spoke to me for the first time in hours, "but he enjoys his flip . . ."

"Like father like son," I groaned.

"Stop feeling sorry for yourself, be thankful for Nedde's recovery. Find time from your other duties to instruct him."

"I do. I catechize. I lecture," Flora, with Nedde in tow, overheard my feeble defense. 'Now all three will join against me.'

"Nedde, tell your father what you'd like him to teach you," his mother beamed.

Springing to the fireplace before Flora could restrain him, he pointed to my musket.

"Teach me to shoot a fox!"

Beth gasped.

"I'll make a pile of fishheads like you do, Father. Then I'll hide and wait for the *wokw ses.*"

"Nedde!" It was my wife's turn to groan.

"Show me how to load and fire your musket and I'll kill the fox myself!"

Fearful that his excitement might delay his recovery, Flora pulled him from the hearth and guided him to the stairwell.

"*Sa no ba wo gan*, Master," she grinned, her charge slowly making his way to bed. "He's ready for manhood."

"No, no!" his mother sobbed. "He's too young."

"Among my people," our Indian commented somberly, "a boy becomes a man when he proves himself in the hunt or at war."

Beth's eyes filled with tears, unready to accept her son's development, sorry she had provoked the crisis.

"We say he is a man when he has found his *manito*—the true spirit that links him with all Mankind, with God, with Nature." Flora's wisdom quieted her mistress who stepped to the mantle, stared at the musket, and opened the Scripture to Proverbs 20:11.

"Even a child is known by his doings," she smiled at us, "whether his work be pure, and whether it be right."

'Lord,' I implored, 'how dares Tabitha Deal accuse these two righteous women of witchcraft?'

*   *   *

Having repaired the extensive damage wreaked on my farm from May's freak snowstorm, I refused supper to nurse myself with warm sack and fell asleep across the fall of my escritoire.

"Wake up," my wife gently stroked my ailing shoulders, "you have a visitor."

With her arm supporting me until my legs regained their strength, we stumbled downstairs in time to see Flora slam the door.

"Who's there?" I freed myself from my wife.

"She rode away," my slave snapped.

"It was Goodwife Deal," Beth explained.

In spite of my condition, I reached for my rapier and buckled it to my side.

"Not tonight, Joseph, she'd have waited if she needed you," my wife declared, unaware of my misadventures with the woman. "She even refused to dismount—isn't that so, Flora?"

The Taranteen's flaming eyes were her only answer, the reason for which became apparent the next day.

"I'll read the Scripture tonight," Elizabeth volunteered as she un-buckled my rapier, "I know just the passage from Isaiah 50 to comfort you."

"The Lord has given me the tongue of a teacher and skill to console the weary . . ." the phrase relaxed me, "and skill to console the weary—*in the morning.*"

"Aptly chosen," I droned as she finished the reading, returned the Bible, and led me to bed.

Sleepily, I was well underway to the Deals the next day when a phrase which had not registered on me the night before came to mind. 'He sharpened my hearing that I might listen like one who is taught,' a reminder that my patience would be tempted by the distraught good-wife.

'Nobody home,' I delighted when my rapier's knock went unan-swered, but a voice within me cried, 'Listen, listen!' When I sharpened my senses, I heard moans from the bedroom window. Dismounting, I opened the great door and called for Tabitha, a tormented groan was my answer.

Again she lay in bed, the scratches healed above her nose, her bedclothes clutched about her neck. Impatiently, I prayed for help.

"Your Indian's imp, that diabolical turtle, came to me again last night," her feeble voice forced me to listen keenly. "Against my will, it made me taste the sabat—unsalted horseflesh," she retched, her eyes still closed. "When the imp left, I was as hungry as if I'd never eaten."

"My slave's imp? You're sure?"

"As certain as I am that you stand beside my bed," her eyes flick-ered, their pupils enlarging quickly. "I rode to your house last night. I . . . I hoped your Indian would touch me and release me from her spell. But . . . but when I kicked at her from my horse, my leg recoiled in midair."

'No wonder Flora was angry,' the demented woman was building an ever-tightening case against my slave.

"She sent her imp to punish me. It stood beside my bed when I got home, although it tried to shy my horse along the road, just as it succeeded twice with yours," I stifled a gasp. "You remember, it threw your wife to the ground and killed her baby and almost killed Nedde last winter . . ."

'Dear Lord, how long must I listen to such drivel without defending myself!' The answer was swift, 'Listen like one who is taught . . . no insult can wound you!'

"Imps frighten animals," she instructed me as she hitched herself upright, the bedclothes still tight about her neck, "like they did Hutch's jade."

'No insult can wound me,' a reply began to formulate in my mind.

"Her imp also dried your cow's milk such that the beast was never herself again and you had her slaughtered."

Unstoppable, even had I tried, she recounted the tragedies of sickness and death among the Farmers, including the current threat to their crops, all of which she claimed were caused by Flora's curse upon us.

"But how can you be sure *she's* the witch?" I played the student.

"She's darkskinned, like the Black Man," her eyes gleamed, "if we're not careful, she'll return our land to him."

My studied look encouraged her: our fleet's failure to storm Quebec, the cowardice of some soldiers at Haverhill, trouble recruiting for the army—all the Devil's doing, with the help of witches such as my Indian.

"Would a prayer rid you of your burden?"

"Not before you're convinced," she relaxed her clutch on the bedclothes, clasping her hands across her middle. "It was I who suffered most. First, when my husband took a broom to me, moreso when the poor man was pilloried," tears streaked her dirty cheeks. "The imp attacked his yard—it's become useless!"

I fought back a smile as she complained that John had long been unable to satisfy their sexual needs, 'A far better reason for your distress than spectral evidence,' but she caught my attention again.

"*Your* witch! She caused that poor Fuller boy to bleed to death and Hutch's son to die so young!" her snarl frightened but alerted me.

'I know I shall not be put to shame,' Goody Deal lowered her hands to her groin and slid prone, 'because one who will clear my name is on my side.'

These unrelated, fortuitous incidents, cunningly marshalled against Flora, could sway many of my flock as had spectral evidence before.

Elizabeth would counsel me to treat the wretch kindly, but I felt stronger measures were called for and so I let her wallow momentarily before I took my gamble.

"*Do* let me relieve you, my dear," I whispered almost inaudibly to disarm her as I stepped toward her bed.

"Please, Pastor, please . . ." she exulted, raising her hands to the top of her bedclothes.

"No need to strip, you craven witch!" I grabbed her wrists and twisted her arms behind her, her legs struggling to free the bed linen, her eyes aflame with hatred.

"No more nonsense!" Another twist and she went rigid. "Keep your cycs on me while you hear me out!"

When her lip quivered, her face so close to mine I was nauseated by her foul breath, I knew I had the upper hand.

"Palms beneath your head, hag!" I forced her to obey and stood erect as if lecturing the children. "I ought to cut your throat for kicking at my Indian last night," she tried to release her hands but a slap on the hilt of my rapier paralyzed her.

"This 'imp' *you* claim torments you, *I* claim you suckle! And willingly at that!"

I could tell I was winning the battle by the terror in her face.

"How else can you explain your blackened nipples . . ."

"My children . . . I . . . I've only suckled . . ."

"And your miserable hemorrhoids? Likcly places for your imp to suckle!"

"No, no Pastor. They're from hard riding . . ."

"Look at you! You call my slave 'darkskinned,' yet your skin is caked with filth. Each time I visit," I yanked the bedclothes off her, shoved her out of bed, and threw her a sheet, "you idle in this dirty, lice-infested nest."

Quaking in the muslin, she was too petrified to weep or stammer.

"An imp must suckle daily—as a witch, you well know that—so you lie idly, awaiting its return. Meanwhile, your poor husband . . ." I drew my rapier slowly to be sure I had her full attention. "Why, if I were to search this room, I'm sure I'd find a hole . . ."

Her head spun toward the window.

"Aha! I'm right! Your imp uses the break in that filthy pane."

Shattered by my attack, her jowls and shoulders dropped, baring her breasts, although she was unaware of her nakedness.

"Suppose I take the tip of this sword, Gamar Deal," I stepped toward her, "and prick a teat." She covered herself. "Come, come, if you're the witch I believe you are, no blood will flow."

"Merciful Lord, help me!" she threw herself at my feet. "Our Father, which art in Heaven, hollow . . ."

"Hallowed," I stabbed my rapier in the floor to silence her and recited the prayer, accompanied by her sobs.

"I promise to return to this matter, Tabitha," she knelt before me. "You will remain kneeling in silent prayer until you recite our Lord's Prayer flawlessly. Pray, too, for God's mercy. His wrath toward people like you, who would deceive Him and harm the innocent, brings a Hell far worse than the gallows."

Her lips began to move in prayer as I sheathed my sword and waited until she finished.

"After I leave, you have work to do. Clean the lice from your bed and wash the linen. Don't dare return to bed, I warn you, unless your husband sleeps beside you. Rise when he does and see to your wifely duties. No idleness! Read the Scripture aloud and diligently, morning and night. Arrive on time for services, take notes, if you wish, but keep silent! Finally, thank Providence that you won't be put in the stocks for having words with my slave without my permission—worse yet, that you won't be tried as a *witch.*"

"You . . . you'll help me?"

"Help yourself! Obey the Lord! Follow His commands." Her demeanor told me my ruse had worked, at least for the present. "Pray the Lord will forgive you for your shameful flirtation with Satan. Pray, too, that John will forgive you for your self-inflicted welts and false accusations."

I felt I was on shaky ground and made ready to leave, but as it turned out, my hunches were correct.

"You *will* return to help me?" she quivered.

"When Providence calls me, not before. May God bless and heal your tortured soul."

When Margaret Rule had been similarly distraught some years before, Cotton Mather chose to treat her with others present. The result of his folly was a blistering attack by Robert Calef. And so, when I arrived home that night, I entered only one line in my diary:

'Visited John Deal's wife.'

*   *   *

"A witch's brew!" I protested against my Indian's smearing my hands and face with the concoction.

"Hush, Joseph, you'll heal well before Cotton Mather's visit. Besides, it's your own fault for letting your horse get away after Jonathan Putnam's marriage. If you hadn't tried to make your way through the cornfields, you'd have returned without a scratch."

"You're not still upset with me, Beth?" A volley from the artillery on Fast Day had plummeted her cherished earthenware pot, a wedding gift from the late John Pride of Salem, onto the hearth, an accident for which she held me partially accountable.

"We're due damages. They compensated John Guppy for his broken glassware, I expect nothing less."

"Well, we *had* to celebrate peace with the French and Indians."

"I would gladly exchange the Treat of Utrecht for my irreplaceable pot. Now, before you complain, read the simple recipe Flora prepared for your wounds."

'A quart of fishworms, washed; add a pound of stewed hog's lard, and filter. Then a half-pint each of oil of turpentine and brandy simmered until thickened.'

"The brandy would suffice, Beth."

"Not on your life! You've got to be healed in time for Pastor Wigglesworth's ordination at Ipswich. Until then, we'll continue the treatment."

Who can say whether I would have healed without the treatment? In any event, I was in good voice as we sang, prophetically, from Psalm 115, "Not to us, O Lord, but to Thy name ascribe the glory," Cotton Mather thoroughly relished the attention he received in leading us.

The delicious aroma of roasting turkey greeted our arrival at my parsonage. Nedde, assigned to watch the bird as it dangled on a cord above the drip-pan, gave my guest only a passing nod. Flora, however, embarrassed me with her distasteful observation. "His *wdup kwan*," referring to the Bay minister's enormous wig. I only hoped he hadn't heard her because I anticipated the advice he would give me about Goodwife Deal.

"It's an act of Providence that you invited me, Joseph," he settled into the chair in my study, "otherwise I'd have had to endure John Wise's blathering about that slanderous tract he's writing."

"Mad!"

"Mad! An apt word for it. I must say, I care not a turd for him! We've a few minutes before your father-in-law takes me to Sa-lem . . ."

Determined to make the most of our encounter, I hastened, "What's really on my mind . . ."

"The sea voyage I face reminds me of the countless prayers and sermons I've offered for our seafarers," I chose not to interrupt him, "let alone the many books I've sent them." I recalled the hortatory letters I had written my oceangoing brothers in '96 and so was unprepared for his anger. "And what, I ask you, has been my reward? Sailors curse, slander, and revile me every chance they get!"

"Perhaps books and sermons aren't their greatest need," I hoped he would leave the matter and respond to *my* need.

"I ask you, who on earth has given more comfort and instruction to the Negroes of our New Israel than I? I deem myself to be the source of their salvation."

"But you insist their blackness means they're Satan's tools . . ." Tabitha had made the same assertion about Flora, perhaps this topic would provide an opening for me.

"Consider women," now he was getting closer to the problem uppermost on my mind. "Who has done more to extoll the honor of their sex, citing time and again the virtue and character of holy women, than have I? And solely for their own profit and honor, I need not assure you." His wig shook furiously as he decried that women spoke basely of him and spit venom at him.

"Joseph! Quick!" Beth's scream called me to the fireplace where Nedde had fallen asleep, spilling the urine-filled dyepot onto the hearth.

"Mop up fast, Flora," I ordered as I made sure the turkey's cord was secure, "before the stench ruins our dinner."

Cotton Mather, slumped in his chair, neither acknowledged my return nor the refilling of his tankard. In a low monotone, he changed the subject to his family.

"My own brothers have been monstrous toward me. They make me feel as Job, 'a brother to dragons,' as have my sons."

'Nedde's carelessness has cost me the opportunity to get Cotton's attention, otherwise I have no complaints against *my* family.'

"And that's not all. The Scottish people—I'm their greatest friend—vilify me. And the many useful essays I've written for our colony's guidance? Met with disrespect, calumny, and aversion. Even the very government I've so forcefully upheld reacts toward me with indecencies and indignities." Disspirited, he wept, "What hurts me most, yes, most, my voluminous writings—designed solely to promote God's kingdom, not myself—have led to my being traduced, reproached, and belied."

'I can surely minister to Goody Deal better than to this sorry man!' As though he had read my mind, he burst, "Can you imagine! My God-inspired, wholly unselfish service to others has only caused *me* to suffer! As if I, of all people, were the greatest sinner." He composed himself, "Joseph, they even refer to me as 'that afflicted minister . . .'

"To be treated as a blockhead, a blemish," he jammed his notes into his coat, slamming my desk's fall so hard I had to repair it the next day, "by Harvard College! I've brought whatever honor one man could upon an institution—albeit never asking for an *undue* honor. What do I receive in return? I'll tell you—debasement, imagine, debasement!"

His worst rebuff was yet to come. When the presidency became vacant, the post was offered to a lesser figure than Cotton, but the man declined it. A second offer was then extended to and accepted by someone else. Thus, Cotton never succeeded to the position once held by his illustrious father, Increase.

"Father's here!" much to my relief, my wife's call resounded up the stairwell.

"Dear Joseph," Cotton Mather pulled me to my feet and embraced me. "Oh, to have had a brother such as you. My company is totally unsought," he admired me at arm's length, "and yet I always make others wiser in profitable conversations such as ours."

Within seconds he was transformed from the downcast, self-pitying complainer to the composed personage most people knew. After thanking Elizabeth for her hospitality, he swept her father out the door. Then, posturing with his back against the jamb, he intoned, "What would *I* give if there were any *one* man in the world to do for *me* what *I* am willing to do for *every* man in the world . . ."

"*Kchi ia,*" I thought Flora would have been so engrossed with the turkey to have paid our guest no attention, but she had seen through his facade to the 'old man' he surely was.

"Not to *us,* O Lord, not to us," my wife chose the Scripture after we had eaten what we could of the odd-smelling turkey, "but to *Thy* name ascribe the glory . . ."

"That just about summarizes what Brother Mather quite unintentionally, I'm sorry to say, taught me today."

* * *

Elizabeth had accompanied me to Salem, determined that the new horse I would purchase was more surefooted than my old one. And that he was as he carried me north across Beaver Dam Brook to the Deals.

'Comfort, comfort,' the passage from Isaiah 40:10 crossed my mind, 'speak tenderly, she has fulfilled her term of bondage.'

If my wife were correct, and Tabitha's gain in weight was really due to pregnancy rather than gluttony, I would have to agree, 'Her penalty is paid.'

"Pastor Green," John met me at the door, "what brings you here?"

"Who's there?" an unusually melodious Tabitha called.

"Reverend Green," her husband answered, "we'll be right up."

The bedroom was immaculate, the linen spanking clean. Not only was the broken windowpane repaired, but each pane gleamed from the sun's reflection on the snow. Surely enough, when Goody Deal rose from stoking the fire, her firm belly confirmed Beth's view.

"I've found comfort in the passage you read me," she squeezed her husband's hand, "from Mark 16:17, 'Faith will bring with it these miracles," she patted her stomach.

"Our children are grown," Goodman Deal explained, "and moved to town as servants."

"The passage ends," she continued, "believers will cast out Devils in My name."

Without the slightest encouragement from me, she then confessed she had been deluded about others, her husband in particular, but most painfully the Lord. As if to assure me of her sincerity, she recited the Lord's Prayer with perfect cadence.

"Amen," we joined her as a wet log snapped a coal across the hearth, drawing my attention to two possets.

"Goose dung?" I diagnosed the nearest.

"Doctor Hale's remedy for . . . for my wife's distraction."

"And this one?" I meant to be gentle, to convey my concern without embarrassing them.

"Part of an elk's hoof, for the same malady."

"There's an emulsion in the jar," she pointed to the mantle.

"I'll reach it for you, Pastor," John volunteered, "it stinks so, she's never been able to swallow it."

'Two drams of assafoetida dissolved in a pound-and-a-half of black cherrywater is enough to bring on a delusion, let alone cure it,' I kept my silence as I stepped toward the chamberpot and motioned her husband to empty the possets into it.

"Tabitha, your faith has freed you from distress, your confession to full convenant with God."

Her husband kissed her tears away while I silently recited from Acts 16:18, 'I command you in the name of Jesus Christ to come out of her.'

"If it is by the finger of God," I lay my hand on her head, her husband's above it, "that I drive out the Devils," I sensed her release as she heard the lines from Luke 11:20, "then be sure the Kingdom of God has already come upon you."

I walked to the fire to warm myself before leaving, marveling at the Lord's divine intervention and allowing the two to share a quiet moment.

"What more can I do to relieve my guilt?" she whimpered.

Until that moment, I believed, together with my fellow ministers, that confession of misdeeds and follies was sufficient, rather than the heretical notion propounded by Anne Hutchinson years before, that good deeds were a better sign of a sinner's return to God. Now I wasn't so sure.

"I'm willing to confess from the Seat of Gloom . . ."

"Tabitha," I feared her public statement might provoke others in our congregation and hastily tried to calm her. "We've moved away from such displays of contrition . . ."

Her husband's sigh confirmed my suspicions but I believed she needed something more tangible to appease her conscience.

"Pray for the Lord's guidance. Rather than invest good works for yourself, act as an instrument for His creativity."

"But, Pastor, *you* have been my healer . . ."

"According to the Scripture," John handed me their well-worn, annotated copy, "Acts 10:38 states, 'He went about doing good and healing all who were oppressed by the Devil," I emphasized, "for *God* was with him . . .'"

"The Lord is with you, my dear," Goodman Deal knelt beside his wife in prayer, oblivious of my presence, and so I left them without further comment.

Smoke, billowing from our chimney, warned me that my wife had chosen to wait for my return rather than retire.

"Sit beside me on the settle, Joseph. Flora, pass us some flip and let's hear what happened."

Pouring a jack of cider for herself, our Indian refilled my jack and sat crosslegged on the floor. Although I acknowledged that my wife was correct about Goody Deal's pregnancy, I felt it wise not to tell either of them about the accusations of witchcraft which had been laid to rest. They seemed satisfied when I recounted Tabitha's confession of having falsely accused her husband and her willingness to forego a public statement to the Farmers.

"It's time for prayers and bed," I announced, somewhat annoyed by Flora's unbraiding her hair, but withholding any censure of her conduct.

"My *po da woz win no*," she befuddled me, pressing her wampum into my hand before she pattered off.

"She calls you her 'counselor," Elizabeth closed my palm around the white conch shells interspersed with purplish quahog clam chips. "I'm afraid she knows there was more to Goody Deal's story than you've told us . . ."

"What am I supposed to do with this?"

"You must keep it. You'd shame her if you didn't."

''But doesn't a gift of wampum call for some exchange?'' I prided myself on having learned something about these heathen customs.

''Traditionally, yes,'' my wife locked her arm in mine as we climbed the stairs. ''An occasion will present itself. Until then, counselor, accept the gift—it may remind you of Anne Bradstreet's words in *The Prologue:*

> ''Men can do best, and women know it well.
> Preeminence in all and each is yours;
> Yet grant some small acknowledgement of ours.''

12 A Fruitful Bough

"Do you mean to say you're paying Katherine Deland *five* pounds a year to teach the girls?" Fruitlessly, I tried to study Michael Wigglesworth's *Day Of Doom*.

"And here's seven-pounds forty-shillings for the boys at Samuel Andrews'," she slammed the account shut.

"You and the children must be provided for," I grabbed her lustfully, tilted her backward on the bed, and kissed her passionately.

Running my hands down her sides, her nipples rose as they rubbed against my chest. I pulled her buttocks eagerly toward my yard, thrilling to the moist warmth of her opened legs as they enveloped me, and secured my position inside her. The June night passed in rapture.

"I'll be underway to Andover-Haverhill before dawn to see about our new farm," I assured my sleeping wife, although I feared my unshod horse might cause me trouble.

Sure enough, as I tried to ford the Shawsheen on my way home, he plunged me into the freezing river and I was forced to travel the remaining twenty miles in icy cold.

"Father will replace you this Sabbath," Beth fed me a dose of squeezed hard boiled eggs mixed with powder of aloes and sugar.

"Read," I coughed.

"Nothing will excuse you . . ." my wife read the letter I had written to my brother-in-law in '96, "if you live in neglect of your duty," she grimaced more in mirth than anger, "and if you say you are not fit then let me tell you that you ought to be fit.''

"I promise . . . I'll be fit. Hand me my *Cambridge Concordance*."

"You're stubborn enough to sermon on tithing again but I'm stubborn enough to deny your request unless you'll let Deacon Putnam relieve you of catechizing."

Using the guidelines suggested by John Tufts of Medford, the deacon introduced the congregation to the New Way of psalm-singing. He sang the first line, joined in the second by the Farmers. I knew it might bring some complaints, but it saved my energy for the sermon.

"Cotton Mather has called us Americans 'The New Israel,' 'The People of the Faith,'" I paced myself, "you will recall that Jacob, Isaac and Rebecca's younger son, was renamed 'Israel' when he accepted the Lord's covenant, according to my first text in Genesis 28:20–22."

While my parishioners searched their Scriptures for the passage, I took the time to clear my throat before I intoned, "Of all that Thou givest me, I will *without fail* allot a tenth part to Thee."

Tabitha nodded approval from the women's side of the meeting house. Without bothering to scan the men's pews, I demonstrated that Jacob's contract meant the Lord would protect, feed, and clothe Israel in exchange for one-tenth of the fruit of its labor. As if to accentuate the point, but really to hide my cough, I upended the hourglass and banged it on the pulpit.

Flora had complained about the maggots in the cornmeal provided for us by some Farmers; my wife about the toughness of the pork; the boys, especially Nedde, about the green firewood; and so I had chosen my second text from Numbers 18, verses twenty-nine and thirty-two.

"Out of all the gifts you receive you shall set aside the contribution due to the Lord," I directed this toward the men, "and the gift which you hallow must be taken from the choicest of them."

Joseph Putnam's head snapped against the pew with such a noise he almost drew a knobbing from the snook. My anger, however, was not directed toward him, his goods always of the highest quality.

"When you set aside the *choicest* part," I stared at my neighbor, Ben Hutchinson, "you will incur no penalty . . . so you will not *die*."

The women kicked their crickets so hard the noise distracted the boys at the pulpit stairs, allowing me to take some deep breaths so that I could continue.

"You shall bring out all the tithe of your produce for that year," my voice had strengthened somewhat as I read the last verses from Deuteronomy 14, "and the aliens," I waved at the strangers' pews, "orphans," I pointed toward the sickly Ann Putnam, "and widows . . . may come and eat their fill."

My wife jerked her head toward me at the mention of widows, but her reaction only encouraged me to conclude my sermon with a stanza from Michael Wigglesworth's *Day Of Doom.*

> "But woe, woe, woe, our Souls unto!
>   We would not happy be;
> And therefore bear God's vengeance here
>   To all Eternity."

Try as I might, I could not restrain a fit of coughing, drops of blood staining my sermon notes.

> "Experience and woeful sense,
>   Must be our painful teachers
> Who n'ould believe, nor credit give,
>   Unto our faithful preachers."

I gripped the pulpit, afraid I might collapse before the Farmers emptied the meeting house. Nedde stayed behind to help me down the pulpit stairs and home to the parsonage where Flora waited with a jack of flip, half of which I drank before I fell asleep, in spite of the fierce thumping on our great door.

"Pastor Green needs his rest, Flora," my wife's voice seemed far away, "tell Deacon and Joseph Putnam to return another day to register their complaints."

Beth soothed my forehead with the gentle brush of her hand, her tears cooling my feverish cheeks, yet I felt my body growing ever colder.

'Give her your counsel. Tell her not to grieve.' Try as I might, I could summon no breath, able only to move my lips to remind her once more, "Think of Eternity," I wondered if she had understood.

*   *   *

"*Kutchim moke!*" Flora flitted from child to child, stroked a cheek, patted a head, never mentioning my name. Even so, the contrast between their stoic faces and the flood of tears that streaked her charcoaled cheeks would have been more than I could have borne without comment.

"Be of good cheer, children," my widow began the family service with a passage from my *Commonplace Book*. "Remember you are mortal creatures," Nedde, unable to restrain Ben, let our slave hold him, "and must not live here always. In a very little time, you know not how soon, you must go to your long home whence you must return no more."

The children had seen me recover so many times before, they found it hard to believe I was gone, but Elizabeth knew I had put all my energy into my sermon, dying two hours afterwards without enough breath to comfort her.

"As your father wrote for his own instruction, and more than once instructed me," she skipped ahead, "those who are religious lead the most pleasant life," she suppressed a smile, "because they are always ready for death."

The distress they felt, she explained, should make them heed my words all the more.

"Think how it will be on your own death bed," Nedde stole a glance at my sheet-covered body, his mother awaiting his attention before she continued. "You will have no regrets, because you had prayed and done that which you knew to be your duty."

'Oh, dear Joseph,' she waited for the message to have its effect on the children, 'I understood when you scurried so about the parish and the farms, you had to do your duty as you saw it or be tormented. I grieve my loss of you. I only thank the Lord I have no regrets.'

My children had reason to squirm—for lying or evading, failing to do their chores or catechisms, blaspheming on the Sabbath—but only five-year-old William, who had replaced Nedde as the family imp, lost control of his bladder and was quickly whisked outdoors by Flora.

"Your past sins, as mine, and your dear father's, the Lord has forgiven," Nedde's relief too blatant, she wagged her finger at him, "but you dare not *forget* your sins or surely you'll repeat them!"

I might have been harsher, but I could not have done better.

"Think much of the Day of Judgment, which your father awaits," she closed my book tenderly, offering it to Nedde to assure him of forgiveness, "then every secret, evil or good, will be discovered. Each of your actions, at whatever time and place, will be openly declared," she had memorized my words, "and we will be judged according to what our carriage was toward God and toward one another."

"Mother, look what it says on the title page of father's book," Nedde, the slowest to learn to read, was the proudest of his skill, "Think of Eternity."

'Think of Eternity, your last words to me, dear Joseph,' my widow's grief was eased by the children's, "Amen."

*   *   *

Because my death had provoked Increase Mather to write an address, the Inhabitants were forced to consider whether to pay to have it and the other sermons printed.

"I'm sure you'll agree," Deacon Putnam began, "to honor our dead pastor, the choicest flower and greenest olive tree cut down in its prime and flourishing estate . . ."

"We'll include your words, Brother," Joseph Putnam laid that issue to rest, "but Increase's address dwells on his *own* ministry, bemoans the fate of *his* family, and hardly mentions *our* late pastor."

"Don't be so factious," Edward reprimanded his younger half-brother, "Mather's 'Address to the Reader' will preface the book."

"So be it," Putt countered, "let the Beggarly people pay for Thomas Blower's sermon or we'll leave it out."

"I suppose Joseph Capen's sermon annoyed you as it did me, Putt, when he warned us not to let our departed pastor's 'instructions and counsels die and be buried in oblivion."

"Well, that final sermon on tithing was uncalled for," Putt defended, "although when Brother Capen accused us of not having profited from the pastor's 'labors and pains,' suggesting that Providence might have taken Pastor Green as a judgment against our 'spiritual barrenness,' I confess I felt somewhat guilty. Read on."

"Although ministers nowadays cannot pretend to cast out Devils or to heal diseases . . ."

Capen's passing remark drew an astonished gasp from Tabitha who pulled her nursing baby aside to stamp her foot in such protest that she drew my widow's attention.

'So, Joseph, *that's* the secret you've kept from me,' she covered her mouth to stifle a sob.

Joseph Capen then chose to elaborate on Deacon Putnam's opening lament, ''Then did our sun go down, and now what darkness is come upon us.'' The good deacon was more concerned for the parish than for me. ''Return to us again in mercy, and provide yet again for this Thy flock a pastor.''

''Let none of you say,'' Capen confronted the deacon, ''after a diffident and distrusting manner, 'We shall never have such a minister again.'' Edward Putnam's crestfallen expression was not shared by the Inhabitants who found the admonition uplifting. ''The same good hand of Heaven that sent him to you, and united you all in him, can do the like again! Unite and accord,'' he charged, ''to be all of one heart and one soul about the choice of another minister.''

Within eighteen months, Peter Clark was ordained, although some complained too much canary accompanied the celebration. Pastor Clark, however, ministered to the Farmers more than fifty years, to be succeeded in 1768 by Benjamin Wadsworth, whose tenure lasted until 1826.

Directing the last of his sermon to my family, the Topsfield preacher mellowed. ''This apostle was no man-pleaser, he feared none but God, and was not afraid of the face of man. He will be known for the weightiness of his teaching and the agreeableness of his manners.''

Had he known how much of my seventeen years' ministry I had spent in fear, fear that the frenzy of '92 might return, fear for my family's safety, fear that my teaching might be too light, fear that I might be too disagreeable, as my wife had often indicated, perhaps he might have spoken differently.

Without taking his eyes from my pregnant wife and family, he exhorted the congregation to be 'kind, tender and compassionate.' As an afterthought, he commented, ''Ministers seem to be under a great disadvantage when they die; inasmuch as when they die, all means of support for the families they leave behind come to an end.''

Having been poor most of my early life, I had made sure that Elizabeth would be provided for—albeit my last tour of our farm killed me. When she sold our farms, she gained over a thousand pounds, with debts no more than two hundred.

''Mark the good man, and behold the upright,'' Deacon Putnam rattled grain from the rafters, closing that part of the service with Psalm 37:37, ''For there is a *happy* end to the man of peace.''

'Melchizedek,' Elizabeth responded inaudibly.

*   *   *

> "In God's House we of late did see
> A *Green* and growing olive tree."

Nicholas Noyes read his elegy from the pulpit steps. This placed a burden on the tithingman because only those in the front pews could see the preacher, having to content themselves with his monotone.

> "But now, alas, we weep to see
> An empty place, where stood that tree;"

He pointed to the pulpit I had occupied for eighteen years.

> "That *Green* and lovely tree whose sight
> Has blest our eyes with much delight,
> For his good nature and his grace
> Both visible were in his face."

At thirty-five, Ann Putnam's face was deeply lined, her body more emaciated each year, but she kept her composure until she heard,

> "*Green* olive trees brought in his bill,
> He dried up floods of strife, and he
> Made brethren dwell in unity."

The snook made a swipe at Ann as a warning against a further outburst. Neither he nor others could have predicted that within the year her body would be buried in the family crypt behind Putt's house.

> "Our Joseph was a *fruitful* bough,
> His virtuous wife was fruitful, too . . ."

Elizabeth flushed at the phrase, wondering if the Farmers might be critical of our fruitfulness, but Nicholas' following verses eased her.

> "They were a lovely, loving pair,
> As most that breathe in common air;
> As if one soul had dwelt in these,
> What pleased one, it did both please."

Restraining any outward show of emotion, my widow prayed in silence for the child she was carrying.

> "They hand in hand did always go,
> Both shunning of the criss-cross row.
> They were so joined, heart in heart,
> Them Death itself could hardly part."

Nicholas had not heard my final sermon, and so his words had an effect he could not have predicted.

> "His dying sermon held almost
> Unto his giving up the Ghost . . ."

Joseph and Edward Putnam squirmed at the reference, their guilt increasing as the passage ended,

> "His Master's work he did so ply,
> He did but just get chance to die!"

Having already exceeded in his elegy for me the high standard he had set in his elegy for Thomas Hooker, Nicholas was quickly tiring.

> "Our Joseph, he is now *alive;*
> His soul, his body doth survive.
> In faith and works if we pursue him,
> Our Lord will quickly bring us to him."

Prophetically, a few years later, Nicholas Noyes choked to death on his own blood, leading some people to believe that Sarah Good's curse had come true.

A commotion interrupted the elegy as the sentinel admitted William Brattle to the meeting house.

> "And though the *Green* and lovely tree,
> Which we lament now withered be.
> The living spring where he did gain
> His sap and oil doth yet remain.
> And by that spring another plant,
> May rise and may supply our want . . ."

Master Brattle, whose stalwart opposition to divination had been my greatest source of strength, could only wonder at Nicholas' final premonition.

> "God of his mercy, give us grace,
> Behold! The *bridegroom* comes apace!"

*   *   *

Our eldest sons, John and Joseph, served as underbearers, carrying my casket to the burial ground. As overbearers, Joseph Putnam and John Deal lowered it into place. The Latin inscription on the upright slab mentioned my having been, "A most vigilant pastor, a man to be held in perpetual remembrance, both for seriousness of discourse and agreeableness of manners."

"Did Brother Noyes' phrase about Joseph's being 'a fruitful bough' offend you?" Putt asked my widow as Flora served the funeral guests a feast of roast pork, lobster, corncakes, and beans, washed down with canary.

"Not at all—our seven children hardly compare with your ten!" She handed my friend a funeral ring inscribed, 'Live to Die.' She then gave him similar rings to deliver to Reverends Blowers, Capen, and Noyes.

Joseph Putnam sired two more children before he died eight years later, one of whom, Israel, brought even greater fame to his already illustrious family.

Sated, some a little drunk, the guests left until only Pastor Brattle remained. As Elizabeth fingered the funeral ring she would offer him, she was reminded of a conversation we had often had.

"You must think seriously about life without me," I had admonished.

"You're too preoccupied with death. Death and tithing, either you offend the Captain or the Putnams!"

"A man, eligible and worthy of you," I would not be deterred from pursuing the issue, "must be your equal in virtue and education."

It was difficult enough to force my wife to attend to the matter when we were alone, but Flora's presence put me at a greater disadvantage.

"Whom do you suggest, Joseph?"

"Nicholas Noyes."

"*Pok ja na hwi ka,*" Flora sneered.

"Stumpy good-for-nothing!" Unfortunately, Elizabeth overlooked

William Brattle's presence during her reverie and repeated her translation aloud.

"Perhaps a sip of canary, Widow Green," he pretended to ignore her comment, "I know how you must feel—I lost my dear wife, also named Elizabeth, four months ago."

"I was just thinking of Joseph's advice about Nicholas, he's still a bachelor . . ."

"*Elizabeth*, how odd it is to hear myself use that name again," Flora refilled his glass, "might I suggest a widower?"

"You flatter me, Brother Brattle," Beth was not nearly as flustered as she made believe, "however, if your proposal holds after I'm delivered of the baby I now carry, due next April . . ."

"Dear Widow Green, be assured you'll hear from me in loving letters . . ."

"If it's a girl, Joseph and I agreed we'd name her Ruth . . ."

"We could be married in December."

The matter settled, William Brattle journeyed back to his Cambridge parish and did not see Elizabeth again until they were married in 1716. Unfortunately, he lived only three months, leaving her widowed for the second and last time.

*   *   *

"Long Nose," our Taranteen threatened William, whom the tithing-man had delivered from skating on Wilkins Pond, "the masked cannibal will kidnap you and spirit you away from here . . ."

"Fetch my Japan box," Elizabeth distracted her slave and hugged the boy before she chased him to bed, "it's in my husband's desk."

Flora returned moments later to squat at my widow's feet.

"Do you remember giving this to your master?" Beth let the wampum dangle from her fingertips. "Refresh my memory as to how wampum came about."

"Among my people was a beautiful maiden who fell in love with a watersnake. Each morning, she slipped away from her tepee to the pond where he lived. Then, right in front of her eyes, he'd slither out of his black-and-white skin and become a handsome warrior. When their day's lovemaking was over, he'd again become a snake and return to the water."

"Let's share a pipe," Elizabeth drew deeply and handed it to the Indian.

"One day, the girl's brothers, suspicious of her absence, trailed her and learned her secret. When the family met to decide what to do . . ."

"Hardly fitting to have one's daughter in love with a snake," my widow took her turn at the pipe.

"They could kill the snake and end the affair . . ."

"Ah, but suppose it were a friend of Gluskabe!"

"The entire family might be harmed," Flora beamed at her mistress' understanding. "They decided that one brother would hide until the snake crept from its skin. Then, while the couple made love, the other would steal the skin."

"And when the warrior was ready to return to his snakeskin?" the pipe had one puff left for Flora.

"He couldn't find it! He remained a man and accompanied the maiden to her village where they were married."

"And this?" Elizabeth held the string forward.

"The snakeskin became wampum," Flora rose to accept what she thought her mistress proffered.

"No!" The Indian slumped in shock. "I'll never part with the gift you gave my husband," aware that she had hurt her slave's feelings, Beth quickly asked, "Is it not your custom that gifts be exchanged as a sign of lasting friendship?"

Realizing she had puzzled her listener, in the way she had often confused me, my widow came to the point.

"You overheard me tell Reverend Brattle I expect a baby next spring. Shortly after that, the trails will thaw between here and Canada and you should find travel easy."

"I . . . I don't understand."

"It's really quite simple, Flora. In exchange for this precious wampum," Beth clutched it to her breast, "I give you your freedom."

'You see, dear Joseph, I was never impressed by John Saffin's argument for slavery,' my widow mused as she lay alone that night, 'Judge Sewall's argument in *The Selling Of Joseph* was much more cogent.'

When, however, Elizabeth was found to have died in her sleep, in

the middle of May, 1747, at the age of seventy-four, it was not Anne
Bradstreet's poems they found clutched in her hands, but my favorite,
Wigglesworth, opened to the passage:

> 'ETERNITY, ETERNITY!
> Oh, were it not for Thee,
> The Saints in bliss and happiness
> Could never happy be.'

Acknowledgements

Many expressions of Joseph Green's views are verbatim excerpts from his writings as are those of John Wise and Cotton Mather, (cited below). During the period covered by this narrative, many ministers circulated their ideas in letters to one another, whether or not their views were ever published in their lifetimes; e.g., Edward Taylor.

Grateful acknowledgement is made to the following for permission to reprint copyrighted materials:

The Commonplace Book of Joseph Green, The Colonial Society of Massachusetts, December Meeting, 1938; Boston, MA.

The Diary of Rev. Joseph Green of Salem Village, (ed. Samuel Fowler), the Essex Institute Historical Collections, v. 8:215–224, 1866, and v. 10:72–104, 1869, Salem, MA.

The Diary of Cotton Mather, (ed. Worthington Chauncey Ford), Collections of the Massachusetts Historical Society, 7th Series, VII-VIII, pp. 705–708, 1912, Boston, MA.

The Works of Anne Bradstreet, (ed. Jeannine Hensley), Harvard University Press, 1967, Cambridge, MA.

The Poems of Edward Taylor, (ed. Donald E. Stanford), Yale University Press, New Haven, CN, copyright by Donald E. Stanford.

Folk Songs of Old New England, (ed. Eloise H. Linscott), The Show Strong Press, Inc., Hamden, CN.

In the public domain are:

Michael Wigglesworth, *The Day of Doom*, (ed. Kenneth B. Murdock), Russell & Russell, Atheneum Publishers, Inc., 1966, N.Y., NY.

John Wise, *The Churches Quarrel Espoused*, 1713, Scholars Facsimiles and Reprints, Gainesville, FL.

John Wise, *A Vindication of the Government of New-England Churches*, 1717, Scholars Facsimiles and Reprints, Gainesville, FL.

Marion L. Starkey, Saugus, MA, author of many books about Salem and its environs, graciously read an early draft of the manuscript and made helpful suggestions, as did Elizabeth Pultz, publisher, Press Pacifica, Kailua, HI. Richard B. Trask, Town Archivist, Peabody Institute Library, Danvers, MA, so valuable to others who have studied Salem Village, inspired the author's efforts. Elizabeth G. Gershman, publisher, Knights Press, Pound Ridge, NY; Jack L. Fitzgerald, playwright and actor, West Hollywood, CA; Paul B. Cross, neighbor; and Larry A. White, playwright and colleague, Los Angeles, CA, read the manuscript and offered ways to improve it.

Two family members, Gaye Sunada, artist, Los Angeles, CA, and Michael B. Wolfe, author and publisher, Tombouctu Books, Bolinas, CA, provided enormous support for this self-publishing venture.

Mahalo nui . . .

Colophon

Cover Design
    Gaye Sunada, Los Angeles, CA
Cover Photographs
    Barry Kaplan, *The Finer Image, Inc.*,
    20 Park St., Danvers Square,
    Danvers, MA, 01923
Front Cover Sign
    Permission requested of the Massachusettes Historical Society
Printer and Distributor
    ARCATA, 15300 Ventura Boulevard, Sherman Oaks, CA,
    91403–3198;
    Thomas Patrick, Senior Sales Representative
Typist
    Judith Yardley, through PAK MAIL, West Hollywood, CA;
    Herb L. Oberman, Manager

The Author

The author's interest in Salem Village began in a doctoral seminar, "The Psychology of Social Change," at Teachers College, Columbia University, in 1946. Three years later, Marion L. Starkey's book, *The Devil in Massachusetts,* Alfred A. Knopf, Inc., redirected his attention from the witchcraft frenzy of 1692 to what she called the "reconciliation" brought about by Reverend Joseph Green. In 1978, he presented a paper, "Cotton Mather at Bay," to the International Society for Political Psychology describing the negative effects of the frenzy on the Bay Minister's career.

Dr. Grace has taught at the Universities of Illinois and Michigan State, after which he combined his teaching with student personnel administration at Grinnell College and the California State College System. After serving as a social psychologist in support of rehabilitation in the Veterans Administration, and as a consultant to the Vocational Service of Rancho Los Amigos Hospital, he resumed his teaching career at Santa Monica City College, the University of Southern California, the Art Center College of Design, Hawaii Pacific College, Chaminade University, and Woodbury University.

He is a Fellow of the Society for Applied Anthropology and a Member of the American Psychological and Sociological Associations. He has published or presented more than seventy research or professional reports.